his in the dark

WWINTERS

His in the Dark

There are two things I've always known:

Magic is real

The gods have no mercy for women like me.

I was born into power, although what little I have is dying. Nonetheless, I've been protected all my life. There are myths and tales that say one day I will come to a fork in a long, long path. Either the light will take me or the dark. I never paid any mind to the whispers and warnings...

Until he crept into my window late at night.

Cloaked in darkness, silent as death. Every inch of me felt terror, and yet I also felt something else. Something I'd never known.

He tasted like sin...and I loved it.

In a single moment, my entire world went dark, and I was nothing more than a captive in the Underworld.

Nothing but *his,* and suddenly all the lore brought a chill to my bones...even if he did light a fire in the most secret depths of me.

Prepare for a dark retelling of Hades and Persephone with spells and war and a love story that would change our world forevermore.

life grew from her fingertips because her existence
knew a being of only death.

I asked Persephone for help
She asked this of me

May we all feel what it is to be truly loved
Blessed be.

playlist

Ashley Sienna & Ellise - Pretty in the dark

Sam Tinnesz - Play with Fire

Neoni - Wonderland

Neoni - Darkside

Billie Eilish - you should see me in a crown

his in the dark

prologue

Hades

WITH THE FIRE CRACKLING AND THE rustling of the sheets, she turns over in my bed. There's a sultry, sinful look in her dark, lust-filled eyes as she peers back at me. The innocence is still there as she pulls the silk threads to her chest, and her pouty lips, slightly swollen from pleasuring me, slip open at the sight of me towering over her.

My Persephone. My queen.

Her chest rises and falls with heavy breaths.

"The blush in your cheeks adds to your beauty," I murmur and kneel on the bed, intent to crawl to her, to spread her thighs and bring her to the highest of pleasures with my tongue, but she hesitates. Her doe eyes go wide. She leans back slightly against the headboard and brings the sheets up higher.

A deep groan of discontent bellows up my chest at her actions. The voices of warning hiss at my impatience.

She will be mine in every way. Every possible essence of her will bear my mark.

Time, the warning echoes in the back of my head. *In time...she will be yours.*

The Fates' foretellings ease the beast inside of me who yearns for her complete submission. Her love, acceptance, and gratitude she has yet to display. Apart from crying out my name only moments ago on this very bed.

I imagine my come still leaks from her cunt. The pleasure still surges in her blood as it does mine.

I thought the deed was done...but there's so much more that must happen.

"Are you sated then?" I question her, intent on fixing the error of my ways. *If only for her.*

She stares at me, her mind no doubt playing tricks on her, and the magic depleting her even more so than it has in the last months of her capture.

"My queen"—I get her attention—"you created that." I gesture to the flames on the back wall.

There's a hitch in her breath. Her darkened eyes widen as the flames reflect in them. "You have power in pleasure. Power that was always meant to be yours," I tell her and ease myself to the back of the bed. Her gaze flicks to mine then back to the raging fire. The flames lick up the wall, leaving black marks in their wake. They will scar and remind her; she herself is a fire no one can tame.

The very thought brings me pleasure.

"Is that not divine?" I ask her in a whisper. "Is it not power?"

Her eyes come back to me, and I know she ponders my question although she's silent. I will break her and remake her in the way she so desperately needs.

She was born a goddess, but prior to me, before I took her against her will, she would have faded. She knows this. How can she not love me when I give her such a gift? When I pine for her and her glory. I fucking worship her, and still she stares back at me as if I am nothing but an enemy. Even after what we just had. Even after all I've done for her.

"It is not my magic," she responds, her eyes turning glassy although there's a spark there, almost defiant. Her spine straightens as the glow of the flames licks along the soft curve of her neck and the ambers glint in the darkness of her gaze.

"It is not what I was created for. I am the goddess of life and there is only death here," she whispers, soft and gentle, her words caressing although they're in rebellion. Does she not know the power in that? The magic that fills the room when she's lost in the role she was meant to play.

The goddess of life can still rule the dead.

The bed groans with my weight as I make my way to her, naked and wanting. As she stays perfectly still, no longer questioning or hesitant but more so in rebellion, my cock hardens. I want nothing more than to hear her moan my name again and again as I give her undeniable pleasure.

Ever so gently, I brush my thumb against her jaw. The softness of her skin is at odds against the calluses that I've earned through brutality. Her eyes close slowly, and she leans into me just slightly. *Progress*. Heat rages through my blood. There is still hope that I will win this war, although the warning from the Fates echoes in the back of my mind as I kiss her. Her blood is hot as she deepens it. Her fists tighten in the sheets as she resists grabbing me, keeping herself from clinging to me.

She will learn. Soon. It must be soon.

The queen of life and the king of death.

I lower my lips to the shell of her ear and whisper, needing her to believe the lie. "Persephone, you were created only for me."

chapter 1

Persephone

The gods are flawed. The prophecy is wrong.
I could never be who they say I am.

A CHILL RUNS DOWN MY SHOULDERS AS I leave the grand main hall with haste. My heart pounds and as I pass the gardens, I'm reminded that they knew before I did. All the tales they tell come true and that turns my blood cold.

The roses wilt and the edges of the grass turn a putrid brown. I stop mid-step and stare back at the faded petals. It is a sign of death when flowers shrivel and do not come alive again, no matter how rich the soil is.

My power is fading. That is reality, and I have no choice but to drown in the despair of it all.

I swallow thickly as my bare feet pad on the quartz floor and my pale pink silk gown flutters behind me, giving away my urgency. I pass by the grand foyer and the din of talk comes and goes quickly as I move past the open doors, my presence not being required.

And why would it be?

Olympus is the home of the gods and goddesses. The heavens that Zeus, my father, shares with the powerful and mighty. I've heard that mortals can't imagine the beauty of this place. It is beyond their depths. There are white spires like clouds, and the rich marble floors are warmed by the heat of the sun. Lush gardens grow in courtyards trimmed with gold. I've heard they don't have water like we have here, every drop sparkling. Everything here is as pure as the gods themselves.

Every presence in this grandeur is worthy of its divinity. For the servants, it's the highest honor to be in the company of the divine and their blessings.

I was divine once. My birth was a celebration. Demeter's daughter would bring fruitfulness as Demeter does with such ease. I was once filled with powerful magic. Not anymore…and he knows. There is no hiding from Zeus. The prophets will not keep their knowledge a secret, for that is why they hear the whispers of the universe. They hear so that they can share what they know.

I fear they will all come to know what was just told to me.

After all, the prophets have been right all this time for everything that has fallen and risen.

The moment I get to my gilded carved door, I close it with my back to the gold painted etches. The thud is barely heard over my racing heart. It is not the foretelling

I wanted, but it is the fate I knew I would receive. I'd still hoped that some miracle would happen in my favor, perhaps even a blessing from the gods who still have power flowing in their veins.

"My lady," Beatrice calls out in surprise as she rises from her knees on the floor. The mortal has a hand on her chest as she takes in my presence and bows with respect. It only adds salt to my wound. For I do not feel worthy of such things.

She's as graceful as anything in Olympus. Dark haired and dark eyed, she makes a calming contrast in her servant's robes. Her Grecian blood is evident. Beatrice's hair, plaited behind her head in a thick braid, shines in the light from the candles. She is surrounded by dozens of small tea lights and tall tapers.

It seems I've caught her in the middle of a ritual. She did not expect my early return.

The pure gold candle holders with white candles coated in a mixture of herbs sits in a pattern on the floor. The flames are bright and tall and in the center of the altar lies an old iron key I recognize.

My heart still beats too fast to be truly calm, but I have interrupted her and I regret that. "It wasn't my intention to disturb your prayers."

My father's disappointment in knowing my own servant prays to another god is etched in my memory. Yet another failure on my part. I cannot provide for those who provide for me. I cannot give them the grace they need from me.

For so long, I thought of Olympus as my home, but now I see how little I belong here. Olympus is grand the way my father is grand. His power reaches every corner of the earth and the heavens. No one can hide from his power, and whenever they seek him, he can be found.

What am I next to that? I am nothing. I have no presence that can fill these flawless rooms. I am as small as one of the flowers in the gardens. Even the flowers have more to offer Olympus than I do.

I do not speak any of this aloud to Beatrice. She already knows the things I fear, and the things that are coming. She is my confidant, and I am hers.

"What is it you ask of Hecate?" I question her, righting my gown and standing taller as I should. My heart still beats savagely from the fears that have only grown stronger.

"Only guidance," Beatrice answers. "I long to see my sister at peace in her dying days, and I struggle with my grief."

"If you wish to go to her—"

"I will not leave you, my lady. I only need to hear of her peace."

"Your sister is merely mortal. She will only be here for a short while. If you change your mind, your departure will be missed but it will be divinely guided and protected." Before I can add that she should go to her sister before she's gone, I catch the agony in her stare and I realize it's for me. I, too, may not be here much longer. Not as a goddess. Not in the castles. I'll be shunned to the forests and lost forever as a garden nymph. So much of what I thought I would be seems so close to being lost forever. Beatrice will lose me as she loses her sister. The choice before her is which one of us to see for the final time.

My throat tightens as I realize her reality. I wonder if my name is in her prayers to Hecate.

"I do not need to go to her; I will see her in other lives. Death becomes us all and it is not an end, merely a crossroad," Beatrice tells me and I rip my gaze away from her, making my way from the atrium, farther back to the broad window with the daybed so I may rest. "What have they foretold?" she asks and her tone is tight with emotion. An anxiousness resides in her eyes. It's been there far too long. I can barely remember a time in which she did not worry for me. That worry has been stronger in recent days, and there is nothing I can say to comfort her. "What did the prophecy tell you this evening?"

The last rays of sunlight outside Olympus are a deep, rich gold, as they should be in the presence of the gods. I gaze upon it with a pain in my throat. I will not be able to look on these sights for much longer. I try to console myself with the thought that I was able to experience them at all, but it does not bring me any comfort. Sometimes I think it might have been better if I had been born mortal. If I had been born like Beatrice, I might never have known what I have lost. What is so close to slipping through my grasp.

"Nothing more than a garden nymph," I make

myself say although it's barely a whisper. "I will not be a powerful goddess."

There is nothing I can say to comfort her.

There was no hesitation or question. That is my fate in Olympus, they made that very clear. I will lose my powers in Olympus. And yet they could only offer one reprieve. *You will be given a choice, and it is only in that moment that your fate may change. Until then it is others that control your destiny.* I stare at the mere human whose sole purpose is to tend to me. She has sacrificed for my comfort in the last decades. I have been the most important work of her life, and I know she feels as if I am being taken from her.

Beatrice glances downward, but brings her eyes back to mine as she speaks again. "Have you told your mother?"

Have I told her? Have I gone to the gardens where she spends her days providing harvest and generously giving and giving to the earth realm? She raised me in those gardens, protecting me like she would protect her own heart.

My mother provides so easily. A single prayer is all she needs and abundance reigns for anyone who thinks to whisper her name, Demeter. That is power I thought I could inherit.

She has never had to fear being cast out from Olympus. The people who pray to her are right to love her, because she can *give.*

I hear the prayers of those who call to me for life, and I can do nothing.

"I have not gone to my mother. It is not a conversation I look forward to having with her." What would she think of me losing my powers? She did everything she could to protect me and guide me, so the fault must be mine.

"Your mother is a great goddess," Beatrice says quietly. "She may be able to offer you wisdom." She stands in her black robe with the lights from the candle still flickering around her in the foyer of my quarters.

"Why do you press me about my mother so?" I question her. "It is not like you to be so vocal."

The smallest pause tells me that Beatrice is choosing her words with great care. She has always spoken carefully but now she weighs every word as if it is the last time we will speak to each other.

"There was something in my cards today," she begins. "A relationship of sorts that would ease your worries." Tarot. The divinity that she seeks is not unlike the Fates.

"Perhaps it is you, Beatrice." I do not need the cards to tell me that. Beatrice has always eased my worries.

She huffs a short laugh as if my interpretation is ridiculous. "I am only human, my lady."

"Do not discredit the power of magic," I tell her, though there is a certain irony in it, as I am the one losing my powers. I do not think magic will save me. It will not save me in time to preserve my place here. If anything does come of magic, it will come too late. The Fates have told me such.

Beatrice sighs. "If only I were of cunning descent. But alas."

"All magic can be learned. I know." I say this without feeling. My powers are weakening by the day, not growing stronger. If there was a cure to find in magic, certainly I would have found it.

"All magic can be learned," Beatrice agrees, in a far more hopeful tone than mine. "You could always turn to magic, my lady. The gods are gifted, but magic is for all of us."

Again I scoff at her answer. "Allow the possibility of magic working," she says. "That is all you must do. Simply allow it."

It hurts to hear her have faith. Hope is the long way of saying goodbye.

"I used to think magic was for children. But then I learned of the gods. You taught me anything is possible."

My throat tightens and I'm unable to answer as I pass her candles with care and make my way to the cream silk settee. As I relax on it, attempting to ground myself, Beatrice continues.

"As long as there have been humans, there has been magic. Love spells were the first, weren't they?"

"Mmm...they're the first written, but I imagine there were others who did not write their intention," I tell her with ease.

"I read the book from Egypt, the oldest book of

magic in Coptic," she says with delight. I imagine it was offered to Hecate; the mother of witchcraft would have such delight with such things.

"And did you learn any spells?" I ask her, genuinely curious.

"There was one for love, but I do not think I crave to use it."

I take her statement in, and I do not know what possesses me to speak at the moment, but I say my thoughts with hopelessness. "I am not much different from mortals, I think."

Beatrice comes to sit beside me, the settee creaking slightly. "You are the daughter of Zeus, king of the gods, and Demeter, goddess of the harvest. The divine is within you."

The last of the day's sunlight fades outside of Olympus as the wary seconds pass. It is no less grand in the dark. Milky shadows and gold lamplight decorate the walls in my rooms. There is endless grandeur outside my windows, the sky and the clouds paying constant tribute to my father. They even honor my mother, who uses her gifts above them and below. They do not honor me. Soon I will be like a flower in a mortal garden, alive only for a short time and offering only a pleasant thing to look at. Beauty is not enough for me to keep my place in Olympus.

"You are not like mortals," she says so convincingly.

"Yet they pray to me to bring life," I say, my frustration growing. "And I fail them."

"They pray because you will bring it." Beatrice puts a comforting hand on my arm. I wish I could take more comfort from it, but all the signs I have seen point to the forest and loneliness. There will be no other place for me. These rooms will not be mine. This place on Olympus will not be mine. "Magic takes time," she says as if it is an answer.

"No." I stare Beatrice in the eyes, and she looks back at me, her mouth set in a line. "They pray because the prophecy foretold my powers. We all know what is foretold does not always come true."

"If that is so, then today is not set in stone, is it?"

It's hard to accept her denial when I can feel it in my bones.

"You are able to bring life," she says, her voice steady.

"Not the life they pray for."

"Another kind, then. There are many kinds of life among the gods and mortals. Show me what you can do, my lady."

My fingertips itch to show both her and me that it is not all drained from me.

"Flowers," I say, reaching for a pot at the windowsill. Even this does not come easily to me now. My fingers rise and I motion in short strokes to raise the seed up. I make a single sprout rise from the pot of earth. It does not seem to want to grow and the small flower that opens has thin petals. "Flowers like this. They are not what people get on their knees to ask for. This is not the life they want from me. Their loved ones no longer breathe, and these flowers cannot help them."

"That is the cycle." Beatrice folds her hands back in her lap and looks at the flower like it means something to the people who ask for my blessing. "And they are for Hecate."

She reminds me this of late. The cycles and that they are for the keeper of the keys, the other side of Hecate. She bears so many talents. The mother. The maiden. And the crone.

"You love Hecate. She is your goddess, not me."

"I love you."

"Pray to someone who can bless you," I tell her, my throat suddenly thick. Beatrice puts her arms around me in an embrace. Her strength is powerful in doing so. I have needed more of her embrace, and I do not know what I will do without Beatrice's warmth and advice. I'm not prepared to be cast out and alone, but no one ever is.

"What is it, my lady? It is not only the prophecy. It cannot be. Did you dream again? If you did, you should have come to me. I would have lit candles for you and stayed with you in the night."

I did dream. It was more than a dream, though. It was a night terror. I was terrified, it is true, but there is something else I do not want to admit to Beatrice. I do not want to admit that in the darkness of that dream I felt thrilling curiosity.

Chills run down my spine and legs all the way to my toes.

"Is that what it is?" She rubs soothing circles on my back, a sign of our closeness. Only the most favored servants may touch the gods and goddesses they serve. Or maybe it is not a sign of closeness, but of how far I have fallen. I will be less than a mortal soon. I will be wandering among the trees, and no one will pray to me. If they do, their pleas will not find me. That is the most upsetting of all.

Beatrice tells me, "I will do a spell for clarity and another for peace."

It will not chase the dream away and…

I do not want her to remove the callings that come to me at night. There is something there.

Because I am not alone in the dream. There is a man in the shadows, with power beyond imagination, even for me. I want to know more about him. I should not have wanted to know, because curiosity like that is dangerous. My mother taught me that long ago. And still, I desire to go to him. To speak to him. To look into his eyes.

There is a calling I cannot deny.

I cannot say if it is his power I feel so drawn to or because I cannot see all of him in the shadows. My mother spent a great deal of time in my early years warning me away from dark thoughts and dark places. Those kinds of places have power, even in Olympus. I listened to her words and took them to heart, but when the dreams began, I could not resist.

Maybe that is why she warned me. Maybe she knew how it would feel to see those shapes in the dark and crave knowing more about them. For a short time, it gives me something to think about other than the loss of my power. It gives me a strange kind of hope. It could be that I am grasping at straws, but I have little else to grasp.

"What is your terror concerning?" Beatrice asks me.

"I don't remember anymore," I answer, feigning disconcert.

It is a lie. I will never forget a second of what comes to me in the night. Certainly not him.

chapter 2

Hades

FROM THE LARGEST WINDOW OF THE TALLEST of towers, in my privacy I can look out over the realms of the Underworld. Its arched facade is picturesque as I gaze onto all that I rule. Every soul I've met and assigned their fate resides beneath me.

I know of the rumors about the place where I dwell. Some of them have a kernel of truth. There are realms where souls go to be tormented, tortured, and live forevermore in pain and agony of thoughts they can never escape. There are realms filled with many fears from their mortal lives—fire and darkness and hunger and cold. Tartarus is one in which screams carry across miles. The mortals that conceive of hell would recognize those places, and some might even say that that is all the Underworld is.

They are wrong. Not every soul deserves to be

tormented. Most souls are far more innocent than they know. When souls are judged, some of them deserve peace in the Underworld. Elysium lies on the other side of my world. There are realms with fair weather and greenery and other souls to smile at, to live in harmony with, and to want for nothing. Where peace is the only existence. My court has made many judgments and the number of people who deserve hell is far smaller than the number who deserve heaven. As it should be, souls enter the Underworld through the River Styx, are judged, then meet their fate. Some may venture to the mortal realm, daring to risk where their judgment will lead them next...but only once they pass through the field that erases their memories.

I cannot do this alone, but my word is judgment. I am just, and my decisions righteous.

The others who decide fates are considerate. But though they are the ones to weigh the deeds of the souls before them, this is my realm, and thus my final authority. It is my responsibility to see that they are not too quick to choose. In the realms that stretch out before my window in shadow and light, there are many regions for souls to go, and it is ultimately my decision to let them continue or change their judgments.

All souls will cross my path, and I will find justice for each and every one of them.

I know my judges took the necessary time. I know how it passes. Other gods choose to ignore the way ages rise and fall, but I do not. I see how it shapes the souls that come to stand before my judges. What they've been through and their perceptions do not always save them from the hells of this place, but I grant mercy where I can find it.

Many of the judges are wise, with experience behind the morality they find they must do. There is no greater evil in them, but they've have more time and made more decisions. That is the way of life for mortals.

They come, they go. Their souls remain for centuries. Very few destroyed. That is for the Fates, the three who clip the golden threads.

As I know, my grip on the iron rail tightens, I do not rule alone, but I am king of the dead, ruler of the Underworld.

And in this room of stone and fine cloth that covers the furniture, with dim lights from torches that crackle with the hiss of fire, I find myself quite lonely. I find time to be stagnant, moving yet not changing. I find this task that I've been given to be one of my own hell. One I will never escape either.

Because we are all given what we deserve.

Although one soul who was judged today would undoubtedly disagree. His screams echo off the ancient walls as I close my eyes and search for it. Most of the sounds can be ignored, as they are only the sounds of souls carrying on in the Underworld.

Other sounds are reassurance that the worst souls who have been delivered to me are where they belong. They are a comfort to me as well as a reminder of what

I suffered, though I do not allow my thoughts to travel to those memories if I can help it. The Titans ruled with pain and unjustly ruled with greed and sloth. They are no more and as I remember the pits I came from, I shut down the tortuous memories of solitude and craze. There is no need at the moment. Not when I am reflecting on another day of judgments and another day of ruling all that is mine.

If all goes according to my plans, more will be mine in a short time. I am not often impatient, but now that I am so close, it is impossible to ignore.

Because of her. Because of the one soul I must have. She must be mine in every way.

A creak behind me pulls my thoughts away from the stream of souls into the Underworld and back to my rooms.

"Fair and just, am I not?" I say and turn. I knew from how Minox's footsteps ricocheted with a heavy weight that it would be him, and it is. Minox is one of the three judges of the dead and my right-hand man. I trust him above all others. His black robe moves around him for a moment after he stops and inclines his head. The hood covers most of his face except his sharp, brightly shining, black eyes. When he is motionless, it is harder to distinguish him from the shadows around him. In contrast, the guard he has brought with him is much more visible. This is not because the guard wears bright clothing, but because he does not have the patience to remain still before me. He tries, but he fidgets.

"My lord. Zeus beckons you." His voice blends with the shadows, too. His timbre deep and his tone barely heard. Many souls who stand before Minox fear him for this reason, but there is more to fear from a person who pretends to be something they are not.

"And what for?" I ask, arching a brow and daring the god of thunder, the king of gods, and the ruler of Mount Olympus to call me. His arena is quite the opposite of mine. For he may play in the mortal realm, but I rule after death and for all eternity.

With that thought, I watch more souls step foot on the Asphodel Fields.

Minox's eyes flicker to mine, but they do not stay on my face. Perhaps he did not look at all. It could be a trick of the light. "He would not say."

"I cannot leave." I raise my hand in a dismissal of these summons toward both of them, knowing that the guard will understand my meaning and begin to turn back to the window. "But send word that I will scry this evening," I add and adrenaline races through me.

I know very well what he craves.

"My lord." Minox's voice stops me. I turn back to him, my hackles rising. Minox has the standing to disagree with me, if he wishes. I count on him to do so when he believes it is necessary. But I do not care for the tone in his voice. "He stressed that it was urgent."

My eyes narrow as I stare at the man who knows I am his liege.

Irritation burns inside of me, a dull anger at the slowly passing time. I do not relish the feeling.

I answer easily, "There is nothing that cannot wait, and I have little patience left for his beckoning. You may go." I give the command to the guard, not Minox.

In actuality, I have no patience left for his beckoning. Zeus thinks of himself as all-powerful, all-seeing, because he spends his days on Olympus. That is all well and good, but I am not lesser because the Underworld is my domain. There is balance in the realms. One cannot exist without the other. There can only be so many mortals alive at any one time and so many gods. The number of souls never lessens. Our world is finite and includes all life.

When the silence hangs between us, the guard allows an expression of worry onto his face. But he nods, and after a few more moments, he clears his throat. "Yes, my lord."

He turns and leaves. Minox and I listen to his footsteps as they get quieter, then fade to silent. It is a silence I do not entirely trust, though I know what it is supposed to mean. The breeze of my realms makes a quiet sound across the window. I wait, pushing down my irritation. I will not let it get the better of me, other than to send a terse reply to Zeus.

"My lord." Minox is far more careful now than he was before. Others may not be able to hear the minute differences in the way he speaks, but I can. We've spent long enough together for me to discern them. "Is it possible he's privy to your night endeavors?"

"That the gates for the realms have been opened?" I assume. A deal was made, and I took advantage. Finding her in a vulnerable position.

Minox nods.

I am fair and just, but I weigh how much truth I want to give him. If I wanted him to have all of it, my answer would be simple. But there are some things that I cannot let others be privy to, no matter how close they have been over the years.

There are some things that must belong only to me.

Like her. *Persephone.*

Even thinking of her name provides a pleasure to my tongue. The image of her, wanting and needing all that I can do for her, thrills me. Her gorgeous locks around my wrist as I fist her hair and wide eyes begging me for more. I need her on her knees bowing before me and agreeing to all that I desire. She is my one gift to free of me this torture.

Minox has not taken his eyes off me. I know I have not given him the information he wants through my expression. I am too skilled in controlling myself for that.

"Possibly," I finally answer although I cannot know for sure.

He unfolds his hands, then refolds them. I would think it was a nervous gesture if I had not known him so long. Instead, I know it to be a gesture of consideration. He is weighing each of his words, more so than he would for any of the souls he has judged in the days that have come before.

"Is that not an act of war, my lord?"

I allow the smirk to come to my face. "Also possibly." A thrum of delight echoes in my blood. It has been so long since war has cast fear and shadows on all the realms, creating an imbalance in the world. I reminiscence on such freeing times.

More silence spreads between us. I watch Minox standing there with all the familiar shadows of my private rooms behind him.

"Zeus was there for you at the end," Minox ventures. "He took you in when others would not."

Emotion swells in me. It is dark and unwanted, and if I did not have such lengthy experience with it, I might react outwardly. But I do not react in any way that Minox can see, although I feel the memories as vividly as if they were still happening. I spent days in darkness in the pits where my father left me. All of the gods lived a life of blessings, but I was alone for years, nearly going mad.

Perhaps I did venture in madness...perhaps I still lay there in this hour.

That is how I know true torture. Of course there is pain. There is cold and hunger and even burning flesh. But all of those things can be survived. A soul can suffer those things for an eternity as long as they have the hope that it will end and they will have the comfort of other souls again.

I did not have that comfort, and that is why I reserve

isolation for the most vile of souls who come before my judges. I know that pain so well that I cannot inflict it on anyone but the very worst. Those who deserve to fall into madness, hoping for a voice to answer them when none will ever come.

Minox is right. Zeus did come for me in the end. And we triumphed together, along with Poseidon, who rules the seas. Each of us given our own realms and the humans who wander on Earth, merely playthings to the gods.

I feel it now, that hope of something more, swelling sharply in my chest and bringing a tightness to my throat that I cannot tolerate in myself. Not now, when I have enough power to keep all my realms ordered as they should be.

My gaze falls on Minox as if none of the memories had made any impression on me, as if his words had not stirred any feelings within me.

"Zeus would be a fool to wage war over what I am after. There are conversations and deals you are not privy to."

"My lord—"

"You will do as I command, Minox. I will not go to Zeus tonight. Tell the guard to carry my message. I will scry when I am ready."

Minox lets out a barely audible sigh and turns away, heading for the door. He leans out, talking quietly to the guard I knew would be waiting outside. "My lord,"

Minox says from the door and bows. He steps back into the hall to let Cerberus enter the room.

I feel lighter, looking at my companion. His paws pad across the floor to me, all three heads of the beast who is my dog bow before me as he whines for my affection and I bend down to let him put one of his three heads in my hand. The door closes, and I lower down fully to my faithful companion.

"You were there, too, my sweet boy."

I notice the tinge of blood on the muzzles of Cerberus's heads. I wet a cloth and lower myself again to wipe it away. When I have cared for my dog, I glance at the bed that dominates this side of my room. There are new chains attached to the wall nearby.

Cerberus wags his tail, pushing another of his heads into my palm. He has six sets of ears, and he wants all of them scratched and all three of his heads stroked. I indulge him, as I always do.

"I will have my queen, Cerberus." Cerberus lets out a quiet bark as if in agreement. As if he knows of her beauty and her power that will change the world forevermore. I know it in the marrow of my bones. "Anyone who stands in my way, in my realms or any other, will perish at our hands." I continue stroking Cerberus's heads and let my mind wander. From here the screams from the darkest depths of hell are not loud but they are still audible. "I have earned her. She has been promised. She is already mine."

chapter 3

Persephone

THE WALK TO SEE MY FATHER SEEMS TO TAKE much longer than usual. Each step on the marble floors echoes. Every heartbeat seems slower and heavier. I can barely breathe as I make my way to Zeus. King of the sky and god of thunder. I peer out into the clear blue skies and pray it remains such a beautiful shade of cobalt even once our conversation has ended. The anger of Zeus brings about storms that flood with no mercy and lightning that terrorizes the sky.

One breath in. One breath out. My delicate and soft cream sheer gown clings to me as I near my destiny. The organza flutters behind me, as if it wishes to escape. And yet, one foot after the other, I persist.

The opulent halls of Olympus stretch out before me, decorated with gold filigree and archways that look out on a perfect sky and gardens that are always filled with flowers. As I get closer to the heart of the court, more souls cross my path. Servants go about their duties and courtiers speak to one another in low voices. They watch me as I pass, but none says a word to me.

With my head held high, I try to remain calm the closer I get to the main hall. Olympus represents my father's power. Every part of it is a reflection of his place among the gods. Every step I take reminds me that I don't have a place here any longer. It has always been so easy for him to rule, seeming to be so effortless, but no matter how hard I try, I can't keep even the simplest of divine magic. My father is on a pedestal above me, more powerful than I can ever dream of being, and with every second that passes I'm more intimidated by his strength.

It's too quiet as I approach the main hall. As I enter through the wide doorway, I'm proven right. The court is absent of its typical celebrations. In the main hall, Nike is not hovering over Athena. She graces the prestigious seat next to my father who sits with his back straight on his throne, lightning bolts propped beside him, waiting for when he may need such chaos to punish the skies.

The dais and the thrones are the most opulent pieces of the court by far. It looks to have been made from the sun itself, if you could take the sun and fashion it into gold. Aphrodite stands in front of Zeus and Athena. She and Athena are sisters of different mothers, but both of them are stunningly beautiful and so powerful. The goddess of war strategy and the arts and the goddess of love and beauty. Although Aphrodite has also been known as a victor of war herself. I wish I still felt worthy of sitting with them, the way I used to. As their sister and their counter. The goddess of life.

They speak to each other, their voices low, and they do not stop their conversation as I enter. No matter how my heart rages in my chest, they do not seem to hear it nor my steps. I hover near the doorway, not wanting to interrupt, but knowing I have to see my father sooner rather than later. I do not wish to shame him nor do I want pity. I have failed and all will know it soon enough. My exit will be swift, if he will allow. I know my mother will fight for my residence, but I do not want war between the gods. I do not wish her to fight for me. My mother would comfort me, protect me, take care of me, but I don't want pity. I need only her to love me even after I have fled.

My palms sweat from nervousness. Does my father know I am losing my powers? Have the whispers of the Fates found their way to his throne?

I just want to know what I can do to bring my powers back—if there is a quest I may complete. My throat tenses and itches with every syllable of the pleas that wish to be heard. For mercy and a way out that grants grace.

If I were being truthful I would sink to my knees, even here at the doorway, because that is the station I am about to have in life. Without powers I am not worthy to stand in front of my father. I do not interrupt the conversation happening in front of me, thankful for the murderous moments that delay the inevitable and yet dying from them just the same.

Instead, I wait, remembering what Beatrice told me: *be careful of your thoughts. They are more powerful than you can imagine.* I wish I could control them now. But they spiral and I have no way to stop them.

I laughed when Beatrice told me that, but now the memory brings fear to my being. I am too aware of how negative my thoughts have become. The thoughts scare me as well, and standing before my father, I am filled with fear for what is to come.

Their voices move over me as I try to quell my panic. Athena is my father's favorite for all to know. Even if he did attempt to kill her mother while she was carrying her. Fate may be cruel, but my father is crueler at times. And still, he rules and he loves us. Although his love is shown in the most brutal of ways at times. Very much the antithesis of my mother.

Athena rises to her feet, holding her shield as if it weighs nothing. Her thick brunette hair spills down her back, held away from her face by a few gold pins. She plants her feet on the dais and looks Zeus in the eye. Her boots are made of a thick leather fit for war and the plate on her gold chest is as well. It is then her owl swoops down to join her, landing on her shoulder gracefully as he drops her Grecian helmet into her hand.

"If you will not aid me, it will take longer, and more lives will be lost."

I peek up at the dais to see my father raising his

eyebrows at Athena. "That is not a problem for me now, is it? The dead are for the Underworld, and they are welcome there."

"You speak of war, sister?" Aphrodite says, arranging her skirts around her feet. She has lighter hair than Athena, beautiful blonde locks and more delicate features with striking blue eyes. They mirror one another in many ways, such as the shape of their chin, but they differ in others. Aphrodite's eyes are a deeper blue than Athena's and they grow darker still.

Athena only attends to our father. "I will return to Sparta, then."

Aphrodite gives her sister a bit of a smirk.

"Perhaps I'll meet you there," Athena answers Aphrodite's expression with a statement that seemingly dares her to meet on the battlefield. Her tone is not threatening, and Aphrodite only smiles. There is a saying that when the gods play, mortals die. Athena is known as the goddess of right and wrong, but there is so much gray in all the realms. Aphrodite has found beauty in darkness, and Athena knows it. The two of them, when paired together, are unstoppable and a force no one could dare to tame. Yet, at times, they are at odds. Such as when beauty is being judged. For the gods have egos just as mortals do.

"I dare say you should." Athena's smile widens. "You to Athens and I to Sparta?" she offers, a flash in her light eyes. I can feel the power in the room heighten. The deep pull in my stomach as every hair seems to pull on end.

The tension comes in waves. It's an undeniable force in the air.

Lightning clashes above our heads, a flash of bright white aids the loud bang that silences the room. "Enough!"

Zeus holds up a hand, and both sisters look to him as if nothing has happened. As if war is merely an outing for them. A reunion of sorts.

"My daughter of life," my father says. I jerk back from the doorway, realizing too late that he has seen me standing here, listening. My heart stops although his tone is welcoming, as if I am a blessing among the irritation my powerful siblings have brought him. *Perhaps he does not know.* "Join us, my dear."

He beckons for me, and I force myself to move in through the doorway as a servant comes in from the opposite doorway with a silver tray. There are drinks for all of Zeus's daughters. Our goblets heavy on the tray. Owls for Athena, shells for Aphrodite, and blooming roses for me. I step up next to Athena and Aphrodite and take mine, my hands shaking. My father is the last one to accept a drink from the tray. He looks at me as he lifts it into the air.

"Cheers to the balance of the world and to those who keep it," he offers, and all three of us accept. My chalice is a brighter silver than the ones my sisters are holding, as if newly crafted, and I wonder if that is on purpose. It must be. Nothing my father does is without a purpose.

I lift the chalice to my lips and drink the divine wine. It is a sweetness mortals will never know, and I will not know again. My heart beats painfully at the taste. This may be my last toasting with my family. There is no such thing as perfect wine in the land of the mortals. They will never know everlasting life. They will never know the luxuriousness of true divinity. It is sweetness beyond sweetness, something completely pure that could never be created by mortals. It could only be gifted to them by the gods.

I try to hold on to my feeling of belonging, thin as it is, for a few moments more.

"What brings you to my presence?" my father asks me. "Not war, I would hope." He glances at both Aphrodite and Athena as he says this, and the room darkens with the tension. They slip on innocent expressions, but as soon as Zeus looks away, Aphrodite smiles again. They are always at their games. Athena and Aphrodite will never tire of wars and battles and mortal arguments, and they will never run out of time to challenge each other. My sisters are true goddesses.

I take a deep breath. "I've come to ask if I may seek the guidance of the seers."

My father frowns and without moving his gaze from my face, he commands to my sisters, "Leave us."

At his tone, Athena and Aphrodite sweep out of the room, as graceful as could be, murmuring softly to each other as they go. I have no doubt they are back to planning the war they want to wage for a test of their choosing.

Their footsteps quiet and once they are gone my heart hammers in the empty room. My father knows. I am almost sure of it. A pure breeze blows outside the windows of the main hall. I can smell flowers and plants from the gardens, the scents almost as sweet and pure as the wine. The flowers give me as much life as I give them, although in this moment the act feels quite one-sided. It is a scent that will never rot into the ground, merely be absorbed back into the earth of Olympus to grow again.

"You are familiar with the lore," my father says as though it is a question.

I meet his eyes and nod. His silver eyes pierce into me. I am all too familiar with the lore. Sometimes, I wish I did not know as much as I do.

"You know of what's to come," he says, nodding, and I cannot help but to nod as well.

My stomach drops and I struggle to swallow, but I try not to let it show on my face. "I wish for guidance still."

Zeus stares at me for a long time. His knuckles turn white as he clenches his hand one finger at a time as if the movement aids his thought. Even the sounds in Olympus feel fitting to the gods. The wind is quiet and sumptuous and the faint sounds of a saint playing the lyre at a distance can be heard in his pause. It is all perfect, like my father. I am the one who doesn't fit.

"Why are you not with your mother?" he questions rather than granting my permission.

Maybe he does not know. The uncomfortable feeling in my gut intensifies, but I make myself stand up straight and continue to meet his eyes.

"My magic seems to be...fickle. Since I've last gone."

His eyebrows rise again. "Fickle? As in, worse than before?"

Warmth drains from my face, and I force myself to answer, "Yes, Father."

Outside the windows of the great hall, the skies dim and go gray. The clouds morph to rainy and threatening. They roll past, seeming to crowd in on me. I wait anxiously to see if a storm will break out, sending more lightning crashing before his throne.

"It has been months of fading; I seek only guidance."

The clouds darken further but no lightning comes. After a few long minutes they lighten again and the sky returns to its former blue, though it is cloudier than it was before. Tendrils of my hair have been blown across my face by the wind, and I brush them back into place as if I did not notice the change in the weather. Surely others have.

My father shifts on his throne, seeming to come to a decision. "You may seek their guidance once this matter with your sisters and the mortal Helen is dealt with."

"When would that be?" I ask, but he has already turned away from me.

Zeus gazes out the window with a look of

contemplation, like I have not spoken. He ignores my question. This may mean that he does not know, or it may mean that he does not care to answer, or it may mean that it does not matter. "In the meantime, I suggest you practice."

My hands clasp to my chest. I cannot stop myself from doing it. I know it makes me appear nervous, but once they are clasped together in front of my heart, I cannot let them go. My heartbeat pounds under my hands, growing more anxious without control or knowing.

Maybe Zeus can feel my fear in the air, because his face softens as he gazes down upon me from his throne. "Go now, my daughter. Your power will strengthen."

What if it doesn't? I want to ask. *Will you make an exception for me even if my presence is a disgrace among the gods?*

I know he won't, and I know better than to ask the question. With how tight it is, my throat would not allow me to, even if I craved to speak the plea. If I were a child, I might throw myself onto the floor in front of him and cry and beg to be saved. It feels as if some part of me wishes to beg him still, but I withhold. It is one thing for gods and goddesses to have quarrels and arguments among themselves, but it is frowned upon to be weak.

I incline my head to my father and back away several steps before I turn and walk out the door. I will turn to the seers and relay what the Fates have told me as soon as I am able. I do not feel as graceful as Athena and Aphrodite. I envy them for how beautiful they are and how confident they are, but I also envy them for the way they can focus on their games with mortal lives. They never have to worry about losing their powers. Their magic is strong and lasting. They never have to worry that their fate will see them cast out from the only home they have ever known, leaving them only with the hope of survival as a garden nymph…or worse, a mortal.

Slightly defeated, and yet still hopeful, I make my way back toward my rooms using a different path, one that takes me through a quiet set of gardens. Clouds still roll overhead from Zeus's changing mood. The breeze lifts the leaves on the trees as I pass.

I welcome the cool breeze on my face and wonder in its pureness. For I may never experience the feeling quite like this again.

There is a pool of still water to the side of the path. Clouds reflect in it, some of them with the gray bottoms of a thunderstorm. I slow my steps, watching the clouds pass over the water, never touching. That is what my life will be like if I leave Olympus. My home will be like a cloud overhead, reflected in the water of the mortal lands but destroyed with a single touch. The smallest ripple will distort what I can see and my memory will fade, the way a mortal's does.

Between two clouds, a darker shadow shaped like a man forms. I am almost past the pool when I see it out of the corner of my eye. My breath hitches and my body freezes. A chill flows through my bones at the recognition. *It's him.* A voice in the back of my mind hisses. I know it is the same man. I know it's him by the shape of the shadows, even if I can't see his face.

With haste, I walk back along the pool and stop at the center. There are the clouds with their gray bottoms and the sky beyond. There is my own face, waving in ripples on the surface.

I watch the clouds' reflection for several minutes, but there is nothing else there. The man is gone, although whatever feeling has overwhelmed me lingers.

chapter 4

Persephone

In the darkness of the night, only the stars keep me company while I sit under them in the large garden near the courts. I can't sleep and I need answers. My mind circles again and again, trying to uncover something I must have missed. Dead flowers sit limply in the grass before me. I lay my hands on them and try to bring them back to life, to make them bloom again. To do what I have done since only a babe.

And yet, nothing happens. My presence means nothing anymore. No amount of concentration brings a spark of power. Nothing has changed in the hours I've sat here while the stars burn overhead. Watching and wanting just as I do.

My eyes are heavy and so is my heart. My hair has fallen out of its braid, but I cannot bring myself to fix it. Strands blow across my face, and I flip them away listlessly.

I came out here with the idea that there would be a miracle. Some of my power would return. Alone in the dark, I would find the source of my power again. I would be able to make a flower return from the dead. I would not let it sink into Olympus to become another seed. It would be mine.

But, as the last hours have proven, I cannot. There is no power that remains. I feel like I may cry, but even crying doesn't seem to have much point to it now. What would tears do? My tears hold no power of their own. I cannot weep over the flowers and expect them to bloom again.

I am a fallen goddess, that is how the stars will remember me.

I rest my chin on my knees and stare at the wilted blooms in the moonlight. There is still beauty in them, I cannot deny, but it exists without me. My mind wanders to what will become of the gardens when I'm gone, but I know my mother, the goddess of abundance and crops will provide for mortals. My tricks that bring smiles to young girls and beauty to plain pastures may be missed, but gardens will flourish if only my mother is asked.

Even those dead flowers have more power than I do. They can become something else, someday. They can form into seeds and grow again without my help. Olympus can carry on in its power and grandeur without me, as it did long before I was born and as it will long after I die as a nymph.

"My daughter."

My mother's voice startles me and I sit upright, a hand on my chest. She stands in the garden with her white silk robe falling gently around her feet and a wrap around her shoulders. She smiles down at me with slight wrinkles surrounding her eyes, like she is happy to see me out here in the garden in the middle of the night. I smile back at her but can only manage a small one.

"Come sit with me." My mother offers me her hand, and I take it and rise from the ground. Her touch is air-like yet powerful. Instantly warmth and comfort surround me. The goddess Demeter is known to comfort, to provide, and to give to those who have little to offer. She is gracious and generous to mortals and in this moment, to me. She guides me to a bench by a round pool of cool, clear water. There is nothing reflected in the water now, only the night sky.

We sit side by side on the bench. "I will plait your hair," my mother says, her voice warm. "As I once did."

Her fingers slide through my hair, undoing the tangles gently, and now I feel closer to tears than I did before. My mother plaits my hair like no one else does. She is balanced like no one else is. She is essential to the way of life with gods and mortals. All is balanced with life and death, old souls and new, those who believe and those who question, the good and the bad. All of it is needed, and when there is balance, there is peace among the gods and with the hands of fate.

Perhaps what is needed is for my powers to dim. Maybe I should surrender and trust in the universe. Tears prick and I remind myself: *Breathe in. Breathe out.*

Demeter is a giving god. She gives easily to the mortals. As goddess of the harvest, she brings a wealth of fortune and provides for many without asking for anything in return. She nurtured me as her most precious gift along with my sister, Chrysothemis, who is also a goddess of the harvest. I have never lived a day without love. And as my mother says, it is the most powerful of all.

My mother begins to braid my hair and makes a soft sound of laughter. "I remember when you were only so tall." She motions with her hand and then returns her fingers to my hair. "You loved the flowers in your hair. You'd grow them only to scoop them up and beg your sister to share them with you, pleading with her to add them to her hair."

"I remember." My throat is tight with how vividly I remember my power. It came easily to me then, and I thought it would never leave. I thought life would always flow effortlessly from my fingers like my mother's power. I thought it was my birthright.

There was no worry. Why should there have been? Nothing in my life had ever pointed to any kind of loss. Now the days are filled with naught but worry.

"I remember the way you laughed," my mother says and sighs, the sound happy. She braids my hair with a gentle touch, exactly the way she used to when I was a child. I close my eyes and imagine I am still a child, still with all my powers, still with eternity ahead of me. Inside, deep within my belly, I swear my power swells with the memory. It is only a moment, but I feel it, and my chest warms with hope until the feeling is lost. My mother finishes braiding my hair and wraps it, her fingers working deftly. She makes no mention of the dead flowers, although they lay plainly ahead of us.

"Mother." She pats at my hair, then rests her hand on my shoulder. I do not turn to face her, but I open my eyes. I search the pool with its reflection of the sky for a man-shaped shadow, but there is nothing there now.

"Yes, Daughter?" she questions as if she does not know, but surely my mother is well aware of my demeanor.

My mother waits patiently, the same way she waits for her crops to mature. She does not rush them along. That is not their way, she tells me. For life knows ebbs and flows. But that is not all of the truth. Some gods know only fruitfulness, in part due to my mother's graciousness.

"What if I wish to be reborn?" I dare to ask in a whisper.

My mother stills. I listen to the sounds of the garden around us. It is peaceful at night, like all of the parts of Olympus that rest. There are no celebrations to pour sounds and music into the garden. It is just us and the plants and the sky above in the late night.

"Why would you ever wish such a thing?" my mother asks eventually, her words quickly spoken as if rushed. "You are immortal. You are a goddess."

"Maybe I am not." My voice is tight and the words choked. It feels sinful to speak the words out loud, but there is no choice now. I cannot hold this burden by myself, and I cannot leave it to Beatrice to face alone. I need my mother to know so that she can be prepared for what is to come. "Maybe I am fated to become a forest nymph."

My mother rubs my shoulder and lets out a breath, steadying herself. "Persephone, you will not become a nymph and live in the forest. You will stay here. With me." Her voice is strong and warm, and I want to believe her so badly. I want her to be right. "You should not worry. Worrying is for the weak," she warns, a terse note coming into her voice. "Fate tells us the fears are not for us and to let them be, as I have taught you. As within, so without. So mote it be."

"Then I am weak, Mother." Tears sting my eyes, and I brush them away. My mother pulls me to her side and puts her arm around my shoulders. "I am weak, because I cannot let this fear pass me by."

My mother's hazel eyes shine with unshed tears as her grip on my shoulders becomes desperate. "And why not?" she asks. "Why not simply let the worry go, it is not for you. You are for the heavens and there is nothing for you to fear. I promise you that, my child. If only you believe me, you will never leave my side. I promise you."

"Because it is already here...the lore." I lean against

her and tell my mother about my faltering powers and how I cannot bring the flowers back to life, and I cannot make things grow the way I should be able to. I tell her about how something is missing in me. Something has gone wrong, and I do not belong on Olympus. The Fates have told me so. I tell her I do not know how to stay.

She listens without judgment, although her eyes are wide with the newly found burden, rubbing her hand up and down my arm and looking out at the small lights in the garden. They look like stars or fireflies. Even in the dark, the garden appears perfect, like the rest of Olympus. Even in the dark, I feel I do not belong here. When I turn to look at my mother in the moonlight, there is sadness in her eyes, but still, she does not judge me.

I take another breath, all of the words spilled out of me at her feet. "If mortals in Elysium and all that is heaven can choose rebirth, why can we not so I may have another chance?"

My mother frowns, a crease appearing in her forehead. She turns, unwraps my hair, and wraps it again, the motion an old habit that will hopefully soothe us both. "I cannot comprehend why mortals choose rebirth. What boredom there must be to leave all that is luxury."

"Perhaps it's about a second chance," I suggest. "About being able to do it all over, but with more of what you're after."

If I were reborn, I would never take my powers for granted. I would practice constantly to keep them at my fingertips. I would learn what they meant earlier, before I started to lose them. I would do everything I could to stay in Olympus.

My mother is silent for a little while. She rises from the bench and walks over to where a patch of flowers grows, picks several, and brings them back to weave them into my hair. This was my favorite part as a child. It made me feel like I was being crowned as a goddess, though I already knew I was one. It made me feel like a queen from one of the old stories.

"I've never heard you speak this way." My mother finishes patting the flowers into place and turns my head this way and that, looking over her work. She releases my face and waves her hand, replenishing the garden with mature sunflowers. It is nothing to her. The stems thicken and grow beneath her finger tips. That is how great her power is, and I could not bring one flower back from the dead. She takes both my hands in hers. "You do not need second chances, my love. For what has happened was meant to happen, and what will be already is."

I stare at my mother, wishing she could understand the fear in me, but knowing that she won't. She is too convinced that our fates are set in stone, and there is nothing we can do to change them. She believes what she wants to believe. And the universe has never dared to challenge her like it challenges me now.

"Thank you for braiding my hair, Mother," I tell her, and I smile instead of pleading with her to understand.

My mother smiles back at me and smooths my

hair with her hand. "Sleep well and know you are always loved." She kisses my forehead, and I can feel her love. The bond between us as mother and daughter is still strong, and in it, I feel a spark of power. "Will you come inside with me?"

"A few minutes," I tell my mother. I want to breathe here in the moonlight and try build as much of a memory as possible. If I am to become a nymph, I want to remember this garden at night, sitting on the bench with my mother, and knowing how it felt to have her fingers in my hair.

She rises from the bench next to me and kisses my forehead one more time.

"Everything will be all right, my daughter. You are meant to be my counter. You have power. Know it is so." Her hand skims my hair, and then I can feel that she is walking away, moving the air as she goes. Her footsteps are soft in the garden, but I know when she is gone and I am alone again.

How can I leave Olympus? How can I live somewhere else? How can I accept what is going to happen if none of it was my choice?

I will find a way, somehow. If my mother has reminded me of anything, it's that. I will find a way, because whether goddess or mortal, that is what is left to us if the Fates are decided. We must find our own place in it.

Even if we're afraid.

And I am afraid.

I keep my eyes closed until I've convinced myself more of acceptance or at least a path to it.

When I open my eyes, there is something new in the moonlight.

I can see it there, and at first I think it may be a trick of the light, my mind convincing me that something is there when it is not. But when I blink, it stays, so I stand from the carved quartz bench and walk toward it, my heart in my throat.

There is something there after all. A small, budded flower peeking above the earth at the end of the row of sunflowers. I bend down and brush my fingers over the dewy petals.

It is real.

A light sparks within me and that small bit of the divine burns in my belly.

My powers are not yet gone. There is still hope. Part of me craves more of it, part of me wishes it would pass and grant me mercy from this torture.

chapter 5

Hades

My andron is a massive room made from polished obsidian with high ceilings, every inch of it gleaming and black. We head to it now and every step draws closer an anxiousness for the night to be done with. The energy is exceptional and the power it gives me is undeniable. It will be empty tonight. It's nearly always vacant unless there is some cause for festivity or a pertinent meeting that cannot wait for the courts. It is the part of my home that's farthest from my rooms and closest to the Underworld, the most public place I can be. It is a place reserved for conversations such as these, which I would rather not hold in my private rooms. I want to be able to leave them behind when they are finished, though I know I cannot really force them out of my thoughts.

I go by way of an outside path, choosing to divide

myself from my private spaces with a walk. The path is empty, as the andron will be. The ground beneath my feet gleams with the flash of silver, though not as smoothly as the floor of the andron. There is no sound other than the air that moves in a mimicry of mortal wind. Through the silence, I can hear all of my realms and all the souls, if only I choose to listen.

Silence is mostly preferred these days, when my thoughts are preoccupied with the image of *her*.

There is no life in the Underworld apart from the souls. Nothing of new life can be made where the dead linger. In Olympus, at the bottom of the ocean where Poseidon rules, and even on Earth where there are only heroes and those sent by the gods for purposes that vary, life can be made. It can be brought forth from the other realms including the Underworld. But the same is not true here. There is a strict tally of souls who come and go, and it is balanced and righteous.

I walk on a path of crushed obsidian that crunches under my boots. My presence breaks the sharp shards as I go, turning it to dust beneath my feet.

"My lord, I will do as you bid," Minox reminds me in the cold night.

With my throat tightening and the black hooded cloaks we wear fluttering in the bitter wind, I do my best to contain my frustration. It will not be helpful to approach this conversation already angry, though I'm not pleased to be summoned by Zeus as if I have the time he does. It's irritating that he keeps his reasons from me as if I am some servant to be ordered to do his bidding. There is a chance, however small, that Minox was right, and I am making trouble for myself by refusing to go to him, but I cannot bring myself to care.

I have already found a way to get what I desire most, and neither Zeus's approval nor his help is required. Surely his ego will be bruised, but I have not time nor energy for consoling such things.

We enter the andron through a side door, foregoing the massive public entrance at the front. The space is empty, as I knew it would be, and cold as the obsidian it's made from. Any shout here would echo off the ceiling, but I do not shout or call. There is no one to call, and I lost that habit long ago.

My reputation is one that denotes I am ice cold, calculated, lacking compassion and empathy at times, but balanced and just. Perhaps my role requires villainy, but I prefer the title of an iron-fisted king.

I take a few moments alone in the emptiness, standing still as the wind blows easily from the outside, and the draught provides a comfort to soothe the eagerness of what is to come. Patience has long been my friend and yet now in this time of need it seems to betray me. I left Cerberus in my rooms. It is only Minox and I who will hear the conversation tonight.

Minox pauses just inside and inclines his head. "My lord."

"Minox, let us get on with it." He's partially aware of what has transpired. He need not know the details. It is only his role to obey. The scar that lines his left cheek flashes with the light that reflects from the obsidian.

He does not say anything further as we walk to the far end of the room. There is a large grate there, taller than I am, and as we draw near I raise my hand to it, commanding the warmth and the flames of divination. A fire springs up in it, the flames flickering orange and black. Smoke gathers above them and floats out toward us, and it only takes a moment for the smoke to congregate in the shape of Zeus's face.

I wave it away with a scowl. It is not the fire I have come here for but the mirror beside the grate. From a distance it appears as black as the walls around us, but when I am close, the darkness begins to dissolve, and it takes the appearance of a common mirror with edges etched in a herringbone pattern.

Minox does not stand behind me, so he cannot be seen in the reflection, only me. My reflection is dim. The mirror has gathered its own smoke, and as it drifts away, it reveals a room in Olympus.

Like most places in Olympus, it is stark white with pale blue details. The mirror makes it look darker than it is, which is a pure, blinding white, as if to remind everyone who looks at it that Olympus is closer to the sun and sky. It does not seem to matter to anyone that the Underworld is just as vast. It is not as if the sky and sun would be in balance without the Underworld. It is not as if anything would continue in the ways it should without all realms.

Zeus steps into view and takes his seat on a throne of quartz, looking at me through the mirror. "Hades." His demeanor lacks warmth, and I return the sentiment.

"Zeus."

He may think of himself as above me. He may be above me, as far as the heavens are concerned. But the two of us are equals. It would be wise of him to remember that.

He toys with his beard as his wrinkled eyes narrow at me. His build is sizable as is his scepter that he taps along the floor. The clang of it echoes slightly in the background. His leather cloak dons the aegis.

"I hope all is well in the Underworld," he says in an even tone.

"It is," I answer simply.

He's not asking if everything is well in the Underworld. He is asking if I want to provide him with a reason for not rushing off to meet him at his command. I do not give him one. We look at each other through the mirror for several beats.

Eventually, Zeus comes to the conclusion that I will not be indulging his curiosity any further and straightens in his chair.

"What we have discussed prior," Zeus begins, "it appears time may be on your side."

My blood runs cold at his admission.

"Is that so?" I ask, adding a feigned curiosity.

"You do still wish for her?" he questions, and I nod.

The vision of Persephone clearly invades my mind and every thought.

"Is this the reason you summoned me?" I ask.

"It is," he says, this time a smile carving slightly on his face.

The conversation continues as it has for the last months, and I lie my way through it. I have found other means to acquire the goddess. He does not need to know, for if he did, all of my plans would be ruined. He does not know what I've done and the depths of my betrayal.

By the time Olympus fades from the mirror, it feels like the fire is no longer in the grate. I burn with anger instead. I stand before the mirror and watch the surface, waiting for my own demeanor to calm.

I am so close to attaining her. So close to a desire I've never felt before. So close...and yet Zeus nearly hindered my plans.

Minox moves closer, his concern apparent in his slower-than-usual steps.

"My lord—"

"Not here."

Not in this room. I need time to gather myself before I speak. Before my command is given in haste. I lead the way out of the andron. Minox walks by my side on the obsidian path. His footsteps make far less noise than my own, though I am far closer to the edge of madness than he is. Anger does not help me keep my realms in balance, and it does not help me remain fair and just, but denying it is as much of a problem as letting it rule me.

I let my fury simmer on the way back to my private rooms as we walk in silence, and the faint screams, cries, and prayers are muted in the back of my mind. He strides behind me through the halls; the guards straighten when they see me coming. The servants scatter, making themselves unseen. Most of what I see are shadows disappearing around corners. It is better that they keep their distance, at least for the time being. I imagine the air itself is thick with my rage.

Finally, back in my private rooms, Minox closes the door and I am more at peace with the decision.

"Cerberus."

My dog's footsteps pitter on the floor as he comes to me, his tail wagging and the ears on all three of his heads raised in excitement, as if I was gone for days and not less than an hour. I kneel on the floor and pet each of his heads in turn, scratching each of his ears. His breath is warm on my face in contrast to the icy anger I feel and gradually I regain control of it. Cerberus shakes his body, delighted with getting so much attention, and I rise to my feet.

Cerberus walks at my side to the windows overlooking my realms. He howls for the edge of all things so he may guard the gates as he so loves to do. He sniffs the air, and I know all too well he craves a run to gather the lost souls.

Minox trails behind me, still silent and waiting. He steps to my other side, and we look out at the realms together.

When I speak, it is not out of the anger I felt in the andron or the desperation that still clings no matter how I try to deny it. It is simply the command needed.

"It is time."

Minox unfolds his hands and refolds them again. "My lord?"

He offers me a moment to change my mind or to clarify. But there is nothing that can stop me from what comes next.

"Tonight she will be mine." I turn to stare into his gaze, "Take her tonight."

"Lord Hades." He turns to look at me, his dark eyes large in his pale face. "Do you mean...? We are ignoring what Zeus—"

"Go in the night and stay in the shadows." I cut him off, unable to dim my rage toward the god of thunder. Tension grows between us as Minox waits for the inevitable. "Seize her."

He is silent to a count of five, unfolding and refolding his hands twice in that time.

I add in an easy tone, "It is an act of war, Minox. You will surely be murdered and tortured if caught."

He looks me directly in the eyes. "I will speak of nothing if I am caught. I will kill myself before such things are possible."

With our eyes locked, I give him a nod.

"Hell awaits you if you are caught," I say. "All of the heavens when you return with my Persephone." I stare off into my realm and whisper, "My soon to be queen."

chapter 6

Persephone

If Beatrice can do this, so can I. A mere mortal. Surely even if I am losing the divine I was born with, magic can aid in my time of need. My mother speaks of it, as has my confidant, Beatrice. And I've seen the powers that have come to her, the blessings she's wished for, and the gifts granted with ease after her rituals.

If it works for her, it will not betray me. The spell I cast will work and my worries will be put at ease.

Those are the thoughts I hold close in my mind as I gather the necessities for the simple spell and carry them to the low altar, the glass clacking as I go. My thoughts are fixed on that altar and on magic, though I do not want to think too far into the coming days.

There is still hope.

My doubts are soft at first. They creep in like weeds

in a garden, growing under the soil and in the night before one knows that they've put down roots. By the time they sprout, they have gone much deeper into the earth than it first appears.

The doubts in my mind sprout like those weeds, budding above the earth and bursting into my mind in full bloom.

What happens if this spell goes wrong? The phrasing on this spell is not specific, nor does it include the true reason behind its workings or even the true reason for its casting, as my particular need is unique.

There is another fear among the others I had not expected to face.

What happens if the spell goes *right?*

What happens if my power comes back in a firestorm that grows beyond my wildest imagination, and it causes great attention and my father's wrath?

A shiver passes through me.

Even with my intentions focused as they are, I cannot predict the outcome. My mother's warnings scream in the back of my head. *Be careful of your thoughts.* Magic happens with a dollop of humor. It is often delivered in a way you weren't expecting and could never have predicted. You'll get what you want, but how and what else comes with it is often unexpected... not always in delighted ways.

Magic is a little like planting an unknown seed in a fertile patch of dirt. One will not know the shape of the flower or the color of its petals until it blooms. One must wait for the greenery to peek above the earth and show itself. One can only hope that the outcome will be good, but there is no guarantee in gardening. It could result in the infestation of shrubbery that shades and smothers the other flowers in the garden. But the seed that you planted will rise. And isn't that what you asked for? What was prayed for even?

There is no guarantee in magic, either.

I arrange the items carefully on my altar, touching each one as if it is something precious. It *is* something precious. The crystals and candle I have brought with me are a part of my magic, just as the altar is. The obsidian sphere is small but mighty, a gift from someone long ago that I cannot remember. The small bottle of smokey quartz chips sits next to it, and as the tips of my fingers brush against it, I pray for the ease of burdens on my mind.

Just as the space around me dwells in magic. Just as I dwell in magic. It is part of me, and I am part of it, too.

"If Beatrice can do this, I can as well," I say softly, letting my mother's certainty smooth my voice. I repeat what she always says, "For the good of all and to the harm of none, I am divinely guided, divinely protected, and I pray to you now and thank you for the blessings you bestow upon me."

I sit on the floor close to the low altar. Seated this way, I am as near as I will ever be to the mortal world and centered within the heart of Olympus. For a flicker of a moment I can feel the prayers from those in the mortal realm, the cries and pleas for me to aid them, and I vaguely wonder if they start their asking with the same quote. And yet I know I have no power to grant their prayers. The thought is only a flicker of a moment, faster than the light of the white candles and it's gone, vanished as I send it away. It is no more that I cannot answer them. "It is no more," I whisper.

I breathe in deeply, feeling the warmth of the air all around me. The safety of my chambers and the safety of my home. I concentrate until I can feel the light of the stars and moon shining through my window.

Then I lay my hand over the crystals positioned to the right side of the altar, the amethyst for power and black tourmaline for protection. Both rough to the touch and yet a soothing balm to my soul.

The heat from my palm seeps into the stone.

My first thought is that it's living heat, seeping into a dead thing. But that isn't right. The crystals are alive, just as I am. They don't have a heartbeat or veins or blood, but they have energies within them, energies that connect to the oldest parts of the world. To before I was born, and they will survive me.

I whisper, "I connect to the void that existed even before there was a world. I am part of the universe, and the universe is magic. I am magic."

I close my eyes and concentrate on the warmth transferring from my palm to the stone. Light transferring to darkness. My head falls back just slightly as a warmth grows in my womb. A dash of power resonates through me as I focus on it, feeling the pleasure of it all.

That is how magic transferred to me when I was formed and born. The universe transferred its magic to me, and I lived, and I breathed, and I was magic. Magic existed long before I was created, and I will dwell in it for as long as I live.

I imagine lighting the unlit wick of the candles that lay on the altar, darkness flaring into heat. It's a transfer of energy, like the same transfers that have been made many times before. I only need to allow it.

Beatrice's words echo in my memory. *The divine is within you.*

"The divine is within me," I repeat out loud. If that is so, then I should not need Beatrice to light candles for me. I should be able to light them myself with my own divinity. I need not tell anyone else of the dreams or the darkness within them. The light is within me as much as the darkness in my dreams.

"The divine is within me," I say again, allowing strength to come to my voice. "It has always been within me. I will allow it to dwell in me and flow from me to the wick. The divine is within me and with me, and I can bring light to the darkness." I do not dare to peek and see if the candles are lit.

Allow for the possibility.

For the first time since I became aware of the fading of my powers, the possibility is there before me. I focus on it growing and I feel it pulse through me, like blood in my veins.

I am a goddess. Not a garden nymph or a nymph of the forest. Not a pale echo of my mother. Not powerless at all. But filled with the power of warmth and light.

"Protect me from all things that wish me harm. Guide me to safety for my powers. Whatever ails me, cannot reach me any longer." I repeat the incantation over and over.

I envision my powers, the life that I grant and the beauty I've aided in. "Bring forth my powers to be my highest self."

Beauty burns in the dark when there is nothing else. Life burns in the cold world when it should not survive. Hope may be the long way to say goodbye, but it is also a way of saying hello.

"I release all that ails me and it releases me as well. There is nothing that will stand in my way from being my most powerful self." A shiver runs through me and I open my eyes. In the dark of my room, the starlight shining through the window, the unlit candle stands before me. It's stoic and straight, its wax still whole. My candle and the altar and me—we are all surrounded with the warmth of magic and the power of the gods.

It is warmest within me.

"It will be warmest within me," I say, giving voice to my hope. Hope must be nurtured as well. I must not let it wither and die.

I will not let it wither and die.

I inhale. Power and magic exist all around me. All I need to do is allow for the possibility. The possibility of a simple transfer. The possibility of ease, like letting water droplets fall from my fingertips into a pool. I can always get more crystal drops of water. The water has been plentiful all my life, and it has belonged to me all this time.

I blow gently on the wick, hope thick in my throat and beating in my breast.

The candle does not light. Inhaling deeply, I ignore the pain in my chest and the doubt that preys upon my thoughts.

"It is warmest within me."

I breathe again, not allowing any more weeds of frustration to creep into my mind. That power still exists. I believe it exists. I believe it exists in me, and I can allow this to happen.

No—I know it exists. I know it in my bones. I know it like I know the solidity of the floor beneath me. This is the cycle. This is hope and perseverance. This is refusing to let death have its way.

This is faith in the gods, but it is also faith in myself. In me, there is possibility, and that possibility comes from magic itself. It gives itself to me freely. I take it freely. Like water droplets falling from my fingers. Like new buds pushing above the soil. They know the warmth is above them. They never doubt.

I will not doubt.

I do not doubt.

Allow it. *Allow* it. I do not know if what I feel is hope or my powers returning. The two may be the same thing.

I take another breath and add the words of the spell written on the crinkled parchment colored with age. I will guide the magic with words from others who sought protection and growth.

"The power inside me craves the light," I begin, the spell taking on a new resonance as I speak the words. "Bring me the warmth of fire and take from the powers to my right."

I blow on the candle. The faintest ember at the wick glows to life. My breath is caught and goosebumps flow over my skin. The skies darken and I repeat the words more confidently and louder.

"The power inside me craves the light. Bring me the warmth of fire and take from the powers to my right." I blow again, and the ember disappears.

I take a deep breath and hold the feeling of the spell in my mind. It is a protection spell. It is a release. Whatever plagues me will no longer harm me. I will be protected and freed. Protected and freed. I vanquish the harm inside of me. I release it. I guide it out. I stare at the budding flame, and I whisper with every need in me, every fear and anger, every hope and love I have for what I know I'm meant to be.

"The power inside me craves the light. Bring me the warmth of fire and take from the powers to my right."

This time, the flame bursts into life on top of the candle, and hope burns bright in my heart.

"The power inside me craves the light. Bring me the warmth of fire and take from the powers to my right."

Tears brim as the warmth from the flame is felt on my face.

It burns. Light in the dark, spilling a pool of warmth onto my altar. My hands over the crystals cast shadows in the dancing flame.

This is the warmth I felt all around me as I came to my chambers. This is the warmth of magic. This is the warmth that dwells within me and calls the flowers to the sun.

I was so hopeless that I was willing to dismiss Beatrice's words before. But she was right.

The gods are gifted, but magic is for all of us. Allow the possibility of magic working. That is all you must do. Simply allow it.

I heard Beatrice's words, but I did not allow myself to understand. Not until now.

I force my next breath to be steady, even as tears prick my eyes. They are tears of triumph. My hand is warm over the crystals. The flame is hot in the night. My own life runs hot through my veins.

"As within, so without," I say, my voice strong and steady. "I am at peace." I blow out the candle, concluding the spell.

What I do not expect is the chill that sweeps over

me. The sudden drop in my chest. I attempt to grip forward but nothing is there.

Everything plunges into darkness. A sweep of bitter cold bites through me.

It is not the darkness of moonlight through the window, shining smoothly in. It is complete darkness, as if I've lost my sight.

My vision is gone.

I blink, my heart racing and my mind whirling with fear, waiting for it to clear, but it does not. The hairs on the back of my neck stand up. I drag in one breath, then another.

I do not wish to release the panic into the air around me. I do not jump up for fear that I will be lost in my own room. But my heart beats faster, as if the power I called on is too large for my body and too large for my control.

I choke on the panic. I've done something wrong, haven't I? I've done something wrong, and I don't know what it means.

I nearly scream out for help. As if a curse has descended in the wake of my spell.

Did I make myself mortal? Did I blow the last of my powers out of me with my breath? Or have I become even more immortal? Have I become something new?

The thoughts race around my mind, growing and spreading until my breath comes shorter. I felt the heat of my palm on the crystals, but now they are like ice under my fingers. Ice. The chill spreads all through my body and to my head, freezing my thoughts.

With no way to anchor myself, I'm lightheaded and lost in the dark. It only grows deeper. I drag in one final breath, then even the darkness is gone.

chapter 7

Hades

SHE'S FUCKING GORGEOUS.

My heart races as I stare at her and the pounding in my chest grows louder and louder. The temptation to have her is realized. I've never felt such lust before.

Persephone lies on my bed, her pale skin almost glowing against the dark silk sheets. Someone with eyes less sharp than mine could mistake her for dead. That's how deeply she sleeps. That's how deeply she *had* to sleep so she could be brought to me. There was no fight, I was told. Lost in thought and casting a spell, it was the perfect time. Her soul open for the taking.

No time seems to pass while I watch her chest rise and fall, each breath a sign of the life that shines within her like the light of the worlds above. The faint clinking can be heard, and I wave a hand to mute it. I need not wake my queen even if she is held there in chains formed from my power.

Faintly, I wonder of her concern when she realizes she is bound to the bedchambers. I wonder if her power will allow her to break them, but the thought is quickly relinquished. She is held here by fate. She will not leave until she submits to this reality.

My chambers, already decorated in a dark, opulent scheme, seem even darker with her brightness in it. A deep hum of satisfaction rises in my chest.

When she is asleep, the chains are like shadows around her wrists and ankles. They do not carry weight, they do not have a feel to them whatsoever, but if she were to fight against them, they'd keep her in place. They darken in color when Persephone stirs, my power tightening on her delicate wrists to be sure she does not escape.

Again an odd sensation stirs in my chest, almost like doubt or regret, but how could I doubt her? How could I possibly regret finally having my perfect match?

Persephone stirs again and my breath stills. It's as if the entirety of the Underworld is holding its breath with me, waiting for her to wake.

A beat of my heart deepens lowly, almost painfully. She will rule them all beside me.

Thump, she is mine. And this world is hers. A gift she mustn't take lightly.

Thump. Every second she lays there seems an eternity. She must wake. She must agree to submit and accept the honor I have given her. She will be perfect. Even if she fights at first, I remind myself, is that not admirable? Does that not add to her allure?

Fuck, my cock hardens, craving the fight. Quietly, I pace back to the window, attempting to rein in the desire that lights its way through my veins.

I have not been able to sit for hours in my impatience. I haven't felt this alive in years. I have *never* felt so alive. Because I've never had her. I've never had a soul so truly mine. My half in this world that I've been condemned to. The Fates are never wrong. They said I'd have her.

I have her.

I *have* her.

The thrill is nearly too strong to contain. Only my years of self-control allow me to hover nearby without touching her. She will wake when she wakes, and the anticipation is delightful. A feeling I've never experienced.

I stalk nearer to the bed, my pulse thundering in anticipation. The sound of my heartbeat drowns out the thick silence in the room. The Underworld is waking for the morning, and I am surrounded by its workings. New souls will be arriving through the River Styx. The dead are at peace in Elysium.

And I am here, waiting for my Persephone, my queen, my wife, my own heaven in this hell. It is much more difficult now that she's within my sight. That is a paradox I did not expect. I was impatient before, but now

I am ravenous for her presence. I crave to see the fear in her eyes. I desire her submission even more.

My patience was hard-won. I will not rush this process. It has been foretold by fate itself, and I will not intervene.

Not when it comes to her waking, at least.

Persephone sleeps for another stretch, her body relaxing against the sheets. Her poor beautiful soul has no idea. The thought is thrilling. The chains binding her to the bed become translucent in the absence of her movement. When the daylight from the windows touches them, they seem to absorb it, turning the light into indestructible shadows.

The chains will keep her here. My power will keep her here. Her submission will keep her here and yet offer her everything else. Power, the entirety of the Underworld with every pleasure. No longer asking anyone, not even myself, for permission. My cock twitches with the excitement of unleashing her. Of watching what she will do and what will become of those who dare defy her.

I swallow thickly and again a near growl vibrates up my chest. Persephone stirs at the sound, and I find myself in a new form of torture. One that offers both delight and despair that I must wait for such things.

I pace around the room, my body demanding movement.

When I arrive at the side of the bed again, Persephone begins to stir in earnest. Her long eyelashes flutter on her cheeks. They are fragile, those thick dark lashes, but they are relentless, wanting to let in the light. She makes a small sound deep in her throat. It sounds like an unconscious protest against waking.

Fuck, every little detail of her is divine. Her gorgeousness lost on all the worlds. I give gratitude that she is mine.

Grateful that she will rise.

In *my* kingdom.

Here, with me, where she will stay forever. Possessiveness lights my blood aflame and the embers of fire dance in the ashes of the fireplace on the far end of the room. Quickly I extinguish them with a wave of my hand. My magic and powers barely contained.

The room itself lacks warmth from the action and I watch as the chill greets her fair skin and she shivers, pulling the sheets up higher as if they can protect her.

My heart has barely settled from the satisfaction of Persephone's arrival, but now it races faster.

Open your eyes, I order her silently. *Open your eyes and let me see into the darkest parts of you…and the brightest. Let me see all of you.*

I nearly raise my hand, I nearly make it a command. But I resist. *I mustn't control her.* The Fates have warned, and being so close to having what has plagued me for centuries, the warning hisses in the back of my mind.

There is so much more to see. I am sure that beneath her smooth, creamy skin, a heart like none other beats. The thin gown she wears tumbles over her thighs, pushed up in her sleep. I do not touch the fabric, though I want to.

She will never know of this torture, none can conceive what stirs within me.

With a steadying deep inhale, I attempt to control the desire. It is like nothing I've ever felt before. In fact, it is beyond desire—it's lust. A deep, unquenchable lust that renews itself like the souls in my kingdom. There are always more souls, and I will always want her more and more and *more* until I cannot want her any more.

I have not approached that limit. I haven't even come close. There is only my self-control left, and once I let go of that—

There will be nothing to hold me back.

Because she's *here*.

In my possession.

She's mine.

At that thought, Persephone's eyelids flutter open, wide and full of shock.

Thump. Her heart beats with mine, both heavy, both of us still apart from the strain of blood rushing through our veins.

And so it begins.

I'm desperate to touch her, and I do not feel desperation often. I wrap the helm of darkness around me, and it covers me in a void that swallows all the light, rendering me invisible. It is almost a living thing, an extension of myself. More an echo of my power than a tool. Within the darkness, I have control.

I command everything about her life now.

Can she feel it, even as she wakes? Can she feel the depth of my control?

Wrapped in darkness, I approach the side of the bed.

Her brown eyes are wide and steadily watch me, although her body remains still. Panic drifts from her frail body. Fuck, the power she gives me in this moment is heady.

If not fueled by fear, I would drink it in.

"Persephone," I murmur, tasting her name. Uttering it out loud for her to hear what it means to me. Her mouth rounds into a shocked O. She gasps, then bites down on her lip, attempting to control herself. The sheets rustle as her fist tightens around the cloth.

Her self-control is nonexistent in comparison to mine. Persephone is a lovely thing. Young in the world of the gods. Pure. Untouched. No matter how much she wants to rein herself in, she will not be able to do it for long.

I relish the idea of breaking her. Of teaching her the art of control.

I relish it even more against this display—against her attempt to have some power, even as she lies in chains forged from my power.

Does she feel them yet? What thoughts ravage her mind in this moment?

Donned by my cloak of darkness, I can watch her all I want, and she will not even know where I am.

Persephone's eyes circle the room, then swing toward

me. Her mouth presses into a thin line, what was fear morphing into anger.

Goosebumps run down my spine. Persephone cannot see me, not with my cloak removing sight from all those in my wake. But she seems to *feel* me, and a fire in her eyes makes me feel that she can see through the darkness and straight into my soul.

I want her to *know* she is looking at me. I want her to know exactly where she is, and who has possession of her now.

Still, I wait. As she rises, Persephone tugs at her bonds, her lips firming even more. Her body trembles a moment as she tests her ankles, making her gown ride up another few inches on her thighs. I want to lean down and kiss that newly exposed skin. I long to mark her with my teeth.

Instead, I drop the darkness that surrounds me, the hood falling back and my vision forming in front of her in a single heartbeat.

This time, her gasp is much louder. Persephone's mouth falls open in her shock, only making my cock harder. Color floods her cheeks. It's a beautiful combination of surprise and anger, and the flush of her skin mirrors the heat within me.

Her body stiffens as she pulls back against the bonds that tie her to my bed.

I've never been more delighted at the defiance in someone else's eyes. *Never*. It's so bright, like a flame, and I want to feed it, to test it until I pinch it out between my thumb and forefinger. And I *will* pinch it out. She will be mine. She burns at my command.

But she burns with her own fire, as well. As sweet as Persephone may turn out to be, as submissive as she will one day find herself, she has strength inside of her. She has *will,* like the many forces of nature.

Her eyes locked on mine, Persephone pulls hard at the bindings at her wrists and ankles. She grits her teeth and yanks harder, the magic darkening and increasing its hold. The sounds she makes are addictive. They grow softer as she realizes that the magic will not release her.

Persephone gives another hard tug, her delicate muscles straining and her face growing red, then lets her arms fall to the blankets, her breathing hard.

I can't help it, I show my delight with an upticked pull at my lips.

"Stop it!" she shouts. "Let me go! My father—"

"Your father will not intervene."

"Yes, he will!" she screams. "You will regret this!"

"He will not. You are to be my queen," I murmur, displeased at the hint of what came before me earlier returning. The concern, the doubt. I must extinguish it before it creeps and buries itself into something else. I keep my voice level, though the words are as good as a promise. It hangs in the air between us like the magic of the chains. She does not understand fully yet, but she will. This is *my* kingdom, and she will rule with me.

"Let me *go,*" she insists, her eyes sweeping around her, the strength dimming so very quickly. *Fight me,*

Persephone, my plea is unspoken and yet, the powerful goddess stirs weakly, searching for escape, but she will not find one.

"As if you have anywhere to run."

Persephone glares at me. "Then why *chain* me?"

Again a smirk threatens but I resist. I hesitate.

If they know she is here, Zeus *might* intervene. Considering the state of our last conversation and what I've done in the cloak of the night. I do vaguely wonder if he's aware yet. And if not at this moment…when? And if he were to intervene, he will not do so alone. It's not his way to approach without several other powers at his back. Zeus is known for playing his little games, and he keeps his people close.

He might gather a few more to his cause and come for Persephone.

As my thoughts race and I debate on what to allow her to know, she lets out a scoff that drips with frustration and disgust, her eyes burning into mine.

Persephone is smart enough to know that Zeus could come for her. It's as if she's reading my mind. Looking into the future workings of my plans.

I saw that anger in her, that defiance. Now I see her quick and cunning mind. Fucking beautiful, if not deadly.

Yet, she's already broken.

She blinks slowly, then stares at the ceiling, her eyes sparkling with tears. I do not think they are tears of despair. Not yet. They are tears of rage.

I reach for her wrist.

She draws her hand to her chest and then flings it out as if to strike me.

I catch her wrist as if it is nothing—it *is* nothing—and hold it halfway between us, my eyes locked on hers and her tension radiating through me. The heat of her skin on mine is electric. The fire rages between us. Persephone's breathing quickens. Her glare is like a torch, bringing fire into the shadows at my core.

Does she feel this, too? The heat that dances between the tension. Her eyes bore into mine and mine to her. She pulls away, and it's then I realize just how little power she has.

Every heave of her breath rings in my ears.

I tighten my fingers around her wrist.

Persephone gasps, her lower lip dropping ever so slightly, fear reflecting in her eyes. This is only a prelude to my true strength, and that gasp is only a prelude to the sounds I'll draw out from her.

"Your magic is weak," I tell her, keeping my eyes firmly on hers. She could close her eyes in an attempt to shut me out. She could try to look away, but she doesn't.

"It's not weak," she snaps, her voice cracking with defiance. "It's as strong as yours. Your chains prove nothing."

It's not her words that strike me, but her bravery. I smirk at her, unflinching.

"Weak," I repeat.

"I'm not." Her voice drops. "I'm *not*. You don't know what I can do. You don't know me."

A huff of a laugh leaves me. I know everything

about her. I've watched her for years now. Pined for her, obsessed with her.

"Show me your power," I command as I release her and take a step back, "Free yourself."

Her eyes narrow. After a beat, she turns her face away. A pain I haven't felt before is sharp in my chest.

Of course she could not free herself. If she had that power, she would have done so already.

I reach forward with my other hand on her chin, I turn her face back to mine.

"Your power is weak," I coax. "But I will help you."

My whispered promise flashes in her eyes. I can practically see her thoughts change before me.

"Who are you?" she asks.

"Hades, lord of the Underworld and your taker."

Her breath seems to leave her. "I will aid you and your powers," I promise her, allowing my admission to sink in.

"In exchange for what?" she whispers although she already knows.

Persephone is no fool. She knows that nothing in the Underworld comes without a cost.

I lean closer. Her eyelashes flutter. When my breath kisses her cheek, her body arches toward me ever so slightly.

"If you submit."

Persephone sucks in a shallow breath. She cannot know that her body arches toward me more with every moment that passes.

The tension steals my breath as much as it is stealing hers. It would take only a moment to lean down and capture her mouth with mine. I let her feel the closeness growing taut between us, alive with heat.

And still she fights.

All she would have to do to submit is to lay down her arm. All she would have to do is stop pushing against me. It is the most delicate fight.

And yet she resists.

"Submit to me," I tell her. It is an order. Anyone else in the Underworld would know it for what it was, but Persephone bares her teeth.

"Never." Her voice is cold. "I will *never* submit."

It takes great restraint on my part to do nothing, because I want to kiss the pulse at her wrist, but I turn my back on her and stalk away.

Persephone does not call after me.

The silence stretches between us, charged with the tension of her every breath.

I can feel that tension behind me and within me—the heat of her defiance—but I ignore it and throw the windows open. Her powers...she will need time to regain them.

Time. Patience, I remind myself.

Cold from outside gusts in. The icy cold dispels the heat on my face.

It will do far more lovely things to Persephone's body.

I inhale the fresh air and let the cool fill my lungs.

Then I turn and leave the room, leaving Persephone exposed to the frigid chill of my absence and the assurance that the room will turn cold as ice.

I will force her to need me. I will force her powers to return as well.

I do not crave her weak. I demand that she be mine as promised. The powerful queen by my side.

chapter 8

Persephone

The chill is barely a thought as I grasp at my wrists and then observe my surroundings. My throat is tight and my body stiff. How the hell did this happen? I can barely remember the chain of events that led me here.

The shackles that bind me are not metal, but magic. That much is obvious. From deep in the pit of my womb I attempt to gather my power, praying for it to course through me, and yet I feel nothing of it. I manage a faint semblance of what used to flourish but it is useless against the chains.

They are as strong as anything I've ever encountered in Olympus. Stronger still, though I do not wish to acknowledge such truth as I scream out and tug with all my might. I do not wish to feel powerless. But as my breath comes in pants and all my might proves useless, I'm left with the dread of what is.

I am powerless.

I have been kidnapped; I have been chained. All to the will of Hades.

Submit, the single word echoes in my mind and a chill flows down my spine. A deep seed of power brews within me at the memory of his whisper.

With a gust of wind, my thoughts are broken, and I turn to the open window.

There is some spell over the window itself, for I can see nothing but dark skies as if in the highest of towers. And yet I know, the Underworld is not empty. It is not vacant. I scream out more than a dozen times, my throat raw and etched with pain by the time I decide the effort is futile.

No one can hear me, and I cannot see a soul from this place.

A shiver runs through me. Does he mean to torture me?

Hades. I nearly whisper his name. The god of the Underworld and the dead. The unseen one. I've heard tales of his brutality and power, but never have I witnessed the man. His dark eyes, nearly devoid of life itself and sharp chiseled jaw that only adds to his dominance. It's the air that surrounds him though, I can feel it beg my body to bow to his. His power is undeniable, as is the fear that burrows itself within me.

Tears prick as I attempt to pull once again and find

it useless. Swallowing thickly, I search the near-vacant room for anything. There exists a carved dresser with intricate detail I can barely make out through my blurred vision. An ornately carved floor-to-ceiling mirror. And a thin silk black sheet on a large bed with an amber chaise at the end, the dark coloring mirroring the ancient wood. The walls shine of obsidian sheen. And the floor appears to be petrified wood slabs.

I attempt to pull from the power of the crystals that surround me, but they betray me, giving me nothing. I feel nothing from them.

A gasp is pulled from my wretched throat as I try to remember my teachings. Though they fail me now, as my powers have failed me.

Someone save me, I plead with the darkness.

Mother, I nearly cry out as my head rocks back. If Zeus will not save me, surely my mother will not stand for such things. I must last. I must only last long enough for intervention.

I know this for certain. Swallowing the lump in my throat, I gather my pride and again search the room, finding the chill has only gotten colder.

The magic chain braids itself together when I rise from the bed. Gently testing my boundaries. I *can* rise from the bed, but it's not much of a comfort. There is no comfort in this room. It's spacious and speaks of wealth, but it is not filled with the kind of things that might tell me about Hades. Very few items at all and nothing personal.

I should have expected that there would not be any sign of a heart. Hades was bold and cruel enough to have me stolen away from my home and bound to the bed with magic. The man cannot have any kind of tenderness to him. There can be nothing *soft*.

Not here where he rules the dead and determines punishment. A god of his power and divinity...

Why would Hades help me find my powers again? The thought riddles its way into my mind. He said he would help me. And the promise of such things...

My mind spirals around the possibilities. Is there a part of me that craves power and strength more than I crave my freedom in this moment?

It tempts me. The promise of my powers. Can he do such things? Is he merely lying to gain my submission?

Time ticks away with no signs of change apart from the wind howling. Hours pass and all I am left with is the pacing and racing thoughts. I fear the heart of me is already becoming divided in these long hours alone. I fear I cannot trust myself to know which cravings are born of the cold and the isolation and the hunger and which are my own.

The craving I have for Hades has never been so strong. It has never felt so insidious. I always knew I could pull myself away from thoughts of him before. I could go to my mother's gardens or walk in the halls of Olympus, bathing in the light, and then I would not be at the mercy of my desires.

Now I am at *his* mercy, and the thought enrages me.

It is him who stared back at me in the dark waters. It is Hades who crept into my dreams. I know now without a doubt.

I only wish it enraged me more. I wish there wasn't so much shameful interest. So much want for this man. Perhaps it is yet another spell he's cast against me.

I do not trust it. I do not trust him at all.

My face heats, even in the cold of the room, and I look down at my hands. The magic chains flicker around my wrists.

If I tug at them, they will eventually tug back, keeping me here.

If I rise from the bed, I have to move slowly and carefully across the room, in order for the chains not to react.

Our conversation rings in my ears, sending more blood rushing to my cheeks.

I will help you.

In exchange for what?

If you submit.

Never. I will never *submit.*

I was proud of myself for how brave I sounded. I was proud of myself for the fight that rose in me.

But now, in the privacy of the room, with my face flushing and my body hot…

Doubt grows in me like the cold in the room. As much as I want to tell myself that Hades feels nothing—that he's cold and heartless and mean—I saw something else.

I saw fire in Hades's eyes. I saw heat and passion and

perhaps even a little amusement. Anger rises within me. How dare he. But the flicker of rage is only that. A flicker.

Shame trickles over my skin. I hide my face in my hands, wishing I could hide from myself.

But there's nobody else here. I am alone, and a captive, and getting colder by the second. I'm lost in the dark. Lost in this room. A plaything for a god who thinks of me as his property. He thinks of me as someone to steal, like a flower plucked from the gardens of Olympus.

Even worse, he was right. My power *is* weak. I have nowhere to run in this realm.

And still, I crave that heat I saw in his eyes. I want to blame it on the cold, but it's not only the cold that has my nipples peaking and my teeth beginning to chatter. It's also because his presence was exhilarating. Exciting. I have thought so much about my waning powers lately that I would hardly let myself consider the dreams I had of Hades and the power I felt in those dreams.

I had some power, too. He did not look at me with cold, blank eyes. He leaned close enough for me to see that I was affecting him. That he desires...

Why me, with my weak powers? Surely a god like Hades would want a more ruthless queen.

The flush on my skin deepens at the memory of his statement.

You are to be my queen.

I can never admit how seductive those words sounded when Hades said them, as if it was fated. My heart pounds. My mouth waters. If I were his queen, I would also be his equal. He would not rule over me. We could rule this realm together.

It could all be lies. Simply a pawn in his game.

The spell comes back to me. I must have spoken it wrong. I must've ruined what should have been my saving grace.

This was *not* the kind of power I meant. I did not mean the kind of power that comes from a man who keeps me chained. I did not mean the kind of power that comes from judgment and death. I meant the kind of power that comes from life. From new flowers and a full harvest. From the love of the people I'm meant to protect.

The one thing I know of the Underworld is that no new life can grow. Raising my hand, I attempt a flower. A single lonely flower to grow between the crack of obsidian in the corner of the room. There is no nourishment, no soil. No possibility for growth. Nothing moves, not within and not without.

I feel nothing. As if my powers do not even exist.

A quiet voice murmurs in the back of my mind—*is it not power to be the only light in the dark? Do you dare to question the will of the gods and the will of fate?*

My throat tightens to the extent that I fear I cannot breathe. I do not know how long it's been since Hades left me here. Hours at least if not the whole day. I stand tall and keep my pace slow until I've reached a table near the windows. A glass pitcher of water rests on it. With my throat aching, I allow my fingertips to glide down the etched side of it. I pick it up and hurl it across the room, an anger brewing inside of me like I've never felt before splashing water onto the dark floor.

The pitcher shatters and a darkness sweeps through me. With trembling hands, I allow them to fall to my side and take in what I've done.

Then, as if nothing had happened, it joins back together, the glittering pieces flickering in the dim light, and the pitcher returns to its place on the table.

I repeat this process with every item that I can lift. The pillows return to the bed as soon as I let go. The thin, soft rug of fur will not tear under my fingers. I pull tufts out of its weft, but it repairs itself.

Any effort to change the makings of the room prove worthless. And yet it only angers me more.

I try my magic.

It's like the candle, refusing to light. My strength drains out of me, and I fall to my knees, dizzy and lightheaded. The rug is the only softness under me. I have spent my life dwelling in the bright, beautiful halls of Olympus, and this dark, cold room sinks into my soul. Frustrated tears burn in my eyes.

I feel as if I've gone mad. I can do nothing but exist with my thoughts in a room I cannot change with a fate that is not one I choose.

Nothing could be more shameful than my loneliness. Nothing could be more shameful than wanting Hades to come back.

Nothing could be more shameful than craving his

attention if for no other reason than information and perhaps a deal.

Because as I kneel on the rug, trying not to cry, one thing becomes clear.

Hades is the one who did this to me.

Not only stealing me from my rooms on Olympus, but also draining my powers so he could do so. My powers began to weaken when he appeared in my dreams. He started stealing those long before he came for *me*.

He did this to me.

Anger lights like a flame in the hearth. It dances with other flames. How dare he! He will pay for his crimes.

I have been so curious about the man in the shadows. I have been so hungry to know more about him. I fear his power and his presence, but I also feared my own desire. I desired him more than I desired anything else, a fact I could not admit even in my own mind.

Hades is a man I knew of but never saw. His face did not appear to me. To know it is him who has done this. The god who came from a pit of bile in the Titan's stomach. A ruthless, cruel, and brutal fighter who speaks of just and righteousness but knows not of humanity.

All the things I have known and the stories I've been told swell into my head at once.

This lore was never hidden from me growing up, but it did not seem real—not the way Olympus seemed real. I'd never laid eyes on the realm. For I was not meant for this place and yet he dragged me here. Where my powers mean naught. Why take me as a queen when I am useless here? Why drain me of my light and then throw me into darkness and despair?

How was I to know that the stories would be so much more?

Prophecies are not always made to manifest. Fates *do* change. The gods swirl their fingers into magic and shift the ways of the world.

But here, in the cold, dark heart of the Underworld, I feel like a child opening her eyes for the first time.

All of it was true. Everything my mother ever told me, every story ever whispered into my ear—it's all true.

And now I will never escape from it.

My sobs overwhelm me. I bury my face in my hands and cry on the rug. My head throbs.

I miss my mother with a palpable ache in my chest. I wish I could hear her voice. I wish I could seek her guidance.

At some point, at the sound of a tinker, I raise my eyes and find that a new tray has appeared on the table.

Someone—or the Underworld itself—has provided food. A plate with bread. A bowl with steam rising from it. A red, shiny pomegranate, cracked open with the seeds offering a delightful image.

I do not go to the table and eat. I do not pour water from the pitcher and drink.

I do not even dare to venture back to the bed.

I fear that if I submit in any way, I have lost a game I do not even know the rules to yet.

I sit alone on the rug with my knees drawn up,

holding them close to my body for warmth. My tears run down my cheeks and dry in cold streaks. My throat hurts. It's raw from the sobbing and screaming and fits. I sit perfectly still, unwilling to act until I'm provided with more information.

I can think of nothing but how much I miss my mother and Beatrice. My heart aches for them and I pray they do not think I've left them of my own accord.

I'm not sure how long it's been when the door to the bedroom opens. With a sharp turn, I face the creak of the hinges.

Hades enters, tall and as calm as ice. Folded over one arm is a blanket. I offer a humorless huff, more than aware that this chill was his intention.

I am no fool and I do not make deals with those who force a bargain that is nothing more than pain and suffering. This is no mercy, this is only his will.

And I refuse it.

I stare at the blanket, my chest aching with how much I wish to be warm, and then I pull my gaze away. Ripping it from the offering.

He moves around the room for a minute or two, his steps eerily patient. I stare down at the tops of my knees, the nape of my neck hot.

The air moves behind me. There is the sound of fabric being rearranged.

I do not turn.

The lights in the room dim. It had not seemed

bright to me before, but Hades has taken almost all of the light.

There is an unmistakable sound, a bed groaning with weight.

"Do you wish to join me?" Hades asks, his voice low.

The arrogance inflames a deep hatred in me. He thinks I will lie with him? For the sake of comfort after what he's done?

I clench my jaw harder to keep my teeth from chattering.

"Fuck you," I manage.

I'm met with a huff of humor that seems genuine and the sound of him gaining comfort on the large bed. "If that is your wish."

My back aches. My knees ache. I'm *freezing*. I attempt to lean back onto the chaise that sits at the foot of the bed, only to find it is gone.

My eyes narrow and indignant hate brews inside of me. I rest my cheek against the wooden bedpost instead, only to find that it loses its composure and my body falls to the floor rather than allowing the bedpost to keep me upright.

Pain flickers within my heart.

He wishes me no comfort or rest at all unless it is on the floor or in the bed.

I turn back to the rug, and find it is also gone.

"You're heartless," I whisper and in return there is nothing. For a bit longer, I sit on the floor in agonizing pain. Not so much physical as mental. Attempting to see his moves before my own.

After a shamefully short time, I get to my feet. My steps are unsteady as I approach the bed. I must entertain him to acquire movement in whatever he is playing at.

I only need a little softness. A little warmth. Then I can survive the night.

The heat of Hades eyes alone is nearly burning as I climb onto the bed and lower my throbbing head to one of the pillows. My body at a distance from his and the blanket. The silence seems to demand that I speak.

"I do not wish to be here, and I do not want to play these games."

Hades exhales next to me. "You have no choice."

"I want my *powers*."

"You will have those back, my queen. You will be powerful beside me."

My queen. The words, smooth and true, make hatred brew within me.

"This is how you treat your queen?" I snidely murmur.

"I offer you comfort, you are the one who denies it."

"Only beside you?"

He is silent for a few moments, and then he says, his tone almost careful, "There are things you do not know."

"I know more than you'd think," I bite back, very much aware of his doings. He made me weak so he could take me. What a coward he is.

I roll over to my back., my mind reeling, my heart racing, my body tense from trying to stay warm.

The soft edge of the blanket lands across my shoulders, and I can't help myself. I let its warmth fold over me and let myself sink into it with a sigh. I do not pull for more of it.

I mean only to rest enough so that I can fight another day. If my actions can even be defined as fighting.

But my exhaustion wins out. The warmth is too powerful. I drift off almost immediately.

For some time in my sleep, the feel of being with a god in bed is different. Something I've never experienced, something hot and heady. A sensation of warmth and even power flows through me as the dreams turn vivid, and I swear a pleasure I cannot place hovers slightly over my sensitized skin.

Never in my existence have I felt such…sensations. Like my surroundings, they're entirely peculiar and tempting in a way that I've not experienced before.

Sometime later, I wake up *warm and flushed* because I've rolled closer to Hades in my sleep. He is solid beside me. His body hot and offering a pleasure I've taken for granted all my life. His scent wrapped around me, seductive and masculine. Anger at the unconscious act comes quickly enough.

It doesn't take long before I realize he's not breathing slowly and evenly, the way he might if he were dreaming.

With a start, I feel his eyes on me, and I look up defiantly to meet his gaze.

He peers down at me, and I *know* the look in his eyes. It's curiosity and lust. It's what drew me to his presence in the shadows. My breath hitches.

"You're a bastard," I snarl to avoid acknowledging anything else I feel.

Touch me. I have to bite back the words to keep them in my mouth.

I shove at him, but I only succeed in pushing myself away. There isn't enough space between us. The reality of being a prisoner, being *held,* being *taken,* floods my mind, filling my lungs with panic and a need to escape that's more animal than human. It's nothing like the gods must feel, and I want to run from myself as badly as I want to run from Hades.

Go, my mind says. *Get away. Fight.*

That feeling spills through me as heat in my chest, cold in my feet, and a strange panic in my arms and legs. I cannot leave. I cannot get up and leave. The chain will never let me go, and I want to be out of its hold. I want to be free.

I pull against the chains on instinct and scream out my rage into the dark, and when I look back down at him, Hades, the unseen, has left me once again, taking the blanket with him.

chapter 9

Hades

With Minox at my side, nearly a shadow of myself, we stride down the hall. Torches burn on the walls, casting flickering patterns of light and shadow on the rough stone floor beneath our feet.

Ages of paths have carved themselves into the worn floor. I've traveled this path in all of the times, the hardships and wars, the depths of betrayal and the rise of power. It is my home and my sanctuary, and yet I feel that it is not enough. That it is a path I've not yet traveled.

We walk in relative silence. The clicking of our footsteps echoes in the quiet of the Underworld. It is late, and my realm has settled around me. A discomfort stirs in the depths of me, churning with anticipation of what's to come with my Persephone.

Her resistance was anticipated and yet the frustration

is far more prevalent. To lie beside her and not enjoy her scent, her warmth, her touch...it is torture, and it is futile. If only she would realize that I would not have to suffer and neither would she. My patience does not exist when it comes to her. Her arrival has affected far more than just many selfish thoughts.

It is the quiet that's different. These halls have not been peaceful as of late. The calm that pervades the hallway now is almost eerie in its contrast. Even the flutter of the flames in the sconces whip loudly through the air.

I've become too attuned to every sound Persephone makes. All the noises that would have faded out of my notice are prominent. Her screams were an unwelcome disturbance to others, though. Others far too close to the god of thunder.

"The witch was able to cast the spell?"

Minox inclines his head. "Yes, my lord. No one will hear her screams any longer."

I give him a terse nod, unsettled from his tone. I've avoided my room all day to focus on the tasks at hand and be present for the questing souls, but that doesn't mean I have avoided Persephone's screams. At times, I think I can hear them even when it is impossible. Her sheer determination is a match for my own will, but she will bend to mine. She must.

"Can you hear them now?" I question him as she cries out profanity from the distance above us. Attempting spells of wrath that are useless. She must know this and yet her rage has not subsided. I fear it only grows with a simmer of hatred that was not there the day before.

"No, my lord," he answers and there's a tone he takes that I don't care for as he stares straight ahead, avoiding my gaze.

It is no one's business how I have acquired my queen.

It's not uncommon for souls to be shocked and grief-stricken when they arrive in the Underworld, but Persephone is not like them. She burns with hatred and there are whispers of the feminine screams from my chambers.

The sensation of *caring* about a spell working to its intended effect—that is perhaps more unsettling than all the rest. Still, it's an unholy mix in my gut.

They may not be able to hear her, but I can. I both revel in the fact that she's here and loathe that she screams in agony. I should know the sound of each breath she takes. I should know the force of each sob that tears from her throat. I should know the rhythm of her heartbeat at every second.

Nothing should be kept hidden from me. Nothing *will* be kept hidden from me. This is my realm, and she is mine to do with as I please.

Regardless of the whispers and the fear and judgment from those under my control.

I should stop *feeling* so much about it, or it will consume me.

"Have you learned anything more?" I question Minox. He's been watching Persephone while I've taken to the courts to calm the disturbance. I may not stay in the room to assure her security all day, but I haven't let her pass the time unobserved.

"She is lonely, my lord. She cannot seem to stop crying." He pauses, as if to carefully consider his next words. "Perhaps...companionship?" Minox offers.

I haven't been able to allow it...I do not trust what I wish to do to her. There's a desire and a temptation that I barely control in her presence. I cannot offer Persephone more *companionship* than I have already given, or I will shut the door to the bedroom and never emerge again. It is not often I fear for what I may do, but the consequences are severe, and the Fates have warned me.

"Or delicacies of another nature?" he suggests in my silence.

As if I have not considered as much already. As if I have not been holding myself back from gifting her delicacies in every flavor possible. Pleasures of the tongue, yes, but also the body. The pleasure of submission. The pleasure of—

We come to an abrupt stop outside my bedroom door.

A scream tears through the closed door, ringing in my ears.

Minox's face remains carefully calm. "This is where the spell was cast. No one outside this line will be able to hear her."

"Good." The single word is uttered beneath my breath lowly as my hands flex and my muscles tense. She wants war, my beautiful vengeful queen. I'll be damned if her defiance doesn't turn me on more than before.

"If you need anything, my lord—"

"I know where to find you." I finish the sentence for him, more angered by the disruption of my thoughts than anything. I pine for her. I've never desired such sinful addiction as I do now.

"Hades!" She screams my name as if a curse. *I fucking love it.*

Minox inclines his head again and glides away, disappearing into the shadows before he has left the light of the sconces.

It can't be unnoticed that his footsteps, without mine, are much quieter than the noise we made when we were together. It must have been me who was so loud.

Was I trying to warn her? Was I trying to inspire that titillating flush of fear down the front of her chest?

Did I want her to hear me coming? Did I want her to tremble, and blush, and try to think of some way to escape, *any* way to escape, before returning to the knowledge that such a thing isn't possible?

Did I want her body to respond to me, slick between her legs, the damp, pink flesh aching to be touched? Did I want her to get wet, thinking of me, and did I want her resolve to weaken just a little more? My cock hardens at every thought. I ache for her in every way.

Have I fantasized, at least once, about how it will sound when she begs for me?

Of course I have. Before she was even in my grasp

I memorized the soft gasp of surprise from her sleep where I stalked her.

Quietly, I enter the room as calmly as possible and close the door behind me. The soft click is all that can be heard over her heavy breathing. Anger simmers in the room, the magic and tension palpable. Persephone has not seated herself at the table, nor stayed in bed. Sometimes, I think of her waiting for me to return, her head held high and her power flowing all around her.

It crackles in the room as she stares at me, her wide eyes red rimmed and her pale skin dull from the chill. The darkness in her eyes has never been so threatening. As if she's nearly a different goddess entirely. If only for a moment. Her eyes narrow and she looks away.

She sits at the center of the dark rug midway between the windows and the table. From here, I cannot see much but the top of her head and the tangle of her hair.

Persephone screams again. It's more of a complaint than a full-blooded scream. Her voice cracking.

I cross the room to her, ignoring the inappropriately fast beat of my heart. Persephone does not turn her head to watch me. She does not even look me in the eye again, although I wonder if the depths of darkness was only a flash…only a sign of what could be.

Thump, thump. My heart races as I get closer and closer to my queen. Heat gathers around every nerve ending.

I stand still in front of her for perhaps a minute, then tap my foot on the edge of the rug.

This is all that makes her lift her eyes. The hazel orbs glisten with unshed tears. No longer the pitch black power that met me before.

Persephone says nothing.

I murmur, resisting the urge to lift her chin and force her eyes to meet mine so I may study them. "You wake the dead, my queen."

She keeps her face tilted toward mine so there is no ignoring the state of her, which cannot be described by any other word than *pitiful.* Persephone's skin is pale. Her eyes are red and swollen. Her cheeks are blotchy from the irritation of her dried tears. Her lips, soaked in the salt, are dry and bitten. And yet, under a thin coat of sadness is rage. I love the rage. I love the sadness. I love the power that echoes beneath them both even more.

"Have you not eaten?" I question, noting she has withered. I cannot imagine she has, looking like this. Persephone shakes her head, confirming my suspicions.

Irritation sweeps its way through me. How can she expect to fight if not caring for her needs? I remind myself that she is not used to the ways of war. A young goddess compared to me. An innocent in so many ways, and although it tempts me, it infuriates me just the same.

That cannot continue, just as the rest of my realm could not continue to hear her scream. With the poison Persephone's been given…

She must eat and nourish her body and spirit. If she is to stand beside me, she must be well.

With haste, I stride to the table in the corner. A bottle of wine and two glasses appear in the center as if sensing my attention. With a wave of my hand, the wine appears in the glasses. Spilling from nothing. It's a delicacy and delight, and the effects of such offerings will ease her tense body. Warm her to my intentions, perhaps.

I note that Persephone appears to not watch me. I will never admit how much I loathe not being able to feel her eyes on my back. I grit my teeth and push those feelings to the distance.

As I lift the glasses, the wine sloshes into the bottom of the glass goblets and settles. I take a sip of the first, enjoying the taste for a moment. Then I carry the glass over to Persephone's place and crouch down in front of her, offering the wine. All she needs to do is lean forward, and I will tip the glass and let the wine spill into her mouth. Goosebumps slip down her shoulder as I stare at her bare skin revealed by the thin straps of her cream silk gown.

Persephone stares at the glass of wine, then looks back into my eyes. I watch her throat as she swallows in defiance.

"Wine for the gods." I move the glass a fraction of an inch closer to her. The rough pad of my thumb slips against the delicate and thin glass.

Persephone glances at it again, then shakes her

head. "I've shattered the glass a hundred times now," she admits. "I do not care for sustenance."

"Come, now." I pull the glass away. My gaze travels along every inch of her skin and I cannot be bothered to have anger within me. Another emotion entirely entraps me. A deep spell of sorts, one of want and pride and weakness. I would bow to such a goddess. I can feel her power buried so deep down. *Come to me, my queen.* From the depths of my soul, I both beg for the taste of what she is, and I remind myself to enjoy each moment that leads to me to the first kiss of her power.

"My queen," I merely whisper. "You must drink."

Her eyes flicker after it. I can tell she's struggling not to keep her eyes pinned on it. *That's* what I want. I want that fire in her back at the surface. I crave those eyes to be dark and hungry.

If Persephone won't accept the wine when it's so easily offered, perhaps she'll come after it with a challenge. A smirk pulls my lips up.

I offer the glass again, but when she doesn't take it, I move it out of her reach, watching her face for any sign that she's truly beginning to break.

The next time I offer the glass, Persephone slaps it out of my hand.

I'm delighted—the speed of the slap, the *daring act*—but I don't let it show. My heart pumps furiously with heated blood and my cock presses against the fabric of the trousers beneath my cloak.

She is not prepared for my speed or my reaction.

My hand wrapped around her throat. The feel of her blood pumping beneath my touch is everything. Fire to my blood. I keep my grip close enough to her chin that she cannot lower her head. Persephone's eyes are wider now and her breathing shallow. Her eyes narrowed with the same hatred as before. They darken and flash with determined defiance. I can feel every heavy pound of her heartbeat. Persephone swallows. Yes, her body remains still. Tense and still.

"You are going to eat," I tell her, my voice soft as I lower my head to hers. My lips so close to hers. "Because your soul will never leave. You have no choice but to be mine."

Thump. Thump. Our hearts compete for the symphony that is silence.

Persephone narrows her eyes. Her lips part. She wets her bottom lip with her tongue, every little movement seemingly erotic. I could kiss her until she was panting and begging with need. I could slip my fingers in her mouth and tell her to suck. She could bite me, and I would fucking love it.

I continue before she can say a word. "There is no way out of the Underworld." Persephone's expression falters. "No one is going to save you but yourself…by choosing to fight."

She blinks, the fear in her eyes turns to a deeper shock, and then denial.

"How can you fight with your powers so weak and your body even weaker?" I have her with that statement. Persephone confirms that this was her question with a tiny, involuntary flinch.

I offer her something no one else did. How could they, when they were so unaware of what she's been suffering. "I will teach you magic. I will give you everything…including your powers back."

The corners of her lips turn down and her eyes soften.

"I know you've suffered loss lately…have you not?"

She remains silent with my question, merely observing me.

"I can make them come back."

"You can't—"

"I can save you from your fate if you give in." *Thump. Thump.* The air turns tense between us, a flash of heat and a knowingness that this moment was meant to be.

Persephone swallows again, the movement delicate under my hand. Ever so delicate. I will think of this when I've left her again. I will think of that gentle movement, and how her bare throat calls for me to squeeze.

If only she knew what pleasures can be had from submission. If only she would let herself understand.

She watches my face so carefully, like she used to do when I came to her in dreams.

"There are things I can teach you, that you could use for your own survival. For your own reign."

Her chin comes up a little. The barest of bits. Our

faces are so close that I could take her mouth without the slightest effort. At this range, with my hand around her throat, I can read the truth in Persephone's heart-beat and even the set of her lips.

I want nothing more than to bury myself within her. The pleasure builds within me.

The tension between us is thick and strong, like the currents that pull the spirits to the Underworld. They are connected to the earth and to the gods from the moment they are born, and they never see the threads that bind them to the beginning and the end of their lives.

Her neck is hot in my grasp. I cannot take my attention from her pulse. My mouth waters with the nearly uncontrollable urge to feel her skin beneath my lips and teeth. Persephone is like a storm about to break. She has no idea how beautiful she would be in her submission and her power. It is only a matter of time until she bends to my will.

She must be able to feel *that*. It is the pull of the thin golden strings. I've tied the two of us so closely together. She cannot escape it.

I want her cold body warming under my touch. Blood throbs in my cock, but I ignore it, choosing instead to breathe her in. To study her as closely as she is studying me.

The will in her eyes is mesmerizing. I stay very still. Persephone could accept me in this moment. She wants the power and the knowledge I can offer her. If she would only let those desires guide her.

I hold my breath in anticipation. It's so close. The moment is within reach.

If she would only give in to it. If she would only give in to me—

But then Persephone's chin comes down. She does not pull her neck out of my hand. She does, however, change the angle—it's a subtle resistance.

"No," she says, and lowers her eyes. That's not a subtle resistance in the least.

Disappointment chills my heated needs.

Perhaps she *does* know what she's doing to me. Perhaps even her tears and her hunger are purposeful and calculated. That sends a frisson through my body. It's not doubt. More a recognition of how powerful Persephone could be if she would give me a fraction of her trust. I wouldn't need much to awaken what I'm *sure* lies within her.

I wouldn't need much at all. Only a sliver of an opening. In all honesty, I had thought Persephone would break quickly. I want to know how long she can resist—the curiosity grows every minute—but I want to be finished with the facade that she's not going to give in at all.

She will.

She has no other choice.

I shouldn't give her another chance to change her mind. I shouldn't find myself willing to bend at all.

This game we're playing won't be won more easily if she sees me as someone weak myself.

I cannot be weak. It is not the god I am. And I certainly won't be weak with her.

"No?" I question, in spite of the strongest instincts telling me to remain silent. To give her *nothing* that would make her think—

Persephone lifts her eyes to mine. For a moment, it's there—that fire, that light.

But just as quickly, it fades back into bleak darkness.

"No," she says, and refuses to say anything more.

chapter 10

Persephone

SURELY HE DID NOT CAPTURE ME SO THAT I MAY perish. The lord of the dead knows more than others what is to become of a goddess who no longer has life within her. Nothingness. That is what I offer him if he merely offers me this. He can turn me into nothing and that is what he will have. I will offer him nothing more.

When Hades realizes I'm not going to say another word, his eyes go black. A deep void of power that lies in the depths of his irises. It consumes me as I stare back. As if seeing through him.

It is clear he thinks he's hiding his feelings from me. The desire and the need to have his hands on me. It is clear what he wants of me.

I do not know him. I do not know how he lives.

I do not know how the Underworld was before I was brought here.

But I *do* know that the small twitches in his expression are a mirror of his mind.

He releases my throat, and I gasp in a breath. The lack of his palm on my throat feels like an immediate loss. I reach up and touch the place his fingers were.

My heart beats fast and hard. His footsteps retreat from me, and I hold my breath again, my mind filling with questions. Will he turn around and come back? Will he move me to the bed? Will he bend me over it, locked in his chains?

Will he lose his patience?

Most importantly the question riddles in the back of my mind, *Do I want him to?*

There's a push and pull within me that's far too dangerous. Like playing with fire. But the bedroom door opens and then slams, and there is silence all around me once more.

I'm alone. Nothing. I make myself nothing.

I remain still, all my senses tuned to the door. I no longer hear Hades's footsteps. He has not called out to anyone. He does not seem to be waiting at the door, ready to come back in for me.

After a minute or two, I let my shoulders slump. I massage the rest of the heat from Hades's palm out of my neck.

I regret it once it's gone.

The windows that Hades threw wide open have

been closed part of the way. There's enough space to let in the blustery air, and it keeps the room cold. The room is dark as well, though I can't tell if that's because I am losing hope or because it is meant to be dark.

It's black outside the windows as well. Late at night. It seemed like Hades was gone for weeks, but if I do my best to remember, there was daylight and then darkness.

Should I keep track of the days and the nights? A prisoner…I've conceded that I am in fact a prisoner.

My muscles ache and my bones crack as I get up from the rug and move around the room, my legs shaking with weakness. I cannot find anything to make a record of the days.

I pause at the table and dig my fingernail into it until it makes a scratch.

While I wait to gather my strength and go back to the rug, the scratch vanishes as if it was never there.

It has been two days at least. Perhaps three. That's what tonight's darkness tells me. I will do my best to remember tomorrow and the day after that, though I do not want to think far beyond another few days.

I could save you from your fate.

"What fate?" I murmur the question I had for Hades at the unsuspecting table. "You have made this my fate. You have made me a prisoner."

The table does not answer. I go back to the rug and sit, curling into a ball and holding myself as tightly as I can.

I could save you from your fate.

Hades's words repeat in my mind. No matter how many times I dismiss them, they repeat again and again. Chills follow the promise.

What does he know of my fate? And how did he know of my powers?

I hunch over my bent knees, resting my chin there. It's so cold, and my stomach is hollow from the lack of food. I've only slept a little, and I can't afford to fall asleep again. I'll wake up next to Hades, and I won't do that.

It is shocking that my mother and father haven't sent someone. They cannot come themselves. The realms aren't open for all to enter, even the gods, but surely—

Surely they should have sent *someone* by now. Some word. Some acknowledgment that they know I am missing and are planning a rescue. If they even know who took me. My heart squeezes at the thought that they may not even know I was taken. They may think I've left of my own accord.

No, no, I refuse the thought. My mother knows I'd never leave her side. Not without telling her. Not without a goodbye.

Someone will come soon. In the meantime, I need to focus my energy on thinking of my *own* plan.

I squeeze my eyes closed and try to concentrate. The cold makes it difficult because I'm shivering so hard. I would do anything for a bowl of warm broth.

Almost anything. I will not submit to Hades.

Maybe a protection spell would work. I don't have my altar, and I don't know if there is power for me to draw on in the Underworld, but I can at least try. If I believe—

If Beatrice could do such things, then it is possible I could cast a spell to help myself even in the Underworld.

The words slip through my mind, faint and hard to grasp.

The power inside me craves the light
Bring me the warmth of fire
And take from the powers to my right

My eyes peer open to observe my right. A sleek obsidian wall.

I repeat, "The power inside me craves the light," to the cold sweeping in through the windows. I imagine being safe and protected. I imagine being freed. I imagine the hunger and cold disappearing. "Bring me the warmth of fire and take from the powers to my right."

"The power inside me craves the light," I repeat, forcing my voice to steady. It's the chains I want gone. I want my body to be my own again. I imagine the heat of a fire that could burn through the magic but leave my skin untouched. I imagine the chains falling away. "Bring me the warmth of fire and take from the powers to my right."

I hope, and I *hope*. I can hear the snap of chains. The metal clanking on the floor.

But then—a noise distracts me, and I have doubt.

The only thing that happens is a hunger pang. My stomach twists around its own emptiness. My throat is dry, every word scratching on the way out.

I'm on my feet before I understand what I've done. I stumble across the room to the table as if the chain itself is drawing me to the bread, and the wine, and the pitcher of water, and the shiny, red pomegranate.

I can't touch it. I cannot touch a single thing on this table, or I will shove it all into my mouth and eat like an animal. I should sit, wait, and be still. I should not give in to this temptation.

But my stomach hurts too much.

I find myself reaching before I can stop myself. I claw into the flesh of the pomegranate and lift out one shining seed.

It bursts between my teeth. Only a taste but such sweetness and divinity lies in its nourishment.

I swallow the juices with a moan, tipping my head back and closing my eyes. It's delectable. I'm not sure if it's the betrayal, the starvation, or the sheer deliciousness that adds to the pleasure. I've never been so satisfied, yet craved so much more, with such a thing.

Before I know it, the glass of wine is in my hand. It's dry and rich, smooth with no bitterness. A small moan slips from me into the glass. I'm sure I appear mad to any onlookers. *Let them savor the vision as I savor the divine wine.* The thought brings a smile to my lips.

I want to gulp it. Vaguely, I'm aware of the craze that's come over me. I want to pour the whole bottle down my throat, but I settle for another mouthful instead, then drop the glass to the table. It lands and cracks in two, spilling wine onto the surface, but as I watch, trembling with the flavors still on my tongue, it repairs itself and waits, upright, for me to fill it with more wine.

The magic...it tempts me. It calls to me. I wish it to buckle under my command.

The temptation has never been greater. My entire body feels pulled to the wine, even as the taste lingers in my mouth. I try to suck more of it down, but it's already fading. There is more here. *More that's meant to be mine.*

The lock on the door *clicks*, hushing the voice in my head. I yank my hand back from the table and rush back to the rug. I'll be damned if I willingly provide Hades the pleasure.

Only I don't stop at the rug. I pad across to the bed and clamber up onto it, pulling the sheet over me like a child hiding from a bad dream. Like those stories the mere humans tell.

It's pitiful. The moment the sheet graces my bare skin, I regret my decision. The desires of the gods are not so far off from mortals, and Hades's intention is obvious. This is what happens when I let my foolish desires get the better of me. This is what happens when I forget to stay strong and start to crumble instead.

With my teeth gritted and the sweet wine lingering on my lips, I stare at the god who dared betray Zeus and Demeter with my abduction. The bastard lord of the dead and ruler of the Underworld.

Hades's footsteps are already in the room before I can even meet his eyes. I cannot get out of the bed without drawing more attention to myself. It is a mistake.

But maybe he will not see that I gave in and tore into that pomegranate. Maybe he will not notice the missing wine. Maybe this is an acceptable sacrifice.

I lay my head on the pillow and close my eyes. Ignoring his presence the best I can.

I feel him pause, noticing his gaze hot on the curve of my body. His intentions slide over my skin underneath the blankets.

I try not to move. Still as can be with racing thoughts as the wine works its own magic. A depth of darkness slips through me and my grip tightens on the sheet.

My breathing gets faster. The tension I feel when he's in the room—when my heart is racing in a warning, *he's here, he's here, he's here*—is too strong to ignore. The scent of him is subtle, but it's there—faint and spicy, like something only the gods could dream of having.

My entire soul centers on his next step.

Will he touch me? Will he reach over the sheet and put his hand around my throat again? Will he lay his hand on my chest to feel my heartbeat? My pulse skips at the idea of his touch, lightning fast and too strong to resist.

And yet I did resist it. I told him *no* to his face.

How many more times will I have to resist? When he can make things so much easier for me? When he promises my powers, and surely, he's demonstrated his.

As many times as it takes, I tell myself sternly. *Even if I have to spend the rest of my life resisting. Even then.*

This god deserves nothing but my anger. How dare he take me, as if I am some possession!

His footsteps retreat, and I exhale a sound of disappointment. I can't stop the noise from slipping between my lips. All I manage to do is make it quieter. Then I press my face into the pillow and breathe long and slow, praying for my heart to slow.

A few minutes later, the bed dips. There are a few gentle tugs at the sheets.

He's gotten into bed beside me. And with him, the heavy presence of a blanket. A soft and luxurious blanket that promises warmth.

I've been too cold to warm the sheets myself, but his heat is an instant presence in the bed. It radiates off him. I will not go to him. I will *not*.

Although I crave the comfort.

It is dark in the bedroom. The low lights that had been on all night are off.

I listen to him breathing.

The sound is welcome after hours filled with only my own screams and tears. After an eternity filled with panic and a night filled with hunger and despair. The sound of Hades's steady breathing shouldn't offer me any comfort, but it does. Perhaps it's the wine. Perhaps it's my own curiosity. Perhaps it's the promises he's offered and how tempting they are.

Hot shame spreads across my face. I close my eyes and try to stop listening.

I can't.

I resolve to listen without caring instead.

I can't.

Another rustling sound. I peek out of the corner of my eye.

Hades has opened an arm to me, his hand nearly touching my shoulder. His masculinity is on full display with his carved muscles. A different temptation sweeps over me. Almost like protection…like a savior. I would only have to turn over, and I would be wrapped in his arms with warmth and an offering I can hardly refuse: my powers. *My magic.* I would barely have to lift my head, and I would be in his arms, his offering.

I close my eyes again. My chest aches, needy and tired. My body wants the warmth he offers. My body is a traitor, because it already wants to bend to his demands, if only to have food and drink. If only to have a taste of the power I'd begun to lose.

Would I be able to stop if I caved? Or would I fall desperately into madness. I've heard tales of Hades's brutality and surely this is weak compared to the stories. I almost tipped the bottle of wine to my mouth and splashed it all over my face in my desperation. Would I be able to hold myself back from Hades?

He sighs in the dark, a deep low sound of almost pleasure. "You will come in the night. It is not shameful."

It is not my choice, I want to tell him, but I cannot bring myself to speak. I fear too many other words would come with that admission. I fear I would tell him of the secret shame that grows behind my ribs and between my legs with every minute that ticks past.

It's the shame of wanting him. It's the shame of

wanting to give in. Everything about this is shameful. To bow down seemingly willingly although I've been given no choice. I have only shreds of my dignity left, and if I do not guard them with everything I have, I will be left with nothing.

"I will care for you," he adds. "Even if you do not care for yourself."

Anger simmers but only dully. As if he knows anything about me to that extent. I do not say a word.

I think, for a few moments, that he will offer me some of the blanket he brought with him, or cover me with it, the way he did last night.

Instead, he rises up from the bed. I lie with my eyes closed until it dips again, then open them and look.

He has brought food on a small plate, and he sits on the edge of the bed, the night lighting his face. My heart races at the regal lines of his beauty. The harsh, handsome face that brooks no argument. The power that sings in the air when he's here. This is his realm, and he *rules,* and yet he sits here next to me, an offering in his hands. Slowly, I sit up to see him more clearly, keeping the sheets clutched to my chest.

My mouth waters. It has nothing to do with the food on the plate.

Hades holds the plate out. Not quite offering it to me, but showing me what he's brought.

"You desire these, do you not?" he asks with the plate of stuffed vine leaves and marinated feta. Some of my favorite bites. As if he knows my cravings.

With strong fingers, he picks up a morsel and holds it to my lips. I desire to take it into my mouth so badly that I tremble from head to toe, but I don't let myself do it. I want to lick the food off his fingers.

"If you eat..."

He lets his words trail off and doesn't finish.

When I open my mouth, my lip brushes the morsel of food. "What will you give me?"

"Nourishment so you can gain your strength."

With those words, it seems to me that he is taking back some kind of deal.

Of course. Nothing he offers me comes without consequences. Nothing is offered without an implicit contract between us. Not even one bite of food. Not even a scrap of warmth.

I pull my head back an inch, clamping my mouth shut tight and raising my chin.

Hades makes a soft sound. Whether it's disappointment or frustration, I cannot tell.

As soon as Hades stands, I lie back down on the pillow, shaking harder with the near miss. I almost gave in. I almost let him feed me. I almost lost.

His footsteps move around the bed.

There's a soft click as he puts the plate on the table next to my pillow.

I do not move.

His footsteps retreat to the other side, and the mattress dips again. He climbs into the bed and turns onto his side, his back to me.

I do not know if he is sleeping when I reach out to take the food from the plate. I eat it silently, one morsel at a time, swallowing without any sound at all. I wish more of it would appear on the plate. I wish an entire tray of delicacies would materialize in the room. I wish I could eat it all night, and all day, and then the next night as well.

When I'm finished, my stomach no longer pains, but it's not full, either. I stare at the empty plate for a long time, wanting more, but I do not move. And I do not cave into his warmth.

chapter 11

Hades

If she does not respond to the offerings, I'll be forced to make her surroundings harsher. She will leave me with no choice. It is not my desire, but I cannot bend her to my will.

I pause for a moment after I unlock the door. Not long enough to make it seem as if I'm eavesdropping, but long enough to hear Persephone's footsteps quiet, flying across the room inside.

I pray she was eating. Her complexion has diminished and without nourishment, her powers are weaker than they were when she arrived. Again, not my desire. She is strong-willed.

The emotion flares up in me like a flame. I have to swallow it back, my expression harder than intended.

I cannot stop thinking about her eating. I cannot stop thinking about color coming back to her cheeks.

Color that is not from crying or raging or screaming. It would be the smallest sign of her acceptance. It would be the smallest sign of her submission. And my condemned soul relishes in her submission. Every little piece of it.

And I cannot put to words how dearly I want it. I cannot say how much I need to see her submission before my eyes.

I know she ate before. The plate was empty when I woke, the delicate pastries no more. Persephone slept on the pillow, unaware that she had stayed in the bed next to me all through the night.

I did not wake her to tell her I'd discovered her betrayal. That's how she will think of it. A betrayal of herself. She tried to keep herself away, and she could not. My failing is my inexperience. I'm not accustomed to company.

If that is betrayal, I am greedy for more of it. I need to take her to that betrayal with my hand in her hair, my grip so strong that she finally understands who has the power in my realm and who *could* have the power, if only—

I cannot think of this *if only*. It is a mistake.

So I do not make that mistake. Instead I pause for another second, giving her time to arrange herself.

The two guards outside my bedchambers keep their attention carefully away. This weakness of mine—her existence—is more than evident I'm sure. I do not keep them here to notice such things, and neither of them breathes a word.

With desire ringing in my blood, I open the heavy door and stride in.

Persephone isn't sitting on the plush rug I've offered for comfort, as she has been. She stands in the center, her hands folded in front of her and her head bowed. She's quiet and submissive, even in her stillness. That is not what I expected of such a strong goddess.

My cock hardens from the sight as I enter but keep the door open. Questions riddle my mind as I am mesmerized by her position. The thin silk fabric is draped delicately over her curves.

Fucking gorgeous. But I do not trust it.

I didn't expect her to break so quickly. From how she struggled and wept, I thought it would take longer. Years perhaps. Decades. An amount of time that would try my patience although for *this*, for *her*, I've done everything I can to be patient.

My pulse beats at the sight of her standing there. She could be a queen, still. Could be strong, still. Could be a goddess, still.

She will. I'll not live in a world where she does not reign beside me righteously and with the same powers as me.

Still, this presentation is...more delicious than the wine I offered her.

She's beautiful with a little color to her cheeks. Her long lashes are downcast, brushing against high cheekbones. Her full lips are no longer dry and cracked as they were.

It brings me to my next offering for her. The sexual pleasure I'm aware she's…not familiar with. I will fix it. I will tempt her. I will educate her as well.

"Persephone," I say. Her eyes flick up to meet me. I hold up a hand and gesture to the guards at my side. "If you are ever tempted and I am not here, there are men outside the door who could satisfy other needs…"

I let the suggestion hang in the air. In the silence, a revulsion twists in my gut. It sickens me to think of her indulging herself with another man, but such measures are necessary. Persephone cannot be allowed to think she is here to be worn to nothing. I want her to play… even in my absence. The thought of men with her, pleasing her, softening and warming her, it gave me great pleasure before this moment. But as the words escape, I question them. What possessiveness has come over me that I would selfishly hold her to a standard I do not express myself?

The only part of her I wish to break is her willful resistance to her own power. I want Persephone to be free of the lies others have told her. I want her to be free to dwell in her power.

I want her craving the pleasure I intend to give her. If she does not crave me at this moment, she may crave others.

For a moment, Persephone does not understand.

She looks at me, her eyes wide, confusion darkening their color.

Then my offer becomes apparent and a fresh blush spreads across her cheeks.

"I offer myself," one of my guards says, his voice calm and quiet, though of course I can hear the arousal underneath his breath. Anger bristles through me. Who would not be aroused by my Persephone? A gorgeous goddess of rare balance. It would be a rare person indeed. He does not step forward, but he is ready—if I gave the order, he would be with her in moments.

Dressed in armor, their presence is for protection, but her desires are to be met with enthusiasm, my orders.

"No," Persephone says quickly, almost with shock as well as fear, then clears her throat. I give no sign of how this pleases me to hear of her denial but still the thought lingers, she is not educated in the pleasures of flesh.

Is this because Persephone has decided to submit to me? Is it because, in her most secret heart, she has given into her desires? I do not know, but I do not give any sign of my speeding heart, nor the flicker of pleasure I feel at her words. "No, thank you, but no."

"The offer stands if you change your mind," I state easily although every nerve ending in me lights aflame. I need her to desire these things.

She casts her eyes back to the floor and swallows hard. Minox, I believe, was right in his suggestion. After all, the offerings have been accepted in her loneliness.

Yes. I *do* think Persephone has eaten. If she hadn't,

she would not be capable of such a deep flush. She would be too weak to stand for as long as she has.

Perhaps she would eat out of my fingers. If not now, then soon.

I am not used to such powerful feelings of impatience, but Persephone inspires them in me.

Still, I keep them on a close leash. I want, very much, to run the pad of my thumb over the deep blush on her cheeks, but I do not. I bide my time, waiting, letting the tension between us increase.

I have not told anyone how strong it has become. I will not tell Persephone that, even now, a current pulls me to her. I am strong enough to resist…for the time being.

As much as I want to touch her, I want her to beg me first. I stand a short distance away, my guards behind me, just outside the door at either side of me, and wait.

Until Persephone lifts her eyes again, daring to meet mine for only a moment or two. It is a breathtaking sensation, and it is only her gaze connecting with mine. It feels like breathing deeply for the first time in months. It feels like bloodlust, only it is not a desire to kill or maim. I feel a deep desire for pleasure and to pleasure her in return.

"Your guards will escort us today." I take one step nearer to her and watch her chest rise and fall faster, though she tries to hide it from me. Her initial instinct is to pull back. I despise it. She cannot hide anything from me. Not here. Not when I spend every waking moment thinking about the pink color on her cheeks and the curves of her body when she moves against me in her sleep. "Although I'm sure they are unneeded, given your state."

The corner of Persephone's mouth twitches with disgust at my comment. Her eyes flicker down to the floor and to the left. She is ashamed, but she is angry as well. The two emotions warring in her are obvious.

She *should* be ashamed for neglecting herself so. A goddess such as Persephone, with so much power just outside of her reach, should be ashamed of her inability to see what I'm offering her. Her power *and* mine. A crown for her head and a place at my side.

Though I must admit that I can admire her spirit. I admire her fight, even if I am certain she will lose. The game itself is…intriguing but not so much as the reward.

And what does it mean to lose? Persephone thinks it would be a great defeat, but I know better. It would be a triumph.

Closing the distance between us, I take another step. Persephone takes a long breath as if to steady herself. Her hands grip one another tightly, then relax.

She keeps her eyes lowered until I reach her and place two fingers underneath her chin. Persephone offers no resistance when I lift her face to mine. The heat of her skin against mine is everything, electrifying and alluring. I need more. More of her. More contact.

There is no resistance except for another flash of emotion in her eyes. Her lips tremble slightly, but she does not speak. I wait to see if my presence will compel her. If my eyes on hers are enough to break her. To bring the future tumbling in to meet us. To bring *her* future and *her* power into their full, uninhibited form.

I can imagine the cries that would come from her mouth when she felt it. I can hear them reverberating in my memory as clearly as her screams, though I have not heard her impassioned moans.

I haven't heard them *yet*. I have not drawn them out of her *yet*.

I will even if it requires sacrificing all of hell and burning it to the ground for her pleasure. Whatever her heart desires, I will discover and I will bend the Underworld to her will.

Time passes slowly as I wait, inhaling the sweetness and warmth her skin creates against mine. Inhaling the flame-like connection between the two of us, burning invisibly through the air and binding us together as surely as the chains bind her to this realm.

I see, I want her to say. *I see that this is not a cage, but a coronation. I see what it is to rule.*

But she does not speak. I drop my hand to my side, and Persephone swallows, her head moving forward as if to capture my touch.

Victory. A small one, but a victory nonetheless.

"I do not deserve your anger," I tell her. This is the truth, and it is time you hear it.

"Are you not the god who took me in the night?" she snaps back, her voice clear and ringing. I do not care if the guards hear her words. They are loyal souls, and the plans of the gods are not theirs to judge. Their tongues will not stay attached if they utter a word and they are aware of that.

"There are others that forced my hand." Although I hesitate to confess such things, I add, "They would have hurt you."

Her eyes narrow, darkening. "Lies." The singular insult nearly hissed.

With my hackles raised, I respond easily, "I tell no lies, my queen."

Her eyes flash once more at *my queen*. Her teeth clench together, and then she bites at her bottom lip, stopping as quickly as she discovers herself doing so. The struggle she faces in her mind is clear in her expression.

Oh, it will be delicious to coax it out of her. She must feel it growing in her. She must know that she craves power, and even more so, she must know that she craves vengeance.

There are those who have betrayed Persephone, but she is not used to such impulses. She is not used to the resolve it requires to seek revenge that is well earned with a wrath deemed intolerable. It requires one to put aside the empathy they hold for other people's weakness. It requires a certain bloodthirsty yet righteous rage, and I have no doubt that if I nurture it in Persephone, it will create havoc on the gods who have done this.

Who would not want to know that their pain had

been avenged? Who would not want to see their enemies vanquished, once and for all?

The gods know I would relish both.

"There is no need to feel conflicted within yourself, my queen. I can offer you the balance you seek."

Persephone lifts her chin. "You speak of balance, but you are still the god who—"

"Who rescued you from danger. You must have known that there was no safe harbor for you on Olympus."

"I knew no such thing," she says with certainty, but the volume of her voice gives her away. It is obvious to anyone that Persephone was keeping secrets when she dwelled in the home of the gods. She would not have craved my presence, would not have accepted it, if she had not been afraid. If she had not known she was near a precipice of abandonment.

They did not want her as she was. I crave her as she is presently and as what she will become. *Mine.*

"You will come to know it," I say, mildly. "You will come to see that you could seek the balance I speak of. It will not take you long, my queen, to see that I am the one who holds it."

"Balance means nothing," she says, though there is a note of curiosity in her voice. Persephone may not believe me now, but she will see. I will make her see. "Imbalance fuels the cycles of what must be."

"What does balance mean to you? Tell me."

"Life," she says softly. "My *life*. And with it, death."

She seems to hesitate, to ponder on the world. My lips threaten to lift in an asymmetric grin. It's telling, her pause. Where there is life, there will be death. And she should rule both. She is destined for it, I know it.

"Your life was not balanced. It was rotting where it lay in the ground. You could not see this because you were not willing to see, but I did, and I intervened. Now I offer you true balance. Your powers and the heads of those who betrayed you delivered on platters for your amusement."

Persephone's mouth drops open, her lips parting slightly. All she must do is allow herself to taste what I am offering, the way she allowed herself to taste the delicacies I brought for her. Once she knew the flavor of power and the flavor of revenge, she would want to glut herself on it. She would find her place of belonging. Where she is meant to be.

"I—" She begins, her hands trembling. "I do not want heads on platters." She stresses the statement although her eyes stay wide with shock. "I do not want to kill for amusement. You are the one who judges. You are the one who sends souls to suffer for eternity."

Persephone's eyes meet mine, suspicious. As if I guide my realm for my own amusement. As if judgment is a child's game.

"You do not know of what you speak," I grit out, not so much insulted by her statement, but more so disappointed with her lack of education.

"You have not told me the truth."

"You have already chosen to believe the lies of others and the lies you tell yourself so you may have what you seek rather than what you are destined to own."

"Why should I not believe others when you've done this?" Persephone cries. "You brought me here. You will not let me go. I am no different from the infinite other souls who—"

"You *are* different." I did not mean to raise my voice, but I must—the anger has burned too hot in me, and Persephone is too close to ignore the heat of her accusations. "You are my queen. And I am not a jailer for every soul who enters my realm."

"But—"

"Those who do no good are condemned to a thousand years of reflecting on their misdeeds."

"That is harsh. That is *cruel,*" Persephone argues and once again her eyes widen. She has much to learn, and the thought strikes a new kind of detest through me.

"It may be cruel, but it is fair. These souls turned their backs on others, so they should be forced to suffer as well. They are left with their thoughts and their memories, looking into the truth of how they failed until they turn their back on themselves."

"And what happens then?" Persephone demands, her voice shaking. "What happens to those who cannot save themselves? Who cannot right their wrongs? Sometimes they know not what they do."

She is thinking of herself. Persephone is young and does not wish to see the truth of her circumstances.

But my words are striking a chord in her. I can tell they are burrowing deep into her mind.

I can tell she will think about them when she falls asleep at night and when she wakes in the morning.

I can tell these thoughts I am planting will only grow.

I can tell she is thinking of herself as a soul condemned to a thousand years of hopelessness, but she is not. She is blessed with a thousand years of power.

If only she would reach out and take it. If only she would fall to her knees and let me give it to her.

"They are simply hopeless. Simply empty. And then they are sent back. To do better..." I take her chin in my hand and stare into her eyes. "Or not."

"That is—"

She attempts to interrupt but I continue. "May they hear the sounds of torture and the pleas from their victims, one at a time, over and over, unable to stop it now that it is done. May they live with the screams and cries, the wails of babes and their mothers' screeches for mercy, over and over again and hear nothing else and feel nothing else but the raw pain and the emptiness of hardships."

"Those who do such things..."

"They are not you. You could not and would not cause so much agony, would you? Would you seek for those who profit on pain to have no justice?"

"I—"

"Yes, I am cruel. Because life requires it. Death is where so much justice is delivered and I have the honor of balancing that pain but there is so much more," I say with my voice low. "There is so much more to the Underworld. So much more of balance and…" My breathing becomes heavy as I stare at her. Knowing the weight of what will be when she is given her throne.

"So much what?" she asks.

But I cannot answer. Not just yet. Not when she knows next to nothing. When she has no idea what power she already has.

chapter 12

Persephone

I stare up at Hades, waiting for his expression to change…for something to change. Tension lingers in the air between us. These souls—these mortals—they get a second chance. What about the gods? Do *they* ever get a second chance? I wish I had the power to go back. I wish any god had that power.

Swallowing thickly, I wait.

I do not wring my fingers together, but I want to. The strength in Hades's touch feels barely restrained. If he wanted, he could take me to the bed and have his way with me, and I would be powerless.

Surprised by my thoughts, I ignore the shiver of desire that moves through me at the idea of being powerless.

It's not right for me to feel that. I *am* powerless. I

am still a captive in chains. Yet it is his hands that stay in my mind, just as his hand is on my chin.

Touch me. He must be thinking it, given his offer of the guards...

"Come," he says, and walks to the door. The two guards who came with him follow without hesitation. The small hairs on the back of my neck stand as I glance at the men. I can barely look them in the eye. Especially the guard who dared to speak up and offer himself. What a fool, a voice in the back of my head hisses, but I ignore that darkness. I ignore the shadows. What lurks there brings out the worst in me.

I stare at Hades and can't move.

"What?" I manage to say, my throat gone dry with the shock.

Hades turns his head. "*Come*, my queen."

A blush rises to my cheeks and I stand, only now noting the chill has dimmed with Hades in the room. I hurry to catch up with him. I didn't expect him to offer to take me out of his chambers. My mind races with thoughts of why. What did I do that made him think he could let me out? Perhaps he's only taking me to the hallway. Perhaps this is only a trick meant to confuse me. To taunt me with his power. But my heart leaps excitedly into my throat anyway. Racing, beating hard, and trying to keep up with every little thought and every little possibility.

Once I am at Hades's side, he puts his hand at the small of my back. Goosebumps rise and I nearly shiver at his heated touch. It takes everything not to gasp. The guards follow us as he sets a fast pace, moving down the hall.

I keep myself poised, but alert. Perhaps the magic of chains does not follow. I wish I could test such things without Hades noticing. Glancing again to my left and right, flanked by the two guards, I think better of attempts of escape.

At least for now.

As our silent footsteps echo in the halls, I take in the surroundings so different from Olympus.

I knew I was in his realm, the Underworld, but the size of the land of the dead only becomes apparent when we leave what must be his bedchambers. Every window carves out cities of souls. Distant lights and noise travels and don't seem to end. As we take a spiral staircase down, I'm given more and more view of so much of what has only been stories.

Every corner of the Underworld houses different souls of different fates. From the unfortunate to those who live in abundance. From the gods and heroes, to those who are damned, and those in between. Ones who suffer with loss for a thousand years in the Fields of Mourning to those souls simply living peacefully now that their human lives have ended.

I cannot imagine the depth of Hades's reign. So much to control. So many souls to judge.

In the back of my mind, I think so much cruelty defined as just.

After a long quiet tour, we walk down a cobblestoned path lined with dark blooms that leads us to the front of his castle.

"This path," I say, pulling one question from the ocean of others in my mind. It feels different here. *It feels familiar.* "Is it—what is it?"

"It is the path by which we see the realm," Hades says. It must not be real the way mortals think of *real,* but it is here nonetheless. I have the sense that the Underworld is vast—far more vast than I'd realized—and that the only way to travel its lengths is by this path.

As we walk, Hades holds out his hand to gesture at a place brimming with greenery and sunlight.

"Elysium," he says. "The souls of heroes dwell here. Demigods and great mortals as well." In the far distance, I can see houses. A town, perhaps. Wide streets with people crossing this way and that. "They may return to Earth, if they choose." I flinch at such a thought.

A glimmering sea and another lush outcropping of green appear.

"The Isle of Achilles," Hades says, hardly glancing at it. "And Odysseus. That is where they dwell."

After a few more minutes, we cannot see the green fields from the path any longer. Instead, when Hades gestures, it's into caverns, so dark I cannot see where they end. Fire brims from outcroppings in those caverns, molten and hot as it lands.

Large shadowy figures in the shadows cry out, their voices like rocks scraping against one another. Something drags and clinks. Metal chains? A chill flows down my spine and my eyes widen with alertness.

"The Titans," Hades says, tone dismissive. "Old gods that Zeus and I overthrew. They dwell in Tartarus with all those who rebel against the guards."

Zeus. The mention of my father brings back other emotions along with the acknowledgment of my predicament. I do my best to cover the feelings and focus on his statement. The Titans… I know all about the Titans from my father's stories. May they suffer for eternity. All but Hecate of course.

I want to turn my eyes away from the prison. "In the dark? In chains?"

"They suffer for all eternity," Hades says. "Eternal hunger. Eternal thirst. They are broken on an eternal wheel. Their flesh burns without ceasing."

I swallow hard, sweat pricking on my forehead.

Light appears on the path ahead of us. "But," I begin, thinking of my faithful friend and her worship. "Hecate."

"Not Hecate," Hades agrees. "Hecate has access to all the realms and retains power under Zeus."

Mother of witches, queen of ghosts, keeper of keys and crossroads, Hecate is the only Titan to rule after the wars. As she should.

Never have I met her, but often I think of her as Mother.

It is not sunlight we step into as we leave Tartarus behind, but a gray, cloudy sky. It is not raining, though the air is heavy with drops yet to fall. It is the light of a stormy afternoon, one where the sun will not come out from behind the clouds, but will set into darkness without ever brightening the fields below it.

"The Fields of Mourning," Hades says, his voice softer. "Those who took their own lives dwell here."

"All of them?" I question. I've heard the tales and I've had questions. But I do not know the details and in my curiosity, I must ask. These thoughts concern me.

"The ones who could no longer bear the sadness of a lost love."

Nodding slightly, I attempt to understand.

"Will they be all right?" I have to ask.

"In time," Hades responds, his dark eyes seeming to look through me in a way I have to avert my gaze.

Clearing my throat, I allow him to continue to lead me. All the while, I attempt to memorize every inch of this place and search for a way out. For the river perhaps.

The light brightens. Sun *does* peek out, but I cannot see where it is from the sky. The next area we pass seems hazy in my eyes, the colors deep and saturated, like jewels. Buildings with tall arches are just visible in the distance.

"The Land of Dreams," Hades intones. "Ruled by Morpheus. He hosts souls while they dream, for he designs the dreams."

As Hades continues to lead me, his hand steady on my lower back, the clunk of the boots from the guards is a reminder that I too am stuck here wherever Hades deems me worthy.

We pass a large gate made of metal that gleams in the light. A tall figure in dark robes, the hood pulled up over his head, stands near the gate, hands folded. He does not look impatient in the least. A smaller figure stands next to him, shoulders hunched.

"Thanos," Hades says. "He takes the souls to Hermes, who guides them to the entrance of the Underworld."

The silent man merely nods. The darkness that surrounds him is uncanny and I do my best to avoid his gaze.

We leave the gate behind. A river winds through the realm, its waters moving under a current.

"The River Styx," I say. I have heard legends of the River Styx. There is not a soul alive who has not heard those stories. It could also be a way out. A glimmer of hope rises in me, and I search within myself.

Hades nods. "Charon steers the ferry, but he only transports those souls who have proper payment."

"Payment?"

"Two coins for his services, and the soul is buried. If no payment is given, they are left to wander the shores for all eternity."

"Two coins? As in they must be buried with them?"

"If they would like help in the afterlife."

That does not strike me as fair, but I keep this opinion to myself.

"And once the soul crosses the river?"

Hades glances down at me. "The soul stands before

three judges. They determine the soul's place in the realm and send them along according to my governance."

"To eternal suffering?"

"Or to eternal peace," he adds, again glancing at me in a way that makes my soul stumble.

"What's beyond the river?" I dare to ask, keeping my voice even.

"Death," is all Hades answers and in his tone I swear he must know the reason I asked. I stare straight ahead, avoiding his pining gaze.

The river falls away, and we come upon more fields.

"The Asphodel Meadows. For souls neither good nor evil." Hades's voice is beginning to sound strained. "They may drink from the River Lethe, which washes away the memories so that the soul may be reborn." His tone is almost one of boredom.

"Is something wrong?"

This time, when he glances down at me, there's a certain sharp anger in his eyes. "No. Of course not."

I look away. "This is your realm, then?"

"This is only the surface of my realm."

I don't know what possesses me. It could be courage, or it could be the past days feeling like an eternity of hours.

"I want to see the rest."

To my surprise, Hades does not deny me. I push away the uncomfortable thought that I am the only one denying myself this freedom.

"Come, my queen," he says and turns on the path.

I ignore the way he addresses me, purely grateful for the change in scenery and smitten by the questions that gather in the back of my mind. This realm is vast and orderly, so different from Olympus, so different from the Earthly realm.

I am not certain how we enter the palace, that stands tall of old stone in the distance. I only know that it's not outside, as the path was. We walk down a long hallway instead, passing arched doorway after arched doorway.

It's odd how the ground moves and how each corridor appears. As if space is not of what I know it to be. One step is nearly a mile.

These are the dens of heaven and hell, I think, and my heart pounds with how close they are. How visible.

My instincts are to run. These rooms are not for me. They are for those who dwell in them. I dare to peek, although something in me holds me back, something frightened.

In one of the rooms, a man tilts his head back, letting out thick, guttural moans. Along the walls are blots of ink, they move and scatter as I attempt to see them. As if they don't wish to be seen. Perhaps they're only for him.

"What's happening to him?" I ask, my curiosity feeling almost filthy.

"It's a manner of psychology, an inkblot treatment," Hades answers, looking in dispassionately. "For torture of pleasure."

"Torture of pleasure?" I question, so unsure of what I've just heard.

He laughs, a short, knowing sound. "Yes." Clearing his throat, he adds, "these rooms are designed for the particular soul. For they are not welcome in the other realms and require special attention."

He takes me through the threshold of another room, and a woman approaches. In a long burgundy gown, her blonde hair braided and swaying down her back. She is beautiful, like my sister Aphrodite, and comes close to caressing my face.

I lean into her touch, unthinking, but Hades's hand on my arm pulls me back. The woman's touch lingers on my skin even after she's walked away.

The room changes around her. The colors on the walls and on the bed warm, making her skin warmer as well. I blink, and she's tangled in the sheets with a man, their mouths open and searching. He turns her over and ruts into her, his forehead leaning against her shoulder. Every bit of exposed skin glistens with how hard they're moving together.

My nipples harden as an immediate reaction. My lips part and my brow rises.

Eventually, she collapses onto the pillows and sleeps.

I blink, and there are two more men in the room with her. The beautiful woman opens her eyes and screams. I jerk backward, but Hades is there, and his presence steadies me enough that I keep watching. With my back to his front, I stare in shock.

One of the men leans down and covers her mouth. The other—

I can't see what he does, or I don't want to see, but there is blood trickling down her skin when he straightens again.

The woman wrenches free, and the first man—the one who was there in the beginning—catches her in his arms. Comforts her.

None of it seems to be a comfort. There is blood on her lips, and she lets out another shrill scream. The other two men have not stopped touching her. They're cutting her. *Hurting* her.

"They wanted to play and scared you?" The first man murmurs. I do not know how I can hear him so clearly when he's speaking into her ear.

"No," she sobs. "I said no. He covered my mouth when I tried to scream again."

In an instant, he viciously murders the two who harmed her. Ruthlessly, with a heavy stone in his hand, the crunch of their skulls and the screams almost muffled.

Shock keeps me still, but so does Hades's grasp. Vengeance. Is this a room of vengeance?

Every time I blink, the image before me changes. It looks real, and close, as if I could reach out and touch her skin, just as she touched me. The first man leans down between the woman's legs and pleasures her, sucking at her clit until she cries out from pleasure. Her lover. Unlike the other two.

She is comforted and loved by him so. Is this a room of heaven or hell?

The man between her legs lifts his head and gives her clit a final lave of his tongue. The woman throws her head back, sobbing or coming. Maybe she is doing both.

He gets to his feet. "Kiss her for me, will you?" he tells another.

A fourth man materializes out of the shadows. He takes his place between the woman's legs and continues licking her, but she doesn't look at him.

She watches the first man, who walks calmly to the two men who had drawn so much blood.

He slaughters them. As if they were not already dead. Chokes the life out of them. One by one, they fall to the floor and lay still. My pulse is a hammer in my ears. I can hardly catch my breath. He brings them back to life, only to kill them once more.

My breathing picks up at the realization. All the while the woman is pleasured by another, watching her lover commit murder.

I notice, as if I'm coming awake for the first time, that Hades's hand is on my shoulder.

"Is this heaven or hell?" I breathe the question, and he laughs, low and pleased. "I love that you have to ask. I suppose it depends on who you are and what your soul is made of."

I tip my face to his, lost for words and lost for thoughts. What has come over me? Something I've never felt before seems to rise in this room. Like magic of fate…like a piece of my soul has found something it was long searching for.

Something it didn't know existed and yet it knew it was missing.

Hades does not push me away as I gasp. As I stare into his eyes wondering if he knows this feeling that's come over me. Slowly, ever so slowly, he kisses me, and his mouth is the only thing that feels real. His lips hot and soft. His touch even hotter. My head goes light and my legs weak as I stand in his embrace.

It's over too soon and I didn't have a moment to even realize what was happening. When he releases his touch, I blame the halls. There are too many rooms, too many visions, and I cannot make sense of them.

It takes a moment for my vision to clear and for me to realize what happened.

The feelings evoked in me are visceral. They're overwhelming and electric. I do everything I can to ignore them.

The lights flicker beyond my vision as he puts his hand to my face and kisses me deeper.

When I pull away, we're back in the hallway outside his rooms. I glance up, and one of his guards is looking at me. He meets my eyes boldly for a second or two, then looks away.

I have the sense that I've traveled a long way. A vast, unthinkable distance. I wobble a bit on my feet, and Hades steadies me.

"This way," Hades says simply, leaving behind what happened as if it didn't. My body trembles as I close my eyes and steady myself. What have I done?

I think he will leave me in his rooms, but instead he leads me down another corridor, the guards following closely, too close for my liking.

We pass through an archway that reminds me of the many caverns of heaven and hell, and I shiver as we go across the threshold. Some of the things I have seen remain vivid in my mind. Others feel more like dreams, as if there's not enough space for my memory to hold them. There's not enough in me to hold onto everything I've seen today. How does Hades do it? Lord over all of this? I watch him as we walk and wonder what occupies his mind as he ventures the halls and creates their reality.

How does Hades hold all of his realm in his mind? How does he rule over such a vast space, filled with so many souls?

I look at him out of the corner of my eye, reconsidering him.

He looks down at me, all traces of the anger he showed before gone. It is like being watched by a predator. A beast whose power is undeniable, and whose rule will not be questioned. My pulse ticks up at the thought that I've already questioned him in more ways than one.

"These are the baths," he says, and gestures just as he did when he was showing me the Underworld. The hot springs are undeniably tempting. The smooth rock and falling waters that steam call to me. The scent of lavender and something else waft to me, drawing me in and calming me before I've even touched the hot waters. Beyond them, the raw cliffs of sparking quartz and pyrite shimmer...there's not an ounce of greenery though. No life present, only Mother Earth in her raw form of stone.

"Bathe. You may take as much time as you wish." With the command given, he turns and walks out. A gesture at one of the guards has him following Hades away from the baths. The other guard keeps his eyes on the floor and goes to station himself near the door. Closing them and giving me privacy for the first time since we've left. The only sounds are my own beating heart and the soothing waters.

Time passes and I stand in wonderment. I turn toward the baths. The pale pink of the salts that wall in the baths shines through a dim light. Creating a calming and soothing feel. The divine oils, scrubs, and soaps sit on a gold intricate tray at the right and just behind the tray lay a pile of lush towels and washcloths. Across an elegant gold chair with rolled arms and a high back lies a cream silk gown.

There is not just one *bath*. There are many pools of inlaid quartz stone and clear water. Some of them bubble. Others have steam rising from them. Vaguely I think of my sister Aphrodite. She would adore these baths. Deep in my heart there is a longing, but one that for some reason feels touchable, if only I wanted.

I will not be able to deny myself this.

I've been so cold, and it seems like I've been cold forever. At the side of one of the pools, I stop and dip my toes in.

The water is deliciously warm. It feels like the sea

heated under the sun all day, and even standing at the edge, all my muscles relax as if I'm already submerged.

I remove my gown after what feels like an eternity. It slides over my shoulders before I've made any conscious decision to give in.

All I know is that I need to be in the water, cleansing myself of the fear and the desperation that came over me. I need the water to wrap around me with its warmth, touching me everywhere and clearing my head of what I have seen.

I step into the water, a sigh escaping me. The visions—or memories—will not last long. The sensation of the warm water holds too much pleasure and relief.

Most of what remains from the tour fades almost immediately.

What does not fade is Hades. His kiss. His touch. Vaguely I remember the river, although it seems much less like an escape now. What lies beyond it is surely not something I wish to see. Instead, as I attempt to organize my thoughts, I think of Hades.

I tip my head back, letting the water soak into my hair, and look at the ceiling high above me as I trail my fingers through the water. It's the perfect temperature to soak in—hot, but not painfully so. It is exactly what I've craved.

Almost what I've craved.

I would like to take my time but scratching in the back wall breaks the moment. Almost like a cracking. I bring my hand to my chest, startled and unsure of what

I've heard. In the silence, the soothing waters murmur, and I cannot hear the sound again. But I swear I heard something, what it is, I'm not sure.

Quickly I dress and search for Hades, only to find him right outside the doors.

chapter 13

Hades

THE SOUL IS HALF-DEAD, ONLY THE REMNANTS of his clinging to the flesh I've damaged. The anger in me is not satisfied. Not in the least as I hover over him, the rage nearly blinding. He no longer cries for mercy. He speaks more of sorrow and regret. Blood pools on the floor, spreading out from what was once identifiable as his body. There can't be much left, and soon it will trickle out onto the tiles, and his soul will be taken for judgment.

Each blow was a soothing balm. The rage could only be held in for so long. He must've known it was coming. What torture it must've been for him to walk beside me, knowing what was to come of his fate but not knowing when it would be delivered.

She bathed and cleansed herself. I sought his punishment to cleanse myself as well. It is not surprising that I struck the first blow the moment the heavy quartz doors closed.

The guard to my right is silent and still. Standing straight and at attention. I barely hear him, focused on the man in my grasp.

He will stand before the judges stained with my disapproval. *How dare he.* That's all I can think. The rage is something I've not known before. One to be untamed and in the back of my mind, my anger is at myself as well. And Minox.

But this soul takes the brunt of it all.

A sound at the door distracts me from the task at hand. I glance up to find Persephone crossing the threshold, her eyes wide, then wider as she takes in the scene.

One moment her pure innocence is easily seen, her gown drifting slightly behind her with her stride, and the next, her eyes full of shock and horror at the sight.

She hovers at the boundary, her toes almost in the pool of blood, her hands trembling. Her hair is beautifully braided; she is freshly bathed and so innocent. Perhaps I should have dealt this judgment elsewhere. Not outside the doors of the baths, but I could not wait. I'd already waited for privacy too long.

"Hades." She speaks my name as if a prayer of despair. Not the way I envision. Her words echo, sounding larger than they are.

"I changed my mind," I tell her without context, and the confusion and horror on her face only aid me in my realization. "You may not seek pleasure in the guards."

I deal one last blow to the thing at my feet and turn to study her more closely.

Pale skin. Pale lips. Her terror is palpable, but it's not her brush with disaster that terrifies her.

It's *me*.

Her brows draw together as I watch her. Can't she feel the pull between us? Can't she feel how a little blood could never break it? Terror won't be enough.

I gesture at the guard, who is hardly a man anymore. "He coveted what was mine."

Persephone's mouth drops open. "You *offered* me to him."

Her misunderstanding is frustrating. "No, I offered him to you, and you did not wish such things."

There is quite a difference. He took it upon himself to present an offer. He dared to fantasize what was not his. Now he shall suffer a loss. Just as I have.

I will deal with Minox later. And my own wayward thoughts.

"This? This was his own doing," I tell her, knowing full well the blood on my knuckles will come clean.

Persephone takes a step back from the spreading blood, but it won't be enough. The blood will continue to pool until there is no more left, and even after the guard's final heartbeat, the circle around him will grow until a servant comes to clear it away.

"I want nothing to do with this," Persephone says, swallowing hard. Her eyes drop to the mess at my feet. "I shall never love a monster like you."

Taken aback from her statement that echoes in the halls of the baths, I steady myself. My anger replaced with something else.

I take a deep breath and calm myself. This…this is nothing. If she is to be queen of the dead, this kind of judgment should not weigh on her as it appears it does. The Fates promised me. They swore to me…

I remind myself of the deal I made before telling Persephone, staring into her gorgeous eyes filled with terror. "You are worthy, and what you knew before is no longer." Her eyes come to mine. "Enjoy what I give you, my queen. It was always yours to have."

"I did not ask for this," she whispers. Her gaze attempts to leave mine, and I position myself between her and the nearly dead soul.

"No one asks for fate." That is the very nature of fate itself. It does not come when gods or mortals bid. It is *fate*. The fact that Persephone is choosing not to understand after a lifetime among the gods tries my patience.

"I choose my fate," she states firmly, as if she truly believes such things.

"Take him," I command the remaining guard, and without hesitation, he drags his former companion away. The metal of his armor scrapes on the stone floor.

"My queen, that is nothing to cause alarm," I assure her, but she stares behind me, watching with terror.

"Why?"

"He spoke when he should not."

She merely shakes her head, staring at me with disbelief.

"As if you are not privy to such displays in Olympus," I comment as shame rises with her judgment. "As if you cannot understand why such acts are needed.

"I—" She starts but cannot finish.

"He was one man. One who spoke when he should not have, coveted where he damn well knew he should not."

"You said—"

"Perhaps it is that you are so beautiful he could not resist."

She parts her lips in protest.

"He knew...I know he did. You denied him and so he perished. It is just."

A shiver rolls down her shoulders.

"Let me make it up to you." I offer a distraction. "Your powers are—"

"My powers do not work here." She cuts me off. Seemingly more distant than before. "I cannot bring life in the Underworld."

With the guard far off in the distance and no trace of the abuse that occurred apart from a streak of blood on the floor, I use a cloth from my back pocket and rid myself of the evidence, still standing between her and the sight behind me.

"There are other powers," I murmur, knowing what is to come.

"I do not *want* others," Persephone screams, and as

the sound is multiplied by the room, the air grows hotter with her anger. My pulse rises with it. This is but a flicker of what I know she's capable of. "I do not belong here," she states. Her lips and eyes darken as she stands before me. A vision of her I've seen flashes before my eyes.

"You *do* belong here. More than you know." It's a promise. This was meant to happen. "Next to me. Reigning beside me. You must learn the ways of the Underworld."

Her hands ball into fists at her sides. She clenches her jaw, her cheeks bright with her fury. "I will never stand beside you."

"Consider—" If she means her words to batter me, she has failed. There is nothing that can dissuade me.

"*You* did this to me." She narrows her eyes, the color dark, almost murderous. "I know who and what you are, and I will *never* obey. I regret what I felt for you. I regret it all."

The thread of my patience snaps. Persephone has been sheltered, yes, but she should not be so bold as to presume she knows *what* I am. She does not know enough to speak to me so, and her anger is both misguided and useless.

Perhaps she is not ready. Perhaps I should not have given her such freedoms. It is my mistake. As I tilt my head, my neck cracks and I do what I can to temper my rage at her thoughtless statements.

Breathing in deeply, I call out for the guards.

The clank of his metal is met with the sound of her

sharp gasp. "Take her to my chambers." I cannot look at her as I give the command.

She doesn't resist. She doesn't protest, and I am thankful for such things. Even if she screams profanities at the men who escort her.

"Do not touch me!" she hisses and that gets my attention.

"You will not harm her," I emphasize to them although they are far more aware than she that they lay beneath her feet.

Her eyes catch mine for only a moment and then she strides ahead with them trailing behind. Disappointment is my only company as I stare back down to my hands, the blood filled in the cracks of my roughly calloused palm.

How could she feel such things for a guard who would put his desires before his duty?

She…is so far from the queen I envision. Yet I feel her power so close.

If this plagues her… If one act of so little consequence yields a reaction from her of this magnitude, how will she ever face the courts? Let alone rule them?

She knows not of his previous life and his debts. She knows not anything of him and yet, she persists in anger and torments me?

I am tired of this lack of progress. I am tired of her focus on what she believes to be true rather than what *could* be true if she would stop railing against it.

The new rage that burns in me is only because of

the memory of the damned soul's quiet offer. Of how he thought, for an instant, I would let him put his hands on her.

And worse—

The sickening question of whether she would want it. I had not known what Persephone's answer would be. I had not dared to hope that she would refuse.

I crave her satisfaction and yet it appears that I am ill-equipped.

I was a fool. There is no such ease with Persephone. She is far too naive, too flighty, to understand that blood on the floor does not always mean a monster is nearby. That fucking *loyalty* does not make a person a threat. That she could be free of her imagined prison if she would accept her true status and her true power. That the ties that bind her would be nothing if she realized she's the one who made them.

It's not long before the other guard returns, and it takes greater effort than I'd like to remain composed. How have I stayed here in this filth with my own thoughts for far too long a time?

"She is safely secured. Shall the doors be locked?"

The magic is still her captor, I nearly tell him but resist. "No need to lock the doors to your queen," I tell him instead. When I am ready, I will give her grace in movement.

"Get rid of half the torches down the left side of the hall," I order him, my voice on the verge of breaking into a shout. "So she's more willing to go right. Give her access and watch her for her protection only."

"Do you think she'll try to escape, my lord?" the guard asks.

I huff a humorless laugh. Escape? I am not concerned of her ability to escape. She cannot and will not without aid. I am concerned her pleas will leave the Underworld and make their way back to Olympus. Secrecy has been an ally the past few days. But the magic will aid me in her silence.

"No. She needs to learn the ways of our realm. Allow her to reign as she should, and she will find her place beside me." I don't speak the last thought out loud, like it or not, this is her fucking fate, and she cannot outrun it.

I walk away from the halls without thought, with only a black anchor clouding my mind. I do not have a destination in mind. I only want to shed these thoughts with brisk movement, but they will not go.

Persephone...my beautiful queen...what am I to do with you so that you will both rule and love me as I love you?

I exhale sharply, trying to release the disappointment. Anger and disappointment have always been strong in me, but that only makes it more difficult to tolerate Persephone's. She does not have anything to be angry about. The things that have happened to her pale in comparison to the life I had before I ruled the Underworld. She is meant for this. She is no victim.

This is a part of her story, and her stubbornness turns her blind. If only she would give in and allow fate to move her as it must.

Slowly, a fear creeps in me. One I've never felt before. I'm quick to acknowledge it and release it, condemning it to the pit of hells where fear belongs.

Minox glides into step next to me, detaching from the shadows without my notice.

"My lord," he says.

"Minox," I say, my teeth gritted. I find I cannot relax them for several beats.

"Where are you going, my lord?"

"I haven't decided," I snap at Minox, though this is not his fault. "I haven't decided," I say again, moderating my tone. "Do you require my presence?"

His hands are folded inside his black robe. His steps have not faltered, even once.

Before he can begin a conversation, I whistle, loud and sharp. I should have called for Cerberus long ago. My faithful companion. A few moments pass, and loping footsteps, along with the *clink* of his collar, grow louder until Cerberus is at my side.

I stop to pet his three heads, stroking between each one in turn until my lungs feel less liable to explode. Cerberus wags his tail and presses two of his snouts into my leg. His black fur shines as a healthy coat.

"Come, Cerberus."

My dog walks along at my side already soothing the agony of impatience, and Minox and I continue down the wide hallway. Cerberus pauses to sniff at several doorways, but stays close.

It is several minutes before Minox speaks again. He takes a short breath before he does, warning me in advance that he intends to say something I will not like.

"It is my humble suggestion that you do not leave her tonight, my lord."

"Excuse me?" This is my realm. I will leave any rooms I wish. I will walk any halls I wish. I will remain absent for as long as I wish.

"I fear she needs your comfort," Minox says, giving no sign of discomfort.

"And what do I know of comfort?" The hot, twisting sensation that shame always brings settles low in my gut like a pool of acid. For it is in the gut of my father that I resided for centuries. Comfort and niceties, social norms…they are not for me. It is not my destiny. The irony that I rule the largest and most delicately balanced realm when I was brought up in dreadful solitude is not lost on the gods.

Minox knows as well as I do that I am the last person who should dare to offer comfort.

I sat for centuries in the pit of a Titan's stomach. I sat alone, in darkness, with nothing but darkness to comfort me. The whispers say it is why I am so cruel. And yet they agree with balance. So many often forget the angels were the most successful murderers. They only exist because they were willing to slaughter ruthlessly. They killed for righteousness and all those who observe choose to forget how they came to be and look at only the glory. Those who do not become comfortable with their darkness and are blinded by the light they crave. One must see both to understand fully what balance truly means.

Although I brought a knowing the gods understood, ruling the Underworld was trying. Surrounded by those in need and judging those who live in worlds so different from my own. The sensation of touch sickened me when I returned to the world. I found it appalling. Disgusting.

Until the visions of Persephone.

She is the first person whose touch does not make me want to rage for as many centuries as I spent imprisoned.

Her touch is all I have ever wanted. And she is the other half to what is required in the Underworld. She will be the queen of the dead. And what an irony it is for her, as in the other realms she provides the most comforting life in delicate flowers that cannot exist in these walls of crystals.

"Do not leave her tonight?" My brow pinches at the absurdity. She does not care for companionship. She does not crave me the way I crave her. And I do not wish to submit myself to rejection so bluntly.

It is brazen of Minox to suggest it. I never wish to be confronted with this lack in myself. How am I supposed to know how to touch her in a way that would bring comfort? I could not bring comfort to myself in all those dark, tortured years and very little has changed since. I remind myself of the warning from the Fates: in time she will be yours. But you must be patient.

"I believe," Minox says slowly. "You wish to give her comfort."

I do not speak. I cannot speak. His daring has gone too far. He has seen too much to continue. Now, at least.

"Leave me," I murmur lowly, barely able to refrain from anger. My wants have never been a concern to others. Never.

"Yes, my lord," Minox says, and melts back into the shadows.

With Cerberus at my side, the hours pass. They do not pass quickly or enjoyably, but they pass with more ease than before. I pay no attention to where we walk. I throw a stick for him in a meadow. I let him roam through wild gardens, sniffing out small creatures. In the distance, the sky cracks along the river. More souls arrive. As souls come, others leave. Choosing the Earthly realm. If ever there is an imbalance, the sky cracks, shattering the weight of what the Underworld carries. Souls who do not wish to return are burned to ash. No longer existing to ensure the balance. The count in the Earth realm echoes in the Underworld. As above, so below. More souls must enter the mortal world. Or else there will be consequences. I do not care for such things, but balance must be maintained.

Night is falling by the time I am calm enough to return. The dusk falls away into dark as I take Cerberus inside.

He looks up at me, questioning.

I pat each of his heads. "Go to them. Come back when you are finished."

Cerberus has many places to visit within my home each day. His favorite place is the kitchens. They are busy all night, as the scale of my home is fit for the vastness of the Underworld. I am not the only one who dwells here. There are guards. Staff. Advisers. Though I spend many hours in solitude, my home is a world unto itself—a palace or a city. Cerberus can find companionship at all hours of the night, and I do not begrudge him his routines. For he is an enforcer and alerts me to those who are not welcomed here.

For if Zeus were to send a god to have prying eyes in my palace, Cerberus would know and therefore I would know. It is a good sign that he is at peace.

He bounds off, and I return to my bedchambers. Though I have ordered the windows shut again, the cold seeps in. That is the way of the Underworld. To Persephone, it will be cold until she learns to find her warmth.

The sconces burn low, and when I enter, I close the door quietly behind me. I cross the room to change and collect a blanket, then approach the bed. I could light the fires, but it will not aid her in finding her powers. *Patience,* I remind myself. *Patience.*

Persephone is already under the sheet. The fabric outlines the curves of her body, and her hair stands out in contrast to the pillow. She does not speak, though I can tell from the way her shoulders rise and fall that she is not yet asleep.

I climb into the bed next to her and, with a motion, extinguish the sconces.

The dark is soothing, whatever Persephone may think of it. I close my eyes and let it cool my thoughts for a few moments before I arrange the blanket over myself.

When I open them again, Persephone has not moved. Stubborn goddess.

I reach my arm out to her and allow myself to brush her shoulder with my fingertips.

She lets out a soft, shallow breath. The sound is a soothing balm. I crave it dearly.

I let my arm rest on the mattress, my fingertips still in contact with her. It is like drawing my fingers through a candle flame. If I let them stay still for too long, it would burn, but for the moment, it is only a pleasant heat.

A heat I would like to watch ignite into the full roaring flame of Persephone's power. No realm should be denied the brightness of that flame.

Frustration begins to return, but I exhale it, then exhale it again, keeping my hand where it is.

"You will be cold," I say into the dark. "You will come to me in the night. You may as well get comfortable now and have a pleasant night."

She lets out a sigh. The tension in her body is like a touch itself. Persephone wants to fight for her independence, but she does not know which battles to mount. I could tell her, of course but she would not listen.

So I let her wage war in the privacy of her mind, even as her body relaxes into my faint touch.

I know when she decides to give in—it's obvious from how her shoulder presses just a little more into my fingertips—but it's several moments more before Persephone can bring herself to roll over.

She turns into my arm and arches her body, pulling herself across the space between us. It is heaven. I've never felt so much pleasure. Persephone settles her head on my shoulder, the heat of her breath tickling my neck, and I wrap my arm around her, pulling her closer. Inhaling her scent is a blessing.

I arrange the blanket over both of us and drop a kiss to the top of her head. It appeases me that she doesn't resist. Despite dwelling in the Underworld for days now, she still smells of sunlight and flowers in the first of their blooms. She smells of the power that has been denied her but that hovers, waiting for her to grasp it.

There is so much we could do together. So much we could be. Her submission would be everything, and it would be nothing, because our combined power would eclipse it. Persephone would be my queen in more than title.

"I do not know what you wish of me." These words are not rehearsed. They spill out of my mouth as if I have been compelled, and have nothing to do with the thoughts whirling in my mind. "I only know I can give you anything you wish."

Persephone tenses, then relaxes into my hold. It almost seems as if she is deciding to be comfortable here. Pretending it is true so it will become true.

"To leave," she says, her voice trembling slightly. "To see my mother."

"Almost anything…"

Persephone is silent.

I wait for her to roll away, to try to put the distance between us once again, but she does not.

Instead, she falls asleep, her body pressed close to mine. And in this moment, I'm given a taste of my own heaven in the walls of this hell. *My queen.*

chapter 14

Persephone

THE BEDCHAMBERS DOOR IS OPEN. A CRACK only, but it is not locked shut.

I stare at it from my usual place in the center of the bedroom, disbelieving. I'm certain it was his intention to tempt me. To his credit, I am ever so tempted. I vaguely wonder what I have done to earn such things. The tour, the baths, the warmth of him throughout the night.

Although my life in Olympus was met with ease and comfort, never wanting for anything, captives were not treated as such by my father. Zeus ruled with a firm hand of lightning for his enemies.

I am reminded though that Hades's sickness is his belief in my attachment to him. As his queen. And with the promise of my powers.

He is deluded surely. But if his state allows me to

roam freely, perhaps there is more of a chance to escape or to call for help. My mother will come. She could never stand for my pain and for my wishes to not be met. I can only imagine her agony in knowing I have been taken against my will. If only she knows.

At that thought, my gaze shifts to the entrance of the room.

The door does not shiver and change as if spelled closed. The door stays open, giving me a view of the hall outside.

There it is. Quiet. Innocent. No one passes by the door. No one knocks on the frame. I cannot see if there is a guard standing by, but I assume there is one...if not right outside the door, then at the end of the hall.

To know that, I would have to go out, and that is where I've drawn the line in my head.

Watching the empty hall is one thing. Taking a step out?

I don't know if it is a sick game or not. If there will be a punishment. Hades does not provide me with instruction. For a god of control, he does not attempt to control me apart from keeping me here. It is maddening.

Days have passed. Nights. I have eaten, and along with the nourishment, a certain clarity has returned to my mind. I can feel my body growing satisfied with its own energy again. The horrible, starved cravings have stopped, though I remain hungry for everything else.

My mother always told me the world is what we make it, what we believe is true is what will be. As within, so without. And so I stare at the door, convincing myself that it is my freedom, that is the right path for me to take. And yet, that truth does not hold true in my gut.

I do not trust this open door.

Even in the daylight, the sight is as forbidding as a dark shadow. I do not trust that it will remain light in the hallway, and I do not trust that the door is open as an invitation.

It feels more like a temptation. More like a trap. Meant to seduce me into going out, only to—

What would happen if I ventured beyond this room? There is something inside of me that promises Hades will not harm me. If it were his intention, I believe he would have done so already. Yesterday, with his bloodied hands, he could have silenced me easily. I believe so much to be true, as much as I believe his brutality is worse than the stories we've been told.

I go a few steps toward it, testing the invisible chains that bind me to the room. They do not pull me back. If I move my arms quickly enough, they are *there,* certainly—bound to the Underworld, maybe? Bound to Hades? But they let me move toward what *looks* like freedom.

No. I simply do not trust that it *is* freedom.

I go back to where I was. With warm food and wine in my belly and energy in my blood, my suspicions are heightened. Days ago, I might have run into the hall, too desperate to think clearly, but now I wait.

For what? A soft voice in the back of my mind asks.

For him, another voice answers. Or perhaps it is the same voice.

For the man who sleeps at my side at night. For the man who holds me close to him so I can share his warmth, although he's the one responsible for the cold. For the man who kissed me as we looked into the heights of heaven and the depths of hell. For the man who showed me eternal torment and eternal rest, and rules over them both.

I bite my lip, considering. I could call for him, I think. There is certainty within me that he would come if only I called. I could make it known that I wish to be in his presence. Would he believe that? Would he come to me, as I wait for him?

I have no choice but to wait for him, whereas Hades can go wherever he pleases.

What would I say if he was here?

Would I ask him what the open door meant?

Would his answer mean anything to me?

And what of my powers? I have yet to do the simplest of things. Ask him for them back. I do believe he's stolen them somehow through my dreams.

Questions float idly in my mind. I wrap my arms around myself. These are not the questions I wish for in this moment. I wish for his warmth. When I have had a few morsels to eat, my body focuses on the cold instead. One problem solved leads to another to be dealt with, and I am cold still.

Answers would help, that voice whispers.

Maybe they would.

Maybe they wouldn't.

I rub briskly at my arms, watching the hall outside these rooms for signs of danger.

There are none. The hall remains a hall. Silent and still.

I turn away and go to the table near the window. Light pours through the enormous panes of glass, but what light is it? After Hades took me along that path, it is impossible to believe that my eyes show me simple reality. The world outside the window is something other than what it seems. Hades's realm contains many lands and many souls. From my place at the table, it looks well-ordered, almost calm, but beneath the surface, it seethes with punishments and torture. And rooms beyond rooms that only have one door house so many souls, many with agony that will last for eternity.

And...it also holds peace, for those who have been granted it.

I nibble a small amount of bread and a glistening seed of pomegranate. The sweetness bursts onto my tongue just as it did the first time I tasted one of the seeds. The food here makes me stop and savor every bite. It does not matter that I am no longer starving. There's something about the food. About the Underworld itself...

Putting a name to it remains impossible. I have thought of it every time I've taken my place at this table. Every time I've looked out the window to the hills of crystals and buildings and land beyond.

If I am getting used to it here...

If that's why the food tastes so rich and finely flavored...

But that can't be. I was born to bring life, not death. I cannot thrive here. It is not my place or fate. I have been told my fate, and I must return to Olympus.

Unless Hades is right.

After I have eaten, the plates and vessels before me disappear and reappear a few moments later in pristine condition. In all the time I have spent eating, I have not been disturbed.

I wonder if that is purposeful.

I wonder if he is watching.

A shiver of arousal runs down my spine and between my legs at the thought. His rough stubble and dark eyes suit him well and urge a darker side of me to play with the fire that lies beneath his gaze.

I try not to feel it. I try not to think of it. But there are things I cannot forget from our walk down the path, no matter how hazy the details become. The blood on that woman's face. Her head tipped back in agony, or such powerful pleasure that it became agony. The way her body moved under the men.

The way the first man killed the one who had hurt her.

The way Hades stood over the body of the guard in that room. His blood spreading on the tile.

My horror should have been stronger. I should have been sick at the blatant ending of a life. And I was frightened, but I was also...

I do not wish to think the word. I do not wish to think of the heat in my face as I stood alone with the body, the scent of blood in the air.

I do not wish it, but the sensation has been imprinted on me, as surely as if I'd eaten it with the food.

No one has ever killed for me before. No one has ever needed to. I know there is an argument to be made that Hades did not need to kill the guard, but he thought it was so, and the man did not live out the hour.

That is what I would have if I ruled beside him.

That is what you already have, that voice says.

"Hush," I tell myself. My pulse has already quickened, thinking of the blood, and thinking of how I should have emptied my stomach, but I didn't. It was, I know, a horrific sight.

And...

There were other elements as well.

I move slowly around the room, keeping my eyes on the door. No one has come, and though the door itself has not changed since I sat down to eat, it seems to beckon me.

Where would I go? I could not find the rooms I visited yesterday if I wished to. I don't even remember which way we turned when we exited the bedchambers. Shock and disbelief has hazed my memory.

One side of the hallway seems faintly brighter than the other, so perhaps I would follow the light.

Or perhaps I would try to discover what hides in the shadows.

A shiver, this one less pleasant, makes me shudder. Seeking beyond my abilities is what got me here in the first place. I should have been protected by the spell I cast at my altar, but instead, it opened a door for me to be stolen.

Unless that doorway was already open.

I narrow my eyes at the door.

I can feel it there, watching. There may be someone hidden from me by magic more powerful than my own. There may be eyes on the back of my neck even now. I do not whip my head around to look. I do not have the power to stop anyone.

I fold my hands together and let my eyes travel slowly over the crystalized gardens below.

I *could* have that power.

Though not here.

This is a familiar path to walk along, as far as my thoughts go. They circle around Hades again and again, returning to his insistence that he could help me. Returning to the blood on the floor. Returning to the offer he made of the guards with that dark heat in his eyes. Returning to his lips on mine. Returning to his arm around me in bed.

Returning, and returning, and returning.

Footsteps in the hall jostle me into awareness.

It's him—that's my first thought—but it is not. It can't be.

The footsteps do not belong to Hades. They are too quick and a bit lighter than his confident, commanding steps. I freeze, holding my breath as they get closer. How many people walked past my rooms on Olympus without me giving them any thought at all? It must have been hundreds. Thousands! And yet now I am wholly attuned to the sound of one man coming and going…

Or whether he is *not* returning. My heart fights between disappointment and an urgent curiosity. If it is not him, then who?

A fair maiden enters the room.

I raise my hand to stop her. It is an old instinct, left over from when I was a child—a simple spell my mother taught me so that I would know it when I gained control of my powers.

The magic behind the spell does not come. Nothing happens, and the maiden is not stopped.

Instead, she raises her own hand in a similar gesture and the lights flicker. My heart leaps, pounding in my throat with immediate recognition followed by immediate suspicion.

A *witch*? Is she a witch?

I feel my teeth chattering then. Feel how the cold has seeped into my bones. It gets more palpable, as if my body is trying to force me to act. As if it wants me to know there is help within arm's reach.

I take a breath, searching for something to say.

"Help me." The words are out of my mouth, and it is too late to stop them. I have no time to consider whether they have sealed my fate.

The maiden nods as if she is not surprised to hear me blurt out this plea. "I am here to do just that. What would you like to eat? To wear?"

"I—"

"I have been told not to offer comfort in terms of the cold, unfortunately." She wraps her arms around herself and glances at the windows. They are open again, if not as far as before. The small gaps seem to let in even more of the cold. I have not seen Hades open or close them, but he must be doing it—giving me the merest hint of warmth, then taking it with him when he leaves.

The woman is tall and lean with reddish hair swept up and pinned on top of her head. She wears dark, flowing robes. Her eyes are the palest blue I have ever seen. Her expression is very calm, as if nothing in the world could bother her, but there is a spark in her blue eyes that betrays the mind behind them.

As if she knows something I do not.

But where does the loyalty of that sharp mind lie? The most obvious answer would be to Hades. No one can come to me without his permission, so he must know of this woman.

He must also *trust* this woman. I want to trust her as well, but I don't trust my own instincts when it comes to my desires. My desire to know more of Hades has been complicated and heartbreaking. My desire to know more of my own magic led me here.

"You can learn magic while in the Underworld?" I ask, finding no other words within me. If this maiden learned to harness her powers, then there is more life than I realized…even her. My mind spins in a new direction.

Magic. In the Underworld. Powers like mine.

I will help you. Those words echo in my memory yet

again. I had assumed all this time that Hades was lying. That what he said was a trick to gain my submission.

I will never stand beside you. I will never obey.

A kiss does not mean I will obey.

When I said those things, I did not believe magic in the Underworld was a possibility. Not unless it was to Hades's doing.

More suspicion floods in. Is this maiden here because Hades is tired of how I have refused to submit? Is she another trap for me to walk into?

I take a deep breath and study her. The light in her eyes is not a hostile one. There is no sign of dislike or disgust in her. I do not know her well, so it is too soon to trust her, but her aura is not one of subterfuge.

Or perhaps it is. My skin prickles with new goosebumps. I will have to reconsider everything in light of this new information. I cannot just *leap*.

"It's cold in these chambers," she says, avoiding the question. "You could make a fire."

"I can't." I gesture to the fireplace. "There is nothing to burn."

She glances down at the floor in a silent denial.

Frustration quickens my breathing. "Why are you here?"

"As I said, my queen. To help you."

"I do not need help if you do not wish to help me escape."

"My queen." The maiden takes a few steps forward, her robes moving elegantly with her. *My queen*...why do they all call me that? Simply to please Hades I imagine. I detest the name but stay quiet so I may observe her.

She glances meaningfully at the open door. Once again, it feels like it is watching me…or like it's calling to me. Is *she* the one calling for me? "You need help more than you know. So much so, you haven't realized the freedom you have."

I do not clench my hands into fists, but the impulse is strong. It is not for this woman to tell me what freedoms I have or do not have. She should not dare to tell me what I know or do not know.

But then—

She dares to speak to me at all, which makes me admire her. She may not be right, but she seems to be speaking honestly.

"I know the door is open. I do not trust it."

"I wasn't referring to a locked or unlocked door." Her eyes meet mine, the light in them brighter now, and an answering light flares in me, like hope. "Please. If you need me, you need only think my name. Silvie."

chapter 15

Hades

Something's different about Persephone when I return for the evening, Cerberus padding along at my side. There's an air about the room that's different as I stand in the doorway and I make my way in, bringing Cerberus with me. Absently I pet his head as I watch her, poised and still and then turn to the crackling lit fire. My faithful companion leans against me for a pat on all three of his heads, then makes a snuffling sound and goes to lie by the fire. The flames are low in the grate, barely there at all, and certainly not high enough to warm the room.

Yet the energy is undoubtedly different. Persephone stands in the center of the room, her hands folded in front of her, as she has many times in the past few days, but her posture is straighter. Prouder. There is an air of anticipation about her. Of challenge. My heart responds instantly, though I do not let this show on my face.

Instead, I move closer, watching her with every scrap of my focus. *Something* has happened today, though I do not know what. I will discover what it was—there is no doubt in my mind. I will ask Minox, if I must.

Inhaling the sweetening tension in the air around Persephone, I pause a few feet away, studying her intently. She lifts her chin and stares up into my eyes, the blush in her face a deeper shade of pink.

Fucking beautiful. At last I put my finger on it. She belongs here. She looks and feels like she belongs here. Like she owns the entire fucking room with her silk cream gown that pools around her, and straight dark hair that only intensifies the color of her eyes. *Gorgeous.* The power that surrounds her is breathtaking.

"My queen," I greet her, not reaching out to touch her. I'm cautious with every move, needing to see her when she's like this. Craving every intimate moment and detail to be carved into my mind. I cannot distract myself with her curves under my palms.

Persephone's chin tips up just slightly, her eyes dancing over my face. "You would give me anything?"

No greeting. Just a tempting statement from her lips. Almost flirtatious. As if she has the upper hand. My cock has never been harder.

Her voice is different. Not the pitch, but the tone. She has asked me questions without preamble before, of course, but there is a certain richness to her words now.

A certain seductive power. Like she already knows the answer and it's because she does.

"That is what I said," I allow.

Her chest rises and falls in a quick, shallow breath. "You seem almost desperate."

I smirk at her truly humorous statement. "Is that what you think?" I want for her, but I need for nothing. She will be mine. And I hers.

Persephone may think I do not notice, but I see the way she readjusts herself, her shoulders going back. *Confidence*. That's what's pouring off her, though I cannot tell if she has convinced herself to feel it for this conversation or if it has come from elsewhere. Somewhere in the shadows, her *desperation* to be freed.

"I think—" She begins, her voice level with only a hint of the way it has trembled in the past. *Persephone's confidence does not reach to the innermost parts of her, then.* "I think my mother and father will discover I am here at some point. I *know* they will."

Again, it's not her words that have changed. It's her belief in them. She has made claims about her father before, but they were made out of fear and desperation. These are not. It is a significant change and raises my hackles, the hairs on the back of my neck standing up straight. It is not a welcome sensation.

"Do you?" I ask, mildly.

"I think you only have so much time." Persephone's eyes narrow.

Of course she is right. Secrets don't last forever. The

tips of my fingers slip over the rough pads of my thumbs as I stand in deliberation. I let none of this show. I have had much longer to practice self-control, though I will admit that Persephone's presence destabilizes it in ways I couldn't have predicted.

"And how much time is that?" I ask her.

The ferocity in her expression increases as my question reaches her, a curiosity reaching her eyes. Almost like it's a game. "I don't believe you know."

I chuckle, a shiver of unease running through me. Regardless of what Persephone believes, her mother and father cannot come to the Underworld.

However, others can come on their behalf.

Has someone told her? Has someone slipped her that tidbit of knowledge without alerting me?

My eyes narrow as I pace slowly and we watch each other. My body responds to her even as my mind ticks through possibility after possibility. Who, where, and when? There are many souls who would have reason, and cover, to visit my realm. Some of them may have the means to access my private rooms. The keeper of keys. Seers and Fates would know and so easily tell as their loyalty is to truth and only such things. There are ways to keep them out, of course, but not every method is foolproof. There is more power in my realm than I can hope to control with absolute authority, so I must remain prepared for my realm's weaknesses—few as they are—to be taken advantage of.

In the silence, Persephone's cheeks grows more

flushed, and the color slips down to her chest. Her eyes search my face again and again with shrewd concentration. It is so different from the days she spent weeping on the rug and curling up into a desolate ball in the bed next to me. The change is one I have craved, yet now that it is here, I find myself cautious in reaching out to claim it for myself.

Cautious *and* ravenous. It becomes harder by the moment to keep my hands off Persephone. I make a point of drinking in the sight of her, collecting as much information as I can without feeling it under my touch.

Persephone swallows, then takes another quick breath. Her hair falls loose around her shoulders. Every individual part of her shines in contrast to the rest. The softness of her hair makes me want the sharp line of her jaw. The strength in her posture makes me want to turn her into languid pleasure, stretched out on my bed... or any surface with room to spread her out for my enjoyment. The hard, focused way she stares into my eyes makes me want the trusting, relaxed side of her that she only reveals when she's deeply asleep.

The duality of the goddess who will rule this kingdom with me. I crave all of her.

"What is it you desire from me?" A sensual note rings in her voice, the pitch slightly lower than it was before.

My cock throbs. "I believe that's obvious, my queen."

A rueful smile quirks the corner of her mouth, then

fades away. "You say that as if you could ever have an equal."

"You think so poorly of yourself." I'd meant to say this lightly, with the same distance between us, but some of my anger finds its way in. "Who put those thoughts in your head?"

Persephone's lips part as if she already had an answer in mind, but she hesitates, closing her mouth again, her brown eyes even more intense as she keeps them locked on mine. The tension between us demands that I move closer.

It feels as if we're balanced on a precipice, and Persephone could fall in either direction—back into her desolate stupor or into the power I offer.

It is so obvious she is meant for the power and the darkness. How can she be so blind?

She takes a deep breath, then moves back half a step. My heartbeat is the loudest sound in all of the Underworld. Will she sink to the floor? Move to the bed? Throw herself against me in a futile attempt to fight?

Instead, Persephone reaches for the clasps at the shoulders of her gown. Without looking away from me, my gaze caught in hers, she undoes one of the clasps, letting the strip of fabric fall gently down to expose the round top of one breast. The gentle sound of the soft fabric falling is nothing compared to the hammering in my chest.

My mouth goes completely dry. I have slept next to her for many nights, but she has never revealed herself to me like this before. I have the strong sense that I am watching something miraculous. Like a fragile flower of the gods opening for the first time.

Persephone reaches for the other clasp and lets it fall, pausing for a few moments in a maddening half-dressed state. It is a promise of what else she might offer me. This *should* be an acknowledgment of her place in my realm—my queen, yes, but a queen who must rule at my side.

I cannot take my eyes off her. It's not possible with the invitation before me. Her smooth skin and gorgeous curves. She's bared to me, and I can barely temper my desire.

Slowly, as if she is beginning to feel the power she holds in this moment, Persephone tugs her dress down and down until first one of her nipples is revealed and then the second. The soft undersides of her breasts meet the light next, and I find that I am not breathing. This is nothing that I could not have taken from her, and yet this slow unveiling is charged with meaning and emotion beyond anything I hoped to experience.

Persephone does not stop.

She continues stripping off her dress, her hands careful on the fabric, bringing it down to her waist and over her hips. The silk clings to her hips for a moment.

"I do not think you care who put those thoughts in my head," Persephone says softly, but I cannot take in her words. I can only take in the dip at her waist and the creamy skin meeting the fabric of her gown. "I know you do not care. You can't take your eyes off me."

I do not answer. My fascination with her is too obvious to deny. I am almost mad with the desire to see her with no clothing on at all. With nothing between us but air. And soon—nothing between us at all; my hands directly against her skin, tracing over that pounding heart of hers. Her pulse quickens, beating in the side of her neck, visible to me though she bears her nerves well.

My grasp on the thoughts I had prior to stepping into this room slips away as Persephone guides her gown over her hips and lets it fall to the floor. It seems to fall forever—for as long as I was trapped in the dark, at least—and then finally the fabric lands.

It no longer touches her.

There is nothing between us but air and crackling tension.

Persephone shifts her weight, lifting her hands to let her hair fall back over her shoulders. Almost no part of her is obscured from me now, save the shadows between her thighs, hiding the soft warmth. What little firelight comes from behind me seems to caress her skin.

I find myself jealous of that firelight. I find myself wishing there was nothing but darkness between us, and that the space itself was nothing.

Persephone lowers her eyes, then brings them back to mine. "Do what you want to me," she whispers easily, "have your fill."

The air between us is thicker than it's ever been,

humming with a sort of desperate tension. Is that coming from her or coming from me?

Her chest rises and falls with her quickening breath and I'm entranced. I cannot deny it.

I take a step toward her, then another, unable to keep myself away. But I do not throw her down on the bed, though I pine to.

Instead, I lift my hand to the side of her neck and stroke my fingers along that fluttering pulse of hers, putting a bit of magic behind my touch. For her to feel what I feel. For her to know her power over me.

Persephone takes a quick breath, and I put more magic in that light, teasing touch. A flame bursts from my fingers. It will not hurt her. It will not burn her. It will sensitize her skin. It will make her come alive in ways I'm certain she has not felt.

She gasps aloud this time. Persephone can feel it—I have no doubt. She can feel my power in the form of fire dancing along her skin and flowing into her veins.

The darkest parts of me beg my body to fall to my knees and worship her, but I do not. I resist the weakness inside of me that craves her companionship.

I circle her, tracing my fingertips along the curve of her shoulder then the dip at the base of her spine, little flickers of flame and power. The shivers and goosebumps that follow in the wake of my touch have a delicate beauty to them. As does the soft gasp and scent of her arousal. She pines for me as I for her.

When I arrive back at Persephone's front, her

nipples are peaked, and she's clasped her hands in front of her. I touch each one of her knuckles in turn. Persephone flips her hands over so her palms are up, and I give the center of each hand a lick of the fire.

Her pupils have gone wide with darkness. She looks up at me, her lips parted, her breath coming faster and shallower than it was before.

The tension is still strong. She's still holding tight to the confidence she found while I was away.

But her desire is growing stronger. Or else that is *my* desire growing stronger. It is becoming impossible to tell the difference.

I choose the former for the sake of my sanity.

I put the pad of my middle finger between her breasts and draw it down over the naked flesh of her stomach. Her belly contracts slightly as I skim my fingertip over her belly button and then—slowly—travel lower.

Persephone is the one who moves in first. She steps closer, one hand rising to the collar of my robe. She curls her fingers around it and holds on, and then—*then*—she inches her feet apart, spreading her thighs.

My cock aches and every muscle in my body tenses with the need for more.

I let my head lean forward and inhale the scent of her hair. Persephone is already in need. Her arousal evident from her flush and the manner in which she trembles before me.

Slowly, with a gentle touch, I explore her folds, finding her wet, welcoming opening and teasing just so.

Persephone does not close her thighs. I circle that place, my cock growing hard and impatient.

Instead, I move my fingers back up through her sweetness and find her swollen clit.

Persephone's lips part with a gasp when my fingers settle over that place, her thighs trembling around my hand in an effort to stay open for me. A few light circles is all it takes to have her panting and holding onto my collar with more force. The pull in the air between us grows stronger as Persephone gasps, and then—

Then there is magic in the air, as if it was always with her, but could not be found. Persephone cries out, her legs barely holding her upright. I tease her clit as she finds her pleasure, then slide my fingers back down and push them inside her to feel the flutters and clenches of her release.

"Oh," she breathes. "Hades—" The sound of my name on her lips is divine.

She clenches down hard on my fingers, her orgasm heightened and extended.

I withdraw my fingers and find her clit with the pad of my thumb.

"Again," I tell my queen.

For once, she does not disobey me. She rests against me, her lips parted and her clenched hands desperate for aid in keeping her upright. Her head falls back, and she loses herself to my touch.

chapter 16

Persephone

HADES MUST KNOW WHAT HE HAS DONE TO me.

It's not only him, of course. It's Silvie, who walked into my rooms unafraid of my status. She looked me in the eye and told me that I had not realized the freedom I had here.

Silvie's words rang in my ears after she left, the ideas taking root like a precious seedling.

It grew surprisingly fast for the Underworld, almost as if my mind had been craving those words, and by the time Hades came back to his rooms the first night after I met Silvie, I felt anew. The crackling behind the obsidian didn't startle me, it felt like it belonged, like the power that rippled through me.

I've spent too much time worrying about the state of my magic and trying to keep the fear of losing my place among the gods and goddesses I had grown up with to let it go all at once.

It was apparent to Hades. His honesty is as brutal as the punishments he delivers so effortlessly.

And yet, he still wanted me.

His touch felt new and tantalizing—not as if I was being forced to bear it, but as if I had invited him in, and he *relished* it. I will admit that I expected for him to lose more control than he did. I expected to be.... ravished. Taken to the bed, at least. I wanted to know what it would feel like. I needed to experience what he has planned for me. And yet he only gave me a taste that sated a side of me that hungers for more, even when limp and unable to cover my body when he was through with his tormenting.

Hades didn't make a move for the bed until I could only draw breath to say *enough, please, enough.*

And then he'd helped me to dress for bed, pulled the blanket over me, and let me fall asleep in peace and warmth. A privilege I once took for granted.

This does not mean I've gained my freedom. I haven't gained the ability to go as I please, away from the Underworld and return to Olympus. But Silvie was right. I have far more freedom than I thought.

More control as well.

For example, Hades leaves each morning and goes somewhere else. The chains do not keep me confined to his rooms. As long as I do not break and run, they allow me to go where I please.

At first, I follow the path we took before, it's thoroughly lit and familiar as well. The hallway outside Hades's rooms has doors out to the makings of what could be gardens, but is crystals instead, and from there it is easy to find the cobblestoned path with the dark blooms growing thickly on either side. I do not know the mechanism by which the path works—all I know is that if I walk on it with the intention of traveling through the Underworld, I can pass by the Fields of Mourning and the Isle of Achilles and the other realms Hades took me to see before.

I find myself burning with curiosity about the other rooms—the *darker* rooms. But I do not visit those places. I tell myself it is because there are too many other things for me to consider, but the truth is that I do not want to visit those places without Hades at my side.

Fear keeps my feet planted on paths I know well. Even if those paths aren't where I crave to be.

I know how that would seem, if I were telling this story to another person. It makes very little sense to think of him as a protective presence, and perhaps that is not the way I think of him at all.

Perhaps it is that the emotions and sensations that move through my body when I am watching those things—*experiencing* those things from such a short distance—were overwhelming in the moment, and if I were to go back…

Well. It is not something I need to think about. I'm too busy making my way in the Underworld. Learning how it operates silently and on my own. There is little to no company for me. And the guards who line the halls are silent apart from the bow of their heads as I pass. The warmth and laughter of Olympus is lacking in the cold castle that I reside in now. I do wonder if it is always like this or if Hades has removed all witnesses for my stay here.

Or at least it was vacant the first few days but now as I set out to wander, I'm aware there is more company than before.

The more I walk on the path, the clearer the realms alongside it become, and the same is true for the halls near Hades's rooms. I could see the hallway outside the open door, but I did not know how many souls dwelled nearby. It is also possible that they had been told to stay away, and now they've been given other instructions.

And when they do…

They bow their heads.

There are more women like Silvie who tilt their heads when we pass each other as I am on my way in or out.

Silvie, I think one day, shortly after I have arrived back from a walk along the path. A few moments later, there are footsteps in the hall, and Silvie enters Hades's rooms.

"Yes, my queen?" she asks. Is there a new light in her eyes? I cannot tell for certain, but she seems to wear a semblance of peace I had not noticed before.

"I would like you to talk to me about magic," I tell

her, as calmly as I can manage. If I *have* this level of freedom, then I will be able to learn from her. If I don't, and it's only an illusion, then it won't matter either way.

"What would you like for me to tell you?" she asks. Her fingers crest on a gold chain that wraps around her waist and over her shoulders, forming an *X* over her chest. It's beautiful against the cream pressed silk with lace edges. It's a dress my mother would love, I think.

I answer without much thought at all, wanting to stop where my mind was headed. "Anything you know."

Her brow raises in surprise and her lips upturn into a smile. "Anything?"

There is something about her words during our first conversation that makes me certain I should start from the beginning. The drain on my powers made it impossible to think of anything but the near future, when I would not be a goddess at all. I should let my knowledge grow in me the way I let her words about freedom flourish.

I vaguely wonder if Hades told her about my magic. I wonder what she knows.

"Whatever you like about magic," I tell her and take a seat on the end of the bed getting comfortable. "Tell me that."

Silvie tells me the earliest stories she can remember about magic and continues to do so whenever I wish for her to come to me. I cannot tell if this is making a change in me, but I listen anyway.

It might not be the stories themselves that matter as

much as the feeling they give me when I listen. In many ways, I feel more secure than I ever have. In other ways, I feel like a child again, my eyes open to all the possibilities of magic instead of the few laid out before me.

As the path has opened my eyes to Hades's home, Silvie opens my eyes to curiosity.

Magic cannot flourish where there is fear.

Listening as if I know nothing, being able to step back and think about magic in a way that's far more innocent than I've felt in a long time… It helps. I have to believe it will help me.

And if it does not—

I *must* believe it will help me, no matter the outcome. No matter what. My mother's voice is echoed in Silvie's stories.

I begin to make a habit of believing it. Each time I go out on the path, I encounter a soul who dips their head when I pass. This is not a sign of mockery. This is a sign of respect. Each time it happens, my curiosity increases.

They know nothing of me other than stories they've been told. And what exactly is that? Do the stories change? Are they real? Or is it simply its own kind of magic?

I listen to all Silvie has to say about magic, then listen some more. She walks with me some days in the dark halls that seem to be brighter as my eyes adjust. I keep my gaze and my mind on what is in front of me, not the home I was stolen from. I do not resist my reality and suddenly I see the freedom she spoke of.

"There is a way, then?" I ask Silvie one morning as she is sitting at the table with me, her hands folded in her lap. "What you mean by all this is that there is...*another* way to have power here."

"Yes, my queen," she answers.

I stare out the window, but I do not see the gardens and the Underworld beyond. It's blurred to me.

There is no life in the Underworld, so I will not be able to use my powers to create. There is only death. I do wonder if Hades made the crystal gardens and the dead blooms that have dried and lined the path for my comfort. At first they were only a reminder of what I lost, but as I watch the garden grow with dried petals that were ash on the mortal realm, I learn to enjoy their beauty.

Maybe *that* is the freedom Silvie spoke of.

But, I decide, there is only one thing to do, and that is to practice magic.

I start by enchanting bells on the doorknob under Sylvie's watch. They will ring if anyone tries to enter and will only allow those who want my highest self to flourish to pass through the threshold. Vaguely I wonder if Hades will be able to enter.

It's a simple spell she says. Three old bells who have seen enough to know what will come. And one little jar that hangs from the rope with the words: *I am protected and guided and safe in these quarters. Only those with who want my highest self to flourish to pass through the threshold.*

"Do you feel it?" she asks me.

"Yes," I answer, although that stirring in the pit of my stomach feels much like what I felt with Hades. The pleasure, the safety, the warmth. I have not felt it before.

When Silvie is gone for the day—or for the time being, as I can summon her whenever I wish—I kneel at the hearth and think of magic, not my powers. They are both divine and worthy. I think of the forces that whirl through the Underworld and Olympus above.

At first, there is nothing. I'm not familiar with this kind of magic. I had thrown myself into studying my *own* powers and only wanted to draw life out of the earth so I could prove that I *had* them—the gifts that I had been granted at my birth from my mother and father.

Now I must reach in another direction.

I close my eyes and try to feel those other sources of power.

It is not lifelessness that I sense all around me, though that is what my childhood would have had me believe. It is not cold death—or not *only* cold death. The souls in the Underworld are not the same as stones left to be battered by weather.

I try to light the fire again. Did it go out before I knelt at the grate? Did it sense, somehow, that I wanted to try my hand at magic? I cannot remember.

It does not take. Closing my eyes, I raise my palms to the fire, my knees against the hard rock. I attempt to light the flames again. "You will light for me. For that is my wish and what I wish is what is granted," I whisper.

I swear when I open my eyes there's a flicker of light, but it's quickly gone and in its place, my frustration. "Would they bow their heads if they could see my failures?" I hiss at the unlit fire. My sense of worth fades as I pace the floor and in that moment, I am compelled to leave. I cannot stay trapped in this room. It's suffocating.

I go for a walk along the path. I do *not* think of magic or the fire or the way it would not light for me. That kind of failure isn't something I'm comfortable with. I let my mind settle on lighting that candle in Olympus—casting that protection spell, which did not protect me. It had seemed like it would not happen, but then…

It did.

The scene plays over in my mind again, what I can remember of it at least. Did the magic work? I felt it. Surely I felt it through every fiber in my soul.

What power did I feel, then? I keep my eyes open as I pass the Isle of Achilles, shining in the middle of the water. I took from the power at my right hand, drawn from the stones, and blew it out with my breath until the flame lit.

I did that because I am capable of magic. Always, I tell myself, reminding myself of Silvie's stories and the lessons they hold. The magic never leaves me. It cannot. It is only the soul who chooses not to believe in it who loses the magic. And yet, it is always right there.

My pace quickens as I harness that feeling, deep

in my womb it emerges as if it was waiting for me to remember.

With a prickling at the back of my neck, I feel someone watching me.

Turning on my heel, there is no one. My heart races and I'm met with an uncomfortable feeling. Like being woken in the middle of the night.

It could be Hades; I have not seen him since he left his rooms this morning.

After a moment, a woman passes me on the path. She stops and turns toward me, dipping her head, so I nod back to her. Curiosity sparks in my chest. Where is she going? Does she have an errand, is it for pleasure, or is she going on someone's orders? What does it look like to *live* in the Underworld, a place where there is no life?

I think to follow her, but I do not. I think to call out and ask, but I do not. For it is the curiosity that intrigues me.

I try to keep my mind open as I return from my walk. There are a thousand questions that could be asked about the Underworld, and I let all of them float into my mind. I don't let myself dismiss any of them, even the simple ones.

Curiosity is like a flame.

Curiosity is its own power.

Quickly, with this feeling brewing inside of me, desperately holding onto it, I rush back to the bedchambers.

I kneel back before the hearth. The low flames that

have not done a single thing to warm Hades's rooms flicker out, fading to nothing as I watch.

The hearth is waiting for me. It's waiting in anticipation for me to direct magic to it and bring the flames back to life. My breath leaves me in a rush as I realize it's there. It's waiting.

With my eyes wide open, I direct the magic into the hearth. Telling it to do as I will.

An ember *cracks* under my magic. My hands tremble and a new flame rises within me. Just as I feel so close to bringing the flames forth, the bells on the door ring, interrupting me.

OLYMPUS

Beatrice

My goddess did not leave me. I know it to be true. From the runes and the cards. From her mother's wails for nine days. She's been taken.

Zeus does not seem as stricken as Demeter. She's searched all of Olympus and reached out to the corners of each realm. No one heard but a single scream in the night.

The courts have gone quiet, and the skies darkened with bolts of thunder.

It is unlike anything that I have witnessed before.

Fear is not my companion but as the days pass with no answers, my concern grows, and tears now flow freely as I mourn her loss.

Where has she gone? I ask again to the cards and once again the death card emerges, but I refuse to think of her soul as gone. It mustn't be right. I toss the deck with worn edges to the side, refusing to believe she is no more. She is my goddess, and I swear I can still feel her and there is pain there. As a mortal, I can barely stand the agony.

The terrors that plague me in my sleeping hours are only worsening.

It is my duty to petition Hecate. To pray with everything I have. The spell must be cast with the plea in my heart.

Wiping my eyes with the small cloth, I lay it down and place a key on where the tears have soaked through. As I smooth it out, my hands tremble. I gather nine black candles for protection and place them evenly in a circle around me, with a single match I light them all.

"Hecate," I pray, "We beg for your intercession. I beg for you to find Persephone. Please. Her loss is my pain."

My voice shakes with the prayer and I bow my body in respect as I continue.

"Demeter searched for nine days. Her mother, the goddess of earth and fertility. She weeps with sorrow. Her father, Zeus, the god of thunder and sky, seeks for union but knows not where to light for the truth of where she lies. Please, I beg you. I beg you please. Goddess of night and mother to all, I cry out to you.

"Find Persephone in the crossroads where she has been lost," I pray, casting the spell with as much power as I can summon. I cast it with the heart of a mother who has lost her child. Who would do anything to bring that child home. She will always be Demeter's daughter, and her agony is felt in the desperate nights. Tears flow and my nose runs as my body rocks, needing the comfort of Hecate.

As I whisper, "please," my warm breath on the cold paved floor beneath me, the screams from the courts are heard.

Demeter's cries of agony and the threats she gives to Zeus. "If I must suffer, they will all suffer!"

The skies brighten with a flash of lightning followed by a thunder that trembles the ground. I close my eyes, fear and rage echoing through me.

"I will let them all die!"

"You mustn't upset the balance! You will destroy everything!" Zeus's voice booms as the sky cracks again. My body tenses as I cry, praying they do not know I still dwell where Persephone once laid.

"If I must be destroyed, so be it!" Demeter shrieks, and I don't dare raise my head to peer out from the window. I don't dare to look.

Demeter screams at Zeus to *do something*. To *find Persephone*. She has withered all the plants that thrived on Olympus. Yesterday, she said she would go to the

Earthly realm. She said she'd take away all warmth and life if no one brought forth her daughter. She rages and in her rage, suffering spreads. The crops are all dead because of her anger, and she shows no signs of relenting.

"Find her *now*," Demeter screams, her voice shaking the walls. She breaks down in tears, her sorrow felt by every god and witness, I'm sure of it. The tears puddle on the ground beneath me and soak into my cheek.

"Hecate," I pray. "We beg for you to find her. Please," I whisper and at that moment, Demeter wails and every candle around me goes out, leaving me in darkness.

"Mother?" I whisper.

chapter 17

Hades

I DON'T ACKNOWLEDGE MINOX WHEN HE appears at my side. Although his dark shadow and presence are felt, he isn't needed. Minox knows better than to interrupt me when I'm involved in a task such as this.

The pleading and scarred man bound to the *X* cross is my task of the moment, and I'm heavily involved. My choice; I needed time to think. I need a physical release as well. I've never cared for touch before her.

Persephone has changed me, and I struggle with my own impulse and desires.

Now, she consumes my mind so wholly that fucking her would only serve to distract me from the things I have seen and the consequences those things will undoubtedly have.

I bring the whip in my hand down on the man's flesh

in five more measured strokes. He screams and pleads but so did those in the Earth realm. And he did not heed the warning. He did not give mercy. Each stroke is duly earned from the soul before me. As above, so below. The pain he brought to others is to be given back to him now.

The righteous justice and balance given is a balm to my soul although it doesn't ease the burden of my thoughts for my queen.

Minox waits.

He is a patient companion, but even his patience is not endless.

"Zeus knows," he says, between strokes.

My muscles tense as a chill runs down my spine.

I deliver one last blow—the man bound to the *X* screams, his voice ragged and on the verge of giving out—then hand the whip off to the man at my other side. He has waited, stoic and silent, for even longer than Minox, and is ready to accept the whip. He does not waste a moment in taking my place. The whip cracks across the man's flesh. Another scream.

Although the man delivering the blows silently weeps. He is next. He so willfully hurt others. Now he will do so again with the vision of himself taking the blows. Then he will receive the pain all over again. There is no heaven in this arena. It is only hell for all who enter this place.

"Is that so?" I question lowly and listen to the sharp whip in the air followed by the strangled cry. The noise seems to become mute as Minox confirms Zeus knows I've acquired Persephone.

I take in Minox's words against the backdrop of my life.

There are 166,000 deaths per day and each of those souls enter the Underworld. Morally righteous souls. Evil souls. Innocent souls. Pained and sorrowful souls filled with regret. Those who welcome death after a life of agony. And those who are at peace and simply accepted what was to come.

I oversee all of them, because both hell and paradise fall underneath my rule. They are both here in the Underworld, which makes them my responsibility. Every soul. Every heaven. Every hell. There are protocols and ease of placement for most. Some require my talent of torture. Those who lived especially heinous lives.

Even those who simply witnessed and did nothing. A thousand years reliving every moment they could have lived a righteous life.

The boundary between paradise and eternal suffering is far less firm than most would suspect. There is gray as far as the eye can see. One's lifetime of a hero is another's view of a villain. The balance is what is necessary. And I provide that.

Paradise exists in the Underworld. *Elysium* exists in the realms of the dead.

Persephone is my Elysium.

Drawing myself out of my thoughts, I survey the realms around me. The whip rises and falls in a steady rhythm, just as it should. Souls enter from across the river and await judgment. Once judgment has been passed by the three demigod ministers, Rhadamanthys, Minos, and Aiakos, appointed by me, those souls take their rightful places. Whether they reside in paradise or suffer in hell or return to mortal life again, they *all* find a place.

If I am required they will inform me. Both of these men deserved special treatment.

I turn away and fall into step beside Minox. I find it difficult to think when I am standing still, so we set a brisk pace.

Zeus knows.

"How exactly did he come to his conclusion?" I ask. I'm not so naive as to think he wouldn't suspect that I would steal her in the night, given our talks. But to know—to know is a very different thing.

"I believe word may have gotten to Hecate," Minox says calmly. "The army of the dead has her gratitude. If she were to ask, they would not lie, my lord. And Persephone's scream was heard clearly. She has ventured down the halls as you wished, which has led to whispers."

A grunt of acknowledgment leaves me as I clench my fist at my side, turning the thin skin on my knuckles white.

Anger rises, hot as the fires of hell. I crave to rain it down on the armies of the dead. I want to find the soul who whispered in Hecate's ear and make them regret it for all eternity.

But I cannot punish them for such acts. For she is a Titan and the mother to all. Their obedience to her is necessary. Although it is very much like a betrayal to me, if I chose to disregard Hecate.

I made the decision long ago that Hecate would not suffer as the other Titans did. She is the first witch, capable of both good and evil. But like me, she recognizes balance and cycles. She sided with me and Zeus in the battle against the Titans. Standing strong, a single Titan against the rest. She freed all realms from the damned reality. We could not have won without her on our side.

The army of the dead is made up of spirits of the unavenged or wrongfully killed who long for retribution. Hecate leads them from the Underworld back to Earth realm on Deipnon, which is the last sliver of the moon before it begins anew. A single night the army of the dead return for justice. She aids in terror but also peace.

I *should not* punish them for such acts. Not those souls. Not those who have already fallen under another's hands and guidance.

For I also knew granting Persephone freedom would lead to knowledge. It is of my own doing that she is here and of my own doing that Zeus became aware.

"And Demeter?" I question.

"It appears it is only Zeus and Hecate for the moment, my lord."

"And does he send word?" I ask.

"For her immediate return or else war will ensue and death of a scale unknown before will come."

My heart races in my chest. My pulse shoots to my temples and pounds there, too. Minox's words are finally sinking in. This is a threat I cannot ignore.

And yet…

I cannot let it cloud my judgment. It is *already* doing so, and it cannot gain any more ground.

"My lord—"

"Leave," I snap at Minox. The anger cannot be quelled. It rises within me to a dangerous degree. How dare he threaten me. How dare he insist she leave me!

Minox bows his head and departs in the other direction without hesitation.

I go back to the *X* on the wall and hold out my hand for the whip. The man who had taken over for me gives it back mid-swing, bows his head, and steps back. His dark eyes are bloodshot and his skin tear stained. I channel all my anger into torturing the bound man, who means *nothing* to me. I would torture infinite souls if it meant keeping my realm secure.

All the souls I *have* tortured did not count.

It is my responsibility to make this man—this *soul*—pay for his mortal misdeeds, but the blows I land on his back have nothing to do with his sins.

They have everything to do with the looming threat of losing Persephone.

I have had *enough* of being threatened. I spent enough time alone in the dark to process all the stages of fury, and when I walked free, I found myself *here*. In cold, ruthless anger.

Anger that now burns, nearly singeing my flesh with its power. It is distorting my thoughts. The rage will translate to action, and I cannot let it guide my hands.

Except for right now. In this moment. In the cell of another's hell I release my rage recklessly.

Whose sins did *I* pay for through all those years in isolation? What right does Zeus have to hold his dominion over my head? *No* right.

He is not in control of her! She is mine! I nearly scream in fury, but the blows are delivered in heavy silence that suffocates the room. One after the other with no pause. The screams no longer come with each blow. The man to my left drops to his knees on the floor, cowering and pleading for mercy.

There is no mercy here. There is only justice.

I breathe in and out and focus on the blows. Blood pours down the soul's back. His screams break as his voice gives out. It will return. That is the beauty—and the horror—of souls in the Underworld. They are made to spend eternity in whatever place is deemed appropriate for them. I could whip this soul down to his bones, and his flesh would reappear, ready for me to peel away again.

I feel a presence enter behind me, but I do not look at her. Soft footsteps. My body stills at the realization. My heart pounding a thin sheet of sweat lining the back of my neck.

My queen.

If I look at her, I will tear apart the Underworld

before Zeus can touch it. If I look at her, I will destroy everything before *anyone* can take it from me, and that is not what I have been charged to do.

"I know what you're capable of," Persephone says, raising her voice to be heard above the screams and sobs.

I raise the whip. Bring it down. Repeat this three times.

I do not look at Persephone, but I *feel* her hesitation.

Perhaps it is not hesitation. Perhaps she is only observing me. Perhaps she knows that I am not myself. Perhaps she knows, despite her fears about her captivity, that I am...not well.

That sends something *like* anger—hot and uncontrollable—through my body. I ignore it.

"Are you all right?"

"I've never been quite *all right*, my queen." My own honesty shocks me. It *disgusts* me. I did not mean to give it to Persephone so easily. I did not mean to lay myself bare. "Go," I tell her. "I have work that must be done."

With a heavy arm, I whip the man again although my rage wanes and in its place creeps in fear. He finds his voice once again, and his screams rend the air.

Persephone does not leave. I can still feel her behind me.

She does not speak, either, but her *judgment* is there, burning into me like her eyes burn into my flesh. *Will it never fucking end? Will I ever be free?*

I grit my teeth until it hurts, but I cannot keep the words in.

"You judge me. I judge them. It is my purpose." I hear her quick inhale, but I do not stop. "You would do well to remember *your* purpose, my queen."

"Fuck you," Persephone says breathlessly.

"You weep for mortals like your mother." I do not contain my own judgment. "But you fail to acknowledge the righteousness of the other side. Of death and darkness. You fear it!"

"Do not mention her name when you've betrayed her so," Persephone shoots back. Her engagement—her attention—is even and soothing, although it scorches me. Her eyes dart over my expression, her head held high. There cannot be one without the other. One cannot know comfort without knowing pain. For me, they will always be bound together. Even now, the *idea* of being comforted by her—the idea of accepting her attention, and her touch, even *demanding* it—rips into me like claws.

"It seems you've found your strength, no?"

"More like my anger." Her voice trembles with her words. I do not think it will tremble forever. I think she will find yet *more* strength, and perhaps for her it will be uncomplicated. Perhaps it will feel like power without the past on its heels. "And I shall take it with me so in my absence you mustn't suffer it."

Her voice *infuriates* me. Her presence in this place turns my vision red. Or is it *my* presence that I find so unbearable? I don't want to be here, torturing this soul. I want to be in my rooms, in bed with Persephone. I want to be somewhere that Zeus can never find, and can never see, and cannot know about.

I have finally found my heaven and all I can see is him taking from me once again. I will not allow it! And worse, I cannot tell her for it would give her hope. Surely she would fight harder if she knew help was coming. I do not wish her to fight me. I need her to love me.

I bring the whip down harder than I ever have on the soul's back. There's too much blood to see the wound I've left.

"Leave me," I order Persephone.

"I've been trying," she says, her voice low and dangerous. The statement is a dagger to my heart.

I thought it was hot before, but I was mistaken. The heat that flares between us is hotter than my fury. It's hotter than the fires that torture deserving souls. It's hotter than anything, and threatens to melt the Underworld into a sick conglomeration of heaven and hell, all of it blended so there is no telling where Elysium once was.

The ground shakes, splitting under my feet. It is a warning. The pressure is reaching into the very foundations of the Underworld. The tension will pull until it breaks us apart. There is far too much power building in Persephone, and far too much anger building in me, and the two *will* meet.

That is guaranteed.

The only question is whether we'll survive it.

"I said *leave*," I grit out, and the cold core of her fear gusts through the heat that's built in this space. It was hot before—the man on the *X* cross has not earned a cool breeze, and will *never* earn one, so long as I am here. But my anger has set the air boiling. Persephone's righteousness is like a match to a pile of dry tinder. This heat is different. It is a harbinger of power that's bigger than both of us. And still, I feel her fear in it. A cold, lonely fear, as if she is seeing me for what I am. For what I could still become. "*Now.*"

Persephone steps forward, into my line of sight. Her eyes are wide—she *is* afraid—but her chin is up, and her hands are in fists at her sides. She's beautiful like this. She's so close to taking her power for herself, and *still* she insists on her suspicions.

Her knowledge?

Fuck. This was not how any of this was supposed to unfold. I had control over my realm and control over my plans for Persephone, and now it is like the strings of fate—out of my reach.

I won't let that happen. I *can't* let that happen.

But even the smallest glimpse of her is enough to turn me feral. I want to throw the whip away and crush her to me. I want to cover her mouth with mine so she can say nothing else. I only desire to work pleasure into her body until she is *mine*. Until she understands that she's *mine*.

And she'll never go back to Zeus.

This is her realm now, if only she would *see* that.

The ground shakes harder under my feet. Persephone glances down at the ground, her lips parting slightly. How much more will it take to make her understand? I wonder if she will break now. Cry. Beg.

But instead Persephone presses her lips together and lifts her chin. "I will go."

As she turns, more words break free. "Don't *ever* threaten me with your absence," I order her. "You know not what you do."

Then I turn my back to her. I cannot watch her leave.

chapter 18

Persephone

I DID NOT WISH TO SEE IT. I KNEW OF COURSE. I can admit that to myself. I've heard the tales. I know the god Hades is. But to witness it…I could never have imagined the pain he so easily delivered.

The cracking is what led me. I swear I hear it more and more down the dark obsidian halls. I know not what it was, but I followed it to the darkest corners and to the ancient wooden door that was parted, granting me entry as Minox fled. It led me to witness the kind of god Hades truly is.

I have never seen Hades like that before. Nor any god. There are fury and wrath, there are stories as well, even of my father and his brutality. But I have yet to witness such things, guarded by my dear mother.

I know as soon as I leave the torture chamber that I

might have made a mistake. I do not know exactly what the mistake *was,* and I do not know how to fix it.

I do not know if I *should* fix it.

There is a darkness I innately wish to fight against, and he embodies that. At the same time…I am drawn to it, but fearful. What plagues me now? Another spell that drains me?

For a few moments, I consider returning to him. To speak freely and demand his attention. I do believe he would assert that darkness against me. That he would listen to me if only to hear me speak to him. There is a power I know I have over him. I do not even know why I stand so against him in that moment. I am tormented myself.

But more screams echo into the hallway. The whip cracks down against a soul's flesh. The man—the soul, whoever it is—lets out an anguished sound, and I picture Hades's face. There was something raw in his expression. Something I had not seen before. Something painful in his words as well.

If I press him, will I learn more or will he push me away? Sure that it would be the latter, I do not go back in. It feels like a delicate balance. One move could ruin everything, and I lack this knowledge of what is to come.

With haste and tears in my eyes, I go back to his bedchambers rather than walking on the path, and pace around in a circle on the rug. The debate in my mind circles with me. I *saw* something about him that I had not known was there.

I wish to see it grow, although it torments me and some parts of me stand against it. I wish to see it rise out of the grounds of Hades's realms and bloom. What shape would it take if it did? I shake my head, trying to settle my thoughts. It is strange to think of him as someone with secrets that could grow and change. He has seemed to be solid and unchanging. Uncompromising.

I pace around the rug some more, then force myself to stand still and breathe deeply.

I'm still standing there when a single footstep in the hall catches my full attention. A warmth runs through me but then a chilling cold. I turn toward it, moving without thinking.

Hades is at the threshold. He stops, studying the bells I enchanted, then brushes a finger across them. The chime they make is light and welcoming—so unlike the rough, almost anguished tone of his voice when I found him at his work.

He lowers his hand slowly and meets my eyes. "Your magic, my queen?"

I swallow a sudden lump in my throat and nod. Dried blood is splashed against the cream vestment under his black robe. I imagine the robe itself is also disturbed in such ways.

Hades nods in acknowledgment. For a moment, the quiet between us is charged with possibility.

"It pleases me," he says finally, then enters, closing the door behind him. Hades goes through to the bathroom and shuts that door as well. Softly, the water runs, and I take it that he's washing away what happened. Although I don't believe I can do so easily.

As soon as he is out of sight, I move, my heart fluttering and my hands shaking. I'm sure now that I am in the wrong. Something I said in that room, or something I did—perhaps even something he saw in my eyes—it was not what I *should* have done. My blood singes with a feeling of betrayal and guilt.

I've been filled with fear and anger, and lately with all Silvie could tell me about magic, and there is something I have missed.

Or something that Hades has kept from me. Something I did not know how to ask about. The conversation we had brought it to the surface in a way I have not seen before.

My nerves force my hands to tremble when the running water is silenced.

And wasn't Silvie right? I *have* found power here. Look at the enchantments on the bells. I have found respect here, too. I am not confined to a cage, but may look upon Hades's realms. I may speak to the souls there.

I do not need to keep anything hidden, unlike in Olympus.

This is a seemingly simple thing, but it hits me like a great gust of wind or a bolt of lightning. I might have been able to convince myself that I hid nothing on Olympus, but what I kept hidden was the most important thing—the failure of my powers. I prayed in secret over those. I did not go to my mother in transparency,

I went in desperation and still refrained from truthfulness. I spent hours trying to force my powers to obey my commands out of sight of anyone. The only person I confided in was Beatrice.

I did not walk the paths there, greeting those I met with a nod and a smile. I hurried from place to place, thinking only of my magic and how I would stop it from fading completely or how I would get it back.

And here…

Here, in Hades's realms…

It is not so different than it *has* been, but it feels like everything has changed. I undress, laying my silk garments over the back of the lone chair, and slide under the plush blankets. The sheets are cool on my naked skin. I do not pull them close to my chest. I just lie there, struggling to calm myself, thoughts buzzing in my mind.

About Hades. About me. About what I crave from him and what he craves from me.

About my purpose. About *his*. About his promise of my powers and about the magic I have found.

The way he said *It seems you've found your strength.* He did not even need to look at me. He sees me in other ways, and I do the same to him, but what I see is startling.

How his eyes went black with an emotion I dare not name when he said *you know not what you do.*

All these thoughts and more speed through my mind. An eternity seems to pass before Hades returns to the room and approaches the bed. His chest is bare, a smattering of hair that I crave to touch above his hardened muscles. The lights in the room dim, which gives me only a little relief. It is not so dark that I cannot see him, although the shadows only outline the curves of his muscles in a seductive way. The corded lines of his arms and the strained veins that promise his powerful touch. They all tempt me. His flesh is divine, my lord of the dead and damned.

He watches me, his shoulders rising and falling as he breathes.

Summoning all my courage, I lower the sheets, baring myself to him as he likes. The air in the bedroom is slightly cooler than the sheets, but my nipples are already peaked. That might've happened when he entered the room. That would not be surprising, because what moves between us is far deeper than hatred.

Hades's gaze stays on my face for a few beats, then skims down over my naked body.

"How angry are you?" I ask. "I do not wish to fight," I whisper the words with emotion I did not realize I had.

He is slow in returning his gaze to mine, lingering over my hips and breasts and throat first as I swallow thickly.

"My love will always be greater than my anger."

My heart hammers once at the word, love. I do not know if he is aware of what the word could possibly mean. He lacks it so. But I know truly what it means, and I feel something there. Something forgiving. Something merciful.

Needing his touch to soothe the uncomfortableness,

for I do not wish to go backward, I hold my arms out for him, then Hades climbs onto the bed. In his masculine form, he allows me to hold him and in return he shifts his body to his side and holds me back. His embrace full of comfort and security.

With a soft gasp from me, he claims my mouth in a hot, possessive kiss, then balances over me. I run my fingertips over his shoulders and down his flexing arms as I moan.

It is like touching a stranger, but it is also familiar to me, as if I have done this many times before. Only for him. This dangerous and powerful god.

I have done this in my dreams, I know. And who is to say that the dreams were less real than this? Hades's realms have taught me that many things that are seemingly impossible—even for gods—dwell in the Underworld.

I kiss him back, tasting him. He tastes fresh, like running through a garden on a clear night. The act is natural and in an instant, the pain and uncertainty is lost. I know not what I feared before or the anxiousness that ran through me.

My body responds as it has never responded before. My hips rock toward his on a wave of desire. It's a new heat, and I feel like I'm coming awake a little more every time he touches me. Every time his strong body meets mine, he is showing me where my own power lies. He maneuvers me beneath him, and I love it.

I wrap my hands around his neck, loving how hot

the skin-to-skin tension is, and hold him closer, arching up toward him. For a minute, nothing else seems to exist but his mouth on mine, his tongue exploring me, and his weight carefully above me, keeping me in place but not caging me. His pulse races underneath my fingertips.

Hades spreads his fingers at my ribs, and I move into his touch, craving more of it. His hand moves down to my hip and moves me with him as he pleases.

The rhythm of it is familiar, too. It is the rhythm of my own desire. Our hips touch. Hades is hard against me, but for these moments, he does not enter me. It is just the two of us, moving together. It takes my breath away. I do not know how he has made it so intimate. Maybe it is not him. Maybe it is the two of us. But kissing like this, moving like this—

It is tender and raw, and I've never felt so close to him or to anyone. I can barely breathe at the revelation. I need this. I need him.

He groans my name in the crook of my neck and my head falls back, loving the warmth and the timbre of his tone.

It makes me crave even more.

I spread my thighs and hook my heels around the small of his back. Hades lets out a low sound into my mouth and presses closer, his cock dragging over my clit. Pleasure unfolds from that place like an entire garden in bloom, and I gasp as it travels down to my toes, making them curl.

Hades makes another sound, this one more curious,

and repeats the motion. The evidence of how much I desire him is between us. It is yet another thing that seems new and familiar and forbidden and sacred at the same time. The wave of pleasure becomes a wave of heat and turns back into pleasure again.

I am not only his *queen* when I am like this. I am also myself. It is the first time in many months that I have felt the power of my own body. And I have needs and desires that no one else has ever brought out in me.

Hades repeats the motion a third time, even more slowly, and a moan escapes me. He says something too low for me to hear, his body pressing even closer, the hard muscles of his abs against the softness of my belly. This is a realm I have not had enough time to discover. My curiosity grows until it is the size of the Underworld, and I feel I must have it all now.

I must know all of him *now*. I must have all the pleasure he can give me *now*. I must know all the ways we can fit together and move together and find pleasure together.

"Please," I beg of him. His answer is only another rough grunt from deep in his chest.

I gasp in another breath, and he lowers his head to kiss the side of my neck, sucking the spot until he must be leaving a mark.

I run my fingertips down the back of his neck to where his shoulders work as he braces himself, one thought demanding to be voiced.

"Love or desire?" I ask. I must know. For my sister

speaks of both things. Aphrodite, the goddess of love. And at this moment, when I feel such things for him, I must know.

Hades lifts his head and stares into my eyes with a depth that seems to see through me. "Unlike you, I mean what I say," he tells me, his voice steady. "I will *always* love you."

My lips part with wanting. I cannot help shivering as the words hit me and sink in. I do not know what to do, or what to say, when there is no doubt in my mind that he has just spoken a plain truth. There seems to be only one path forward.

I kiss him quickly, pouring all my emotions into it. Hades groans into my mouth, and then, without breaking the kiss, he repositions himself over me and notches his cock to my entrance.

He breaks the kiss, his eyes closed in peace before opening them again with a striking primitive need. "You're prepared for me," he says, his voice full of lust. "My queen."

"I need you," I confess to him in response. "My king." I offer him the respect of his title as I offer him my body. Knowing who he is and even so, I desire him.

I spread my thighs wider, although my body tenses. Never have I done this. He sinks into me slowly and my lips part. The slow stretch and slight pain is nothing compared to the overwhelming and instant pleasure. I cling to his shoulders, gasping at the sensation. There is power in taking him inside me. His breath hitches as he buries himself deep, pushing forward until our hips are even. My head falls back and I close my eyes, relishing the feeling.

Then, the only sounds in the air are my breath and his. Every nerve ending is lit aflame as if he himself is fire.

I close my eyes, letting my body adjust to him as he rocks against my clit.

"You were made to take me," he whispers at my neck as he pulls out slowly and then slams himself back into me. My nails dig into his flesh as the wave of pleasure crashes against me. "You were made for me to have like this," he murmurs in reverence and does it again and again. Each thrust forcing small gasps of pleasure from me.

I have never felt so exposed and so covered at the same time. The width of his body between my thighs is perfect, but heady. I'm nearly dizzy from the intensity of him, and his words, and our need.

The shock of it fades quickly and it is replaced by an intense craving. My clit throbs. I need for him to *take* me. Not just enter me, but *take* me.

"Yes," I breathe into his mouth, and work my hips.

Hades lets out a growl, rutting recklessly so I cannot rock myself on his length. "Is this what you want?" He slams into my body, and I press into the mattresses, screaming out pleasure.

"Please," I beg.

It is the last word I say for some time. Only sounds

come out of my mouth. Sounds that I cannot stop and do not want to stop, because I can feel nothing but him.

Hades fucks me like I am his queen—body and soul, possession and partner, and fills me with pleasure and heat. I am lost in the hard strokes and orgasms that continue to peak until I am all wrung out. Until my body can give nothing more. I scream his name as I climax the highest of highs and love every moment of his devouring of me.

Hades captures my mouth again as he pumps his release into me. Thick and pulsing. Claiming me as I have claimed him.

Even then, it does not end. There is too much energy between us to stop. I kiss him until he is hard against me again, and it does not matter how sensitive the softest parts of me have become. I need more.

The last thing I am aware of is his arms around me and his heart beating hard and him groaning my name as if a prayer itself. It is this sound that lulls me to sleep.

chapter 19

Hades

I'll never have enough of her. To have her once, completely and wholly knowing what's to come plagues me. The thought of losing her…I can't bear it. Of her choosing to stay away if given the chance. Deep in the marrow of my bones I fear she would. That I haven't provided enough to keep her. Or worse, that they take her from me and her father holds her captive as punishment. I cannot leave the Underworld. If she is taken…I will live an eternity of hell without her.

The thought that preys on the weakness of my mind is that I truly believe I would deserve it. The loss of her and torture of her absence. I betrayed. I have been cruel. But I cannot and will not stand for such things.

I need to meet with the Fates, so I send word, making clear that the request is an urgent one. And one of secrecy.

Only after consulting the Fates will I meet with Zeus. There will be negotiations I'm sure of it. I'm aware of the sentencing following betrayal of Zeus. But I am also aware of so much more as is he. I will not enter a discussion with him unprepared. I will need every weapon possible at my disposal, even if those weapons are only information.

I sense a disaster looming on the other side of the conversation, though I do not know what form it may take. I do not think it is because of this meeting, or the Fates themselves.

These thoughts consume me as I pace the halls. My faithful dog beside me. Occasionally he whines and I stroke his heads. Offering comfort.

How angry are you? Her voice whispers that question into my ear over and over, but it is drowned out by the sounds she made when I pleasured her. She had not had a man like that before. I could hear it in the low moans and the higher gasps.

I cannot close my eyes without thinking of her sweet mouth against mine. The way she moved against me and shuddered in ecstasy is branded into my memories. It is torture to stay away from her, but I must, because if I go to my rooms, I will not leave the bed.

How would I cross the threshold and leave her there? How would I pass by the enchantments she made for herself? All I want to do is lose myself in her touch and the curves of her welcoming body. I crave to discover what sounds she makes when she is on her stomach on the bed with her legs spread wide, or kneeling above my face, or clinging to the headboard.

My cock grows hard thinking of her, and I close my eyes and pace around the hall where I am awaiting a message from the Fates.

Love or desire?

How can I make her understand that it is desire borne of love? That the desire I feel for her grows stronger with each part of her that she reveals to me. It is only *going* to grow stronger the more I love her.

Because I *do* love her. The days and nights I watched her, I escaped to her slumber. I know of her in every way. And that which I do not know, I'm anxious and curious to discover.

It is not something I wanted to admit to myself. It was growing in me long before I realized it had surpassed obsession. By the time she asked me that question, my cock nearly touching her sweet, wet entrance, it was far too late to stop it.

Far too late.

I go to the carved window of ancient stone and look out, seeing almost nothing. The pull to her is so strong it almost overpowers my determination to meet with the Fates. If they do not reply soon—

Then I will wait. We cannot be caught naked, in the throes of passion, if Zeus attempts to attack the Underworld.

When he attempts to attack.

Minox appears less than an hour later. His dark cape

dragging along the obsidian floor. Darkness under his eyes I've not seen for ages. The depths of what has been done is known to him alone. Regret seeps into the back of my mind.

The Fates will meet with me. I only need to come to them.

I do not hesitate once I receive this word. I leave immediately, anxious for their consult.

The Fates are not met through a mirror, as I spoke with Zeus before. I stalk along the path in my realm, careful not to be seen, until a branch shows itself to me. It is not the same every time, nor does it appear in the same place. Still, I recognize it the moment I see it.

I follow that branch until I reach what appears to be a simple, yet well-built dwelling in a forest glade.

The moment I step through the threshold, it is as if the forest glade does not exist.

No. It exists somewhere in my realms, but the room that can be found beyond that door is not *in* the forest glade. It is not even in one of my realms. It is not in Zeus's realm, either, or the mortal realm. It exists between all the realms and could be considered a kind of neutral ground. So that all may access the Fates.

I march in feeling as if I am going to battle. The dark velvet of my cloak is blown back by the gust of harsh wind. As if I will have to fight to come away with the information I need to protect my queen.

And I *would* fight. I would tear down any realm if that is what it took to keep her at my side.

I ignore the unease in the pit of my stomach as the door closes behind me, and I move to the center of the room.

The space is one that could be recognized across centuries. A bright white room, cloaked in protective light. A white marble floor. Walls that disappear into shadows beyond where they reside. It is not a *place* the way mortals would think of it. If I were to walk toward those walls, they may change, shifting in their appearance. It is not for me to know what their true appearance may be, or if the walls *have* a true appearance. That is only for the Fates.

The three sister goddesses wear gold silk garments much like the threads of fate they weave. Their obsession with the threads of every soul is necessary for order. Their knowledge of what is to come is inescapable. For humans, Clotho spins the thread to begin their lives in the mortal realm, Lachesis measures the thread, and it is Atropos who cuts it, ending their life. For the gods and demigods, there is power still in the Fates. With how the threads are woven and where they lay on the boards.

This place—and the work of the Fates—exists outside of mortal time, and even time on Olympus or in my realms, and the atmosphere reflects that. The air is still. If I think of windows, they appear in the corner of my eye, but they do not look out on familiar realms. Their images change frequently, and the thoughts of the sisters thicken the air.

They look out on the mists of time, which might

look like anything if one stared long enough. I cannot imagine anyone who would come here would care about what was outside the windows. There are more important things to discuss.

I do not bother looking. I've come for answers and I pray they have them for me.

I stand in the center of the room. The Fates sit on three chairs across from me, clad in their delicate gowns that speak of bygone eras. Or perhaps they are from future eras that only the Fates have glimpsed. I do not know, nor do I ask. They look back at me with placid, youthful faces.

Here, where the Fates take audiences, they change subtly the longer I watch. I do not let my mind dwell too deeply on how they look, though my eyes snag on the changes, trying to make sense of them.

No sense can be made.

I push aside the strange stillness of this room—this *space*—and bring what matters to the tip of my tongue.

"Does Zeus know, or does he not know, that Persephone resides with me?"

The Fates glance at one another as if they are communicating thoughts with only a look. The one in the center—her dark hair is the feature that stands out most—meets my eyes.

"Zeus believes, but he does not know entirely," she says, although the words seem to come from all of them at once. The smooth, regal voice is soft, but fills the room. It does not echo, though there is little else in the chamber. Perhaps there is, but I cannot see it. "Ignoring him is not wise."

"I am not ignoring him."

"Are you not?" they ask, and their glare seems to dare me to lie to them.

"No. I am making the necessary consultations. That is prudence, not avoidance."

"So you have come to us." The Fates rise from their chairs and stand together, the hems of their gowns turning hazy, much like the mists of time. I remain where I stand. There is no wind inside this chamber, but their gowns move as if in a breeze. They reach for each other's hands, touching and pulling back. "You believe a change will come about when you meet with him."

"I know it will."

I do not offer more of my thoughts on the matter. Things always change when two forces meet with opposite desires.

Love or desire? Her question resonates through me, as if the Fates have pulled the question from my memory themselves.

I feel Persephone's absence in painful longing, watching the Fates stand together. I need her beside me. It is a desire I will not allow myself to feel in this place. My emotions are too strong as it is, and they are balanced against those years of isolation. It is not like me to wish for the touch of another, especially one so casual as what the Fates are sharing now. Yet I find myself wanting it.

Only from Persephone. No one else.

I do not flex my hands against the urge, but it is there.

For a few moments, it seems the Fates are waiting for me to speak. Perhaps they are remaining silent to encourage me to do so.

I do not speak, I wait for their consult as they pick through my mind. I think of my hands on Persephone's skin. I think of her heels in my back. I think of how she tasted, and how she sounded, and how she took me into her body and let me find pleasure there. I did not think it would be like it was between us. I did not expect to be able to let myself get lost enough to have such a powerful release.

My mouth goes dry remembering it. Dangerous to let my mind wander at a moment like this, but the Fates must decide that I am not going to continue.

"Do not underestimate the power of the goddess." I am not sure which one of them speaks. It could be all of them. It could be none of them as the voice seems to come from deep within my mind. "The more support you give her, the less she will need from you. The more powerful she will become."

Those words do not inspire desire in me. They inspire pure irritation. The less she will *need* from me? Why do the Fates insist on misunderstanding me? Why can't they see *these* threads when they can see so many others?

"I do not wish for my wife to require my hand," I say

sharply. "I wish for her to desire it above all else. Is such a partnership in your visions?"

The Fates shiver, as if a stronger breeze has come through the room, but I do not feel a change in the air. I would welcome it if I could.

"It's a dangerous game you're playing," they say, a warning edge in their tone.

I laugh. It cuts through the stillness and echoes back at me. "Yet we're playing it, nonetheless. Such is the way of gods."

The sound of whispers fills a room. Is it the Fates or souls out of time? What are they discussing? I cannot make out a single word. The Fates themselves shift in their places, their hands brushing against one another's, eyes on me.

"Zeus would win if it came to a war," one of them says. "Only in the sense that you would be trapped in a hell of your own making."

The voice splits in two. "The dead will be the undoing," another adds, tone sharper. "For all mortals will perish."

All mortals would perish. My eyes widen with what they predict. It is not possible for the mortal realm to be barren. Demeter. The singular goddess's name echoes in my mind and a chill flows down my arms.

"*And*," says the third, "the Underworld will be no more than ash."

The voice snaps back together. "—with the screams of the souls that once were."

The ominous foretelling is not what I had hoped for. New fear creeps through me.

I feel it all down my spine. My arms. My legs. The dread does not stop until it has filled every place in my body that is capable of feeling it.

"I will not give her up," I state. Knowing the pain that will come of me. Perhaps we are all meant for pain.

"We did not say you must give her away."

"Your words are not clear."

"You should avoid war, my king," the Fates say as one. "For the fate of all. War will end us as we know it."

"How?"

"That is not for you to know. It simply must be."

My anger rises again like a flame that will never be extinguished. It is useless. "I want to fight for her, to protect her, to keep her."

"If you fight to keep her, you are not the only one who will perish."

"What must I do then?"

"Meet with Zeus, it is the start of her destiny. Offer her the seeds of the Underworld. You may tempt her with them, but she must consume them of her own will."

"And what will come of the meeting?"

"Demands and anger. Threats and betrayals."

A grunt leaves me. "What do I leverage? What can I offer? Give me something, I beg of you. You see the path to what I desire."

"You must release what you resist. You must allow

Persephone to rule her fate and only then may she choose you."

"I will not let her go."

"It will not be your call, my lord. You must offer her the seeds; you must allow the future to unfold without your control."

A furious rage consumes me. "Do nothing but give her seeds? That is your will?" I question with a trembling tone that darkens the room. "There is no point then in discussing matters with Zeus."

"You must or she will die."

My throat is dry with their tellings.

"If you fail in any of these ways, she will die."

"Do not resist. Release and allow her to follow her fate. You prayed for a queen to stand beside you; she will enter fires of her own making. She must become what you have both asked her to be."

"And what can I do!?" I scream the question, feeling lost without actionable cause.

The Fates echo in unison, "What you resist will persist. Tempt her with the seeds and allow fate to unfold without your control."

And with that, the light closes around me and I'm left in the cold darkness of the forest, with little but anger and doubt that fuels a thunderous scream to billow from me. It is only after the ragged scream has left me that I look in my fist to find the seeds. A gift from the Fates.

chapter 20

Persephone

I know not much of my powers here. Only that growing new life from naught is futile. Silvie tells me I have more power than I know and perhaps it is because there is something in this realm that I have a gift for, and I do not know of it yet. I'm reminded of my mother, who was told of my powers, teaching me. Was she told more? Does she know? Does anyone know? The Fates did not prepare me for this, and I wonder if they play with the threads of gods.

Sylvie sits across from me at the old oak table in the corner of the room, various materials gathered in front of her in a neat row. I have my own collection before me. We're making witches' ladders in the light of the window. Yarn. Feathers. Both came from a small wicker basket Silvie carried in with her this morning.

She says it's her favorite thing to do. To weave like the Fates, spells of wishes and protection.

I wish to know my powers here. To know what is possible, to know where my powers lay in this realm... I wish to be my highest self and earn the title of queen of the dead if I must stay here.

I concentrate on another knot. Another feather. We have been working in silence, because Silvie made clear that *some* silence was required. Concentration, really. In order for this work to have any power, it must be done with intention, with emotion, and with the power within.

My intentions are not simple.

Be stronger than any one who prays for me to bend to their will, I think, and tie another knot.

Be more powerful than I can imagine, I think, and add another feather. *So powerful no one would ever dare harm me.*

Discover every bit of magic I can bend to my will so that I may rule myself and no god can force otherwise, I think again and again.

With the mere thought of gods ruling over me, I glance to my right. The fire crackles beyond it and as it does, Sylvie's eyes glance up to the flames and then to me. She's quick to look away, as if she knows what I think.

My mind keeps returning to the bed and being in it with *him*. I had not expected to feel power in pleasure. I had expected to be...made smaller, somehow. I thought giving myself to another would be more like letting him *take* me. Take part of me. Claim it as his forever.

It *does* feel like Hades has claimed a part of me as his, but only because I offered it in exchange for a piece of him. Only because I wanted him to claim it. Surely that is a kind of strength, too. Did I find it because it was already within me, or did I find it because he taunted me with those words?

It seems you found your strength, no?

And I had said...

More like my anger.

I make another knot. Add another feather. The ladder grows as does my desire.

If I could go back and have that conversation again, I might use another word.

I might say *more like my passion*. That is how it feels to me now. Like passion, which can seem like anger if it burns hot enough.

It certainly burned hot when we were moving together under the protection of the covers. So heated I could hardly keep my mind above the sensations. So hot that many times, I did not, and I let them overwhelm me. The feeling is addictive. I crave more of him. The feeling and his power.

Maybe that is a kind of strength as well. Maybe it does take courage to let pleasure claim a part of you, because once you have done so, you cannot forget it.

I will never be able to forget that moment. When

there was a shift within me. When I felt such things that cannot be undone.

Concentrating on pleasure and strength nudges my thoughts into another realm. I make the decision to speak only moments before I do.

"I have a friend I miss," I tell Silvie. "I wish to send her a message."

Silvie frowns down at her witch's ladder. "I cannot aid you with that."

"I don't think that's true," I say lightly. "You have helped me with so much. Surely you can help me with a message." I don't look her in the eyes. Not yet. I am careful as I speak to her with this request.

Silvie laughs, her cheeks turning pink. "I know only what I know. Sending messages to places other than this one is not within my power. I am confined to the realm, my queen."

I had not considered her magic is confined to the realm. What I know of the Underworld are only stories, because whispers are not known to be true. Communications are limited between Hades and Zeus alone. Hecate knows. But she is silent in most ways. A light dims within me as I think of my mother and of Beatrice. Perhaps I can persuade Hades. He seems to enjoy pleasing me. The dull flame brightens at the thought.

"I see. We should find out what lies within my power." I tie the last knot on my witch's ladder and stand up, Silvie's eyes following me. "You have told me many stories, but I do not think I have done my part. I haven't practiced enough or tested beyond simple spells."

"You have, my queen," Silvie says quickly. "You have done the work of years in a short time. You may see them as simple, but a single flame can turn an entire kingdom to ash."

"In my mind, but not so much with magic."

"What do you call those bells on the door, then?"

"A *little* practice." I smile at her, and she smiles back. "Those are evidence that I *am* trying, but you have guided me again and again to the fire. Let's imagine we are there for the first time."

Silvie looks skeptical, but joins me at the grate across the room. It's then that the door creaks, gathering our attention. Cerberus enters the room. Such a regal pup with his three heads, all eyes on me. He trots toward me, and I pat his heads to greet him before he takes a preferred spot in the corner of the room.

I watch him as he makes his circles and lies down.

"Well then," Sylvie says with a huff. "You have gained more power than you know."

"What do you mean?" I ask her before she returns her attention back to the grate.

"He does not allow anyone beyond Hades to touch him."

I search her eyes to see if such things are true and find sincerity there. "I did not know."

She nods, something changing in her eyes before she says, "Back to our task at hand?"

Nodding, I take in a steadying breath.

The flames are low and do not give off much heat. "This is the fire, my queen," she says slowly. "Magic can be worked here, as fire consumes, and its work is shown in flames. These are flames." She points, and I laugh. Silvie's mouth twitches, but she keeps her expression serious. "The way to approach magic such as this is by concentrating on the flames and the work they must do. How high do you see them, how hot can you feel them, what colors dance within them? You must see it in all ways. You must know it to be your vision. I will put them out for you."

Silvie waves her hand, and the flames burn out. Envy burns within me at her power. She controls the fire so easily.

"Now," she says, her voice hinting at laughter. "Concentrate on the work."

"The work?" I ask, as if we have not talked about this before.

"Yes. The fire consumes the wood, turning it to heat and flame. That means that the power you send must…understand the intention."

They are the same words she has said to me before, or very similar, but they reach my ears differently.

I concentrate on the empty grate and the power that *must* exist in the Underworld, even if it is different from the power of bringing life. At first I envision taking from the floor beneath me. The black obsidian and sparkling pyrite. Vaguely I hear a scratching sound, and I welcome it this time. Whatever craves for me to hear it, I listen. With my hand outreached and my head falling back, I allow my mind to think of the flames and of their purpose. It's heat. My eyes close and the vision comes without conscious thought and I think of Hades's hard length, of his hips rutting between my legs, of my growing desire, the mere *intention* of letting him fuck me as he desires and how the flames of his power wrap around me.

An ember *cracks*. My eyes open in an instant and I stare at the wood. Imagining the flames that match the beauty of what I had in that moment. I wish to see my own desire in the flames. My lips part and I will it to give me that pleasure.

And this time, a small fire catches, the little flames dancing there before us for several beats and just as I begin to enjoy them, they sputter out again.

"Your powers are progressing," Silvie says breathlessly. "That is more than I have seen you achieve before."

Humming in confirmation, I attempt to hold onto the fact that I made fire. Never have I before and I find comfort in that. "They *do* seem to be progressing," I agree, trying to keep my voice from showing too much emotion. "Thanks to you."

Silvie scoots closer, both of us on our knees, and squeezes my hand. Both of us look into the grate. No flames now, but there *had* been. They were there. I made them.

"My queen," she says. "Have you had your wine today?"

"Not yet." Wine is for the gods and divination.

"Perhaps we'll have a glass and try again after?"

With a smile, I acquiesce although when I look back to the grate, I envision the flames, and I swear I hear the crackle again. We go back to the small table. Silvie pours the wine into two goblets with a proud smile on her face. We lifts the cups and clink them together, then drink. It's a true celebration, though it is only the two of us standing side by side at the table together.

Silvie exhales, lowering her glass. "Do you know, my queen, that there are spells for things such as...love and peace?"

Her statement sends a shift through me. As if my very being knows her statement to have purpose.

"I have heard of them, but I thought they were mostly myths." I take another sip of my wine. The flavor is rich and full on my tongue. I savor it before I swallow. "The kinds of magic one hopes for, but can rarely use."

Silvie reaches over to her chair and takes something out of her basket.

It is a book bound in smooth leather with an intricate pattern embossed into the cover. Silvie holds it out to me with both hands, and I take it just as carefully, my fingertips slipping over the texture.

I meet her eyes, my heart racing. Silvie nods.

I balance the book in one hand and open it with the other.

The aged pages inside are covered in writing. These are ancient words. Spells that are so old they have become viewed as myths. I run my fingertips over the writing. The page feels warm with power. Or is it the heat of my intention in my hands? I think it might be both.

"Love and peace," I say softly. "The spells for those things can be found in this book?"

"Yes, my queen. And balance. We know so much of hate and violence, but they only exist because of the balance we protect."

Spells for peace and love. I know there is no new weight on my shoulders, but I feel it regardless. These spells would take much more power than lighting a fire for a few seconds. They would take more power than I have ever dreamed of having or trying to use. For they reflect onto others. To their minds and actions. Like sirens in the ocean and the fairies in the woods. Although the creatures I speak of are mysterious and dangerous.

Silvie exhales as if she needs to speak the words more than she needs to breathe. "I do not think it will be Hades who saves us," she says.

It takes me a few seconds to absorb her words and

lift my eyes from the book to hers. She looks at me steadily.

"Save us?"

"From the fallout of what he's done to be with you," she answers.

"You think it will be my mother? My father?" I question her, not knowing if either will ever find me here.

The corner of Silvie's mouth turns up slightly. "I think it will be you."

A chill runs through me as Silvie inclines her head and leaves. Her steps are the only thing I can hear as I watch her go. I close the cover of the book and lay it on the table.

It takes a few moments before I can think clearly. Surely I am not meant to save anyone in this state. I swallow thickly, removing the thought entirely from my mind. If I am to be queen of the Underworld, and Hades believes it as truth, then there is something I will do.

With the thought echoing in my mind and the chill having an unrelenting grip on me, I return to the grate and concentrate my power into it. The power of the queen of the Underworld.

The flames spring to life without hesitation. My eyes widen, almost in disbelief, but I refute the notion, and instead I tell the flames what I want of them.

I sit before them and watch as they dance, letting my gaze settle on them, considering the power there. I wish to play with it, to grow it, to feel the warmth and desire Hades gives me. The power I took from him. I know I did such things even if it was not my intention. For I am more powerful today than I was before.

What appears in the flames comes slowly. At first, I think it is just shadows, but I keep my eyes soft, and the image clarifies.

In the flames, I see my mother, crying. Dread slips into my blood and my lips part with a pain of seeing her cry.

Tears stream down my face slowly, but it stopped mattering to me long ago. What difference does it make if someone sees me? None. If I must cry, I will allow it. And in this moment, the absence of my mother but knowing her pain is too much for my soul to bear. I wish she could see me light the fire. I wish she could know the power I feel in this place.

Tears flow from me as I watch her scream and thrash against my father, who wishes to calm her. His sorrow is evident, and I cannot stop my emotion, but I am grateful for it and do not care if anyone sees it. The flames are swept away by the wind and my mother is gone. But it doesn't take long for the fire to play before me another scene.

In the vision, there is a knock at the door and it opens to reveal Zeus, a servant hovering by his side. He steps across the threshold with the servant and takes in my quarters in Olympus, which is spacious with graceful wood floors and plaster walls. These may seem like mortal touches to others, but they are mine. Beatrice's love for them grew on me years ago.

My father gazes to the plants that once grew here. I see them the way he must.

All the flowers have died. The fruit has withered and spoiled. None of it grows anymore. None of it bears life.

Zeus looks back at me; I swear he sees me. I can feel his eyes on me. And I can see in his eyes that he thinks I have met the same fate. A coldness of death flows through me as the back of my eyes prick with tears.

But no—I am still present.

I watch him blankly, feeling nothing except grief, raw in my chest. It occurs to me that I should stand to greet him.

I stand, but no words leave my lips.

"Demeter." Zeus clasps his hands in front of him. "Many gods come. They bring many gifts."

"They are not my Persephone," she replies. "Bring her back to me!"

He lifts one hand. "Demeter—"

"How am I to know she's well?" She rasps, her voice etched in raw pain. "How am I to *live* without her?"

I wish to scream to her, but my voice is silent.

"Demeter," he says again, but she does not care to hear what he has to say. She does not care to see his face.

The feelings break loose like a plant bursting out from a seed and racing toward the sun. One with many thorns that cuts and tears at my insides.

This feeling—this horrible, bleeding feeling—wretches through me as my mother answers my father.

"If I must suffer, so must all. So will *you*." With that the fire goes out and I'm left stunned wondering if what I witnessed, even the hissing of my mother, was real.

OLYMPUS

Demeter

I slam the door in Zeus's face and pace away, the anger simmering within me. A full moon has passed and there is no word! How could they not have found my daughter? There is betrayal and I know it so. I have been still for many hours, and now I feel as if I will burn alive if I do not walk. *Move*. If I do not do something.

How dare he come to me without her. *With gifts?* As if anything could replace her? *Come to me with the severed hands of those who stole her from me!*

Is this what it feels like to go mad? I used to think that the great abundance that surrounded me would shield me from such madness. I gave so willingly, wanting those to have fortune I possess.

But there is no abundance without Persephone. There is nothing without Persephone. Nothing without my daughter.

Covering my eyes with my hands, I press my palms to my reddened eyes.

I am supposed to be the goddess of abundance. I am the goddess who gives of the harvest so that the Earth can keep turning. So that mortals can continue in their cycles. So that the realms work as they should, in accordance with the Fates.

My gaze settles on a sliver of quartz that falls from the chiseled wall. It shook free as the door slammed. A thin sliver with rough edges.

"All will feel this pain," I whisper, dropping my hands and throwing the words at my window. "It does not leave me, so it will not leave you." I carve a sigil into the wooden floor. The ragged rock digs into my flash and blood drips to the tip of the crystal, filling in the etching.

The sigil; agony.

This pain will *never* leave me. Not until Persephone is with me once more. This pain consumes me like fire, but it does not bless me with light. It is only scorches the loss.

"Agony," I pronounce. I do not know who I'm praying to. All I know is that I will not pray only for the return of my daughter. "I want *agony*. All mortals shall suffer crippling agony, and may they blame it on *you*, Zeus. May they blame it on your incompetence. May they blame it on your lies. May they blame you for all their suffering. May you *pay*. May all feel the agony of loss. May it be felt as if it was their own." I stare down at the carving and whisper, "Until she is returned, all will feel my pain. So mote it be."

chapter 21

Hades

Agitation grows within me. From the message of the Fates to the god of thunder's demands. I cannot meet with Zeus through the mirror this time.

No—he will not accept a meeting through an intermediary that keeps such distance between us.

I would rather have much *more* distance between us. The desire to end him is strong. If only I remove him, no one would know. But the Fates' tellings pull me back.

He must sense as much, because he is satisfied with meeting where the Fates dwell.

Between realms. Neutral ground. I follow the path to their dwelling place with my teeth gritted and my eyes focused straight ahead. My hands do not move from their clenched position.

We will meet. We will discuss what has happened.

And afterward, Zeus will attack the Underworld or he won't.

Oh, there's no need to pretend. He will move against me. The only thing left to be decided is the method.

Or perhaps he's already made up his mind.

For the Fates to warn me not to fight… I fail to heed their warning in my mind, but I close my eyes, having faith that they see another way. They see her with me. That is all that matters.

I follow the path to the dwelling, stride up to the door, and go in without knocking.

My blood freezes as I gaze upon the dwelling. Zeus waits inside. His long white robe and golden cloak are at odds with my darkly mirrored attire. His golden silk to my thick velvet. The stark white to my pitch black. I take a moment, as the door closes behind me with a soft click to note the darkness under his eyes and the growth of his beard. He is plagued and for a moment I feel certain sympathy for him.

"Hades," he greets me and in his tone, there is desperation. My head tilts as I answer him, "Zeus."

Zeus sits in the center chair, but gets to his feet. A quick glance at the walls says they are more solid than they seemed before.

Perhaps that is Zeus's wish. He wants them to seem like the walls of Olympus. As if he owns this place, too.

He does not.

The Fates are nowhere in sight, though their

influence is all around us in the stillness of the air, as if they're watching.

Zeus tampers his scepter on the old floor and his crown, a wreath of olive leaves, slips slightly. A challenge, of course. I can tell from his eyes that he is sizing me up. That he did not think of this as a meeting between equals, perhaps. That he thought this would be a chance for him to issue commands

If he thought so, he is discovering now that he is wrong. This is not a meeting between equals, nor one where he is free to issue commands.

I am more than he is. I am more than he will ever be.

Because I have Persephone.

She is what makes me more. She is what keeps my back straight and my mind focused. Together we will rule. The Fates told me so, if only I allow fate to be.

I clear my throat and pull a chair back, taking a seat across from where he was. My own crown of celestial bronze doesn't slip as I lift my chin in gesture of him retaining his seat.

The silence stays heavy between us for some time before Zeus lowers his chin just slightly and he retakes his seat. He was already looking into my eyes, but now his gaze has a different intent.

"You have her," he says. It is not quite a question.

"How is it that you come to ask?" I ask, my tone just as light.

Something flashes in his eyes, and he spreads his

hands in front of him. "I did not know, but I was hopeful she was in your hands."

"*Were* you?" A glimmer of hope lights within.

"It will be easy to acquire her back." The glimmer is quickly vanquished by his statement. I rub my forefingers against my thumb, watching him, waiting for more but he does not offer it.

There are no words to express the rage I feel at his easy words, but I let nothing show. I let it burn inside me.

"I will not return her," I answer and all air leaves my lungs.

There is a pause while Zeus takes this in, reacting only with a blink.

"I do not wish to be on opposite sides of a war with you," he says.

"There is, perhaps, a deal to be made here," I offer. There is no deal that will include me handing Persephone over. One does not *hand over* a queen.

Zeus shakes his head. "You stole her. The terms have changed."

"Have they?"

"What of Demeter?" Zeus questions, his brow furrowing. "What of the loss she has suffered?"

Ah—that is the change in the terms, then. Demeter's sadness. Her demands. She has impressed her wishes upon Zeus.

Whatever Demeter feels, it will not sway me.

"Inform her of what you must. I will not live without Persephone."

Zeus lets out a short scoff, a break in his usual control. "War is what it will come to." His voice rises in disbelief. "*War,* Hades. I cannot stop her! You have not seen what terrors she's already unleashed!"

"I will suffer the losses of war then," I say simply. And the warnings of the Fates hiss at me. Consuming me. Demanding my words to be taken back.

"The losses of war could be beyond—"

"It would be *nothing,*" I interject, cutting him off with more feeling than I had intended to show. It is difficult not to show *more,* but I resolve to keep a tight leash on my voice. "Nothing at all compared to the loss of my queen. We do not need to fight. Do not take her from me. She is at peace in my realm. She is a queen. She must stay."

Zeus's expression shifts. It is a slight change, but I am watching for it. His eyes widen subtly and his lips part as if he cannot decide what to say. He controls it within a heartbeat, but I have already seen.

It's fear. That's what is written on his face. A small part of me wants to gloat at this small victory. Zeus *should* have known he was fucked from the moment he entered this room. He should have known what Persephone meant to the realms of the gods and the Underworld—and to me.

But of course he did *not* see, did he? So often, it is his habit to dismiss what is right in front of him, only to be shocked when it slips out of his grasp.

Zeus takes a heavy breath, his expression slipping

back into calm even as his hands tighten around his scepter.

"Hades," he begins, as if dealing with a stubborn child. "You can choose from any and all. There are multitudes, if only you would—"

"I chose her." My own control is fraying. I wish to end this discussion and return to Persephone. I wish to let out the frustration I carry locked deep inside, near all the wounds that have not healed from the past. That *may* heal from the past, if Zeus would stop trying to take my queen from me. "I *choose* her. It is done. She is mine."

Another moment of silence, this one heavier than every silence before. Zeus's eyes burn into mine. The fire in my chest has nothing to do with Zeus.

"The bonding ritual is done?" he questions and my heart beats heavy in my chest.

This time, he *is* asking, with a note of hope in his voice. He *hopes* there has been no bonding ritual. He hopes he still has a fucking chance.

I will crush that hope beneath my heel.

"It is done," I lie smoothly. I pray he cannot hear my racing heart.

Another long silence descends on the room. I do not look at the windows to see if the mists of time have arranged themselves into another form. I do not look at the walls.

I watch Zeus.

He watches me.

"Simply leave us be."

"I cannot."

"I cannot let her go," I answer, and I hear the warning yet again: what you resist persists. The hissing of the Fates clouds my judgment and for a moment, I think Zeus may have heard something as well.

Make your choice, I will him, swallowing thickly. I have made the choice that matters most in all my years. There is no backing away from it. There is no returning to how things used to be.

Unless…

I brush away the warning of that voice in the back of my mind. Unless *nothing.* There is nothing in all the realms of existence that could turn back time or erase my feelings for Persephone. If Zeus is waiting for some sign of that, then he will be waiting for the rest of eternity.

Finally, Zeus answers, "You leave me no choice, Hades."

"There are plenty of choices, Zeus. She is a daughter you were willing to lose. Don't forget that."

"You do not understand the anger of Demeter."

I narrow my eyes at him. Does he *mean* this? Does he mean for me to cower because of the anger of *Demeter?* Such a giving and kind goddess. One who bestows blessings to those who do not even ask it of her? He can bend to her whims all he wants. It does not mean anyone else has to follow his lead.

And it is not as if hers would be the first anger I faced. The first wrath I suffered. Far from it.

"The goddess of abundance? Of harvest and fruitfulness?" I scoff. "The goddess of—"

"You have stolen her daughter." His voice is deadly low.

"You knew I would have her."

"It is not as we discussed," argues Zeus. "I cannot tell Demeter what transpired."

Well. If Zeus wanted it to be another way, perhaps he should have fucking planned for that in advance. It is no worry of mine.

"Demeter will find peace when she hears her daughter is well and loved."

"Hades." *Now* he is trying to convince me. Appeal to some better nature he believes I have. "You do not know the anger of a mother torn from her child. She cannot come here. But Persephone can return."

"No. I do not know the anger you speak of."

His lips part again, hesitant for a moment.

"Nor is it my concern," I continue. "You will fix this."

"I cannot—"

"Need I remind you, Zeus, *you* are the one who started this." My blood turns to fire as I remember his words.

Zeus nods, seeming to forget himself for a moment. It is not like him to accept responsibility for agreements he has made. Why would he when it is so much more convenient to toss the blame on others? It is probably Zeus's habit on Olympus, where those around him have no choice but to shoulder whatever he throws at them.

"You do not want me to finish this, Hades," he warns.

I lift my chin. It is impossible to straighten my back any further. "I recommend that you confide in Demeter swiftly then. Persephone flourishes here."

His tone echoes disbelief. "In a realm with no new life! She cannot be herself in the Underworld. Not as the goddess she was."

"She can as the goddess she is now!" I bite back.

"With what power?" he questions, and my words leave me. For I know what I have taken from her, but I wish to give her so much more.

He huffs. "If you truly loved her, you would feel the pain she has from the loss of the gift of gods and the loss of her mother and life as she knew it."

Silences stretches between us as I attempt to deny the truth he speaks. "I have never claimed to be a selfless god."

Zeus glances at the windows, as if he might reach out through one of them and bend the mists of time to his will. That is surely beyond him, and if this problem could be fixed by doing so, there is no need to discuss it with me first.

Perhaps he is only thinking of a way without war.

Is there some path he could take that I have not considered? Thoughts riddle in my mind. Perhaps I offer a gift. Persephone accepts the seeds, and I will grant something for her mother. A letter, a vision, a way for her worries and loss to be soothed. Before I can speak, he interrupts the silence.

"I need her returned," he murmurs, his gaze piercing my own.

I cannot accept her loss. I do not reinforce this by repeating myself. I have been perfectly clear.

Zeus meets my eyes once more, a glint there that speaks of determination. "Let me see her."

"No." My refusal is echoed in my mind with a chorus of agreement. *No*, the voices in my head say.

Zeus will not have my invitation. No matter what excuse he fumbles for to get it, I will not give it.

The urge to be with Persephone grows stronger. I need her where I can see her. Where I *know* Zeus has not gotten to her through some other method.

"I can only confide in Demeter with truthfulness if I can see Persephone myself."

This is laughable, but I do not offer him humor. Bring her here within his grasp? Let him talk to her? Let him try to convince her that *his* way is the only one?

There is not a chance in any realm of that.

"Since when has truth been a requirement for your persuasion?" I ask him.

Zeus's mouth thins into a grimace, and then his expression breaks into the anger he has been attempting to subdue all this time. Outside the windows, a bolt of lightning cracks through the mists.

"Let me see my daughter," he demands.

"Not at this moment; perhaps shortly." I lift my eyes to his, "There is another way. I know it."

"Time is not on our side," Zeus warns.

"I require it." Abruptly I stand. "Tell Demeter what you must. I will speak to Persephone." With that, I leave him. Ignore his screams of profanity and the thunderous bolt at my back that the light prevents from harming me.

chapter 22

Persephone

Hades is not in the bed when I wake, although I can feel that he was here last night. He left me to my own devices yesterday. I fell asleep waiting for him. Loneliness is all I have for my company this morning.

I wonder why he avoids me. Have I done something? Is there something that plagues him? Has he realized I've taken from him as easily as he took me from my own home?

It is completely different to be in bed with him when we are not at war.

I will always love you.

Some part of me wants to argue against the proclamation he made. It wants to argue that *love* can mean many things. My eyes drift to the bound grimoire on the table where I left it. It might not mean he wants me to stay here, for example.

If he loved me, would he not wish me to be with my family? Would he not regret the pain he causes me of losing my mother forever?

But—no!

I open my eyes and get out of bed before I can let those thoughts spiral too far.

I wash my face and dress simply, my mind caught between thoughts of Hades and the loneliness he's left me with, choosing one of many pieces that appear in the wardrobe of the dressing room in the baths. Then I go out to the grate to practice my magic. If I concentrate hard enough, the flames disappear...

And I can make them come back again. I play with the fire now. It knows me and I know it.

It is only one fire and only in this grate, but I love the sensation of having it *work*. For so long, I was filled with fear that I would never have powers at all and would become a nymph, wandering about the gardens aimlessly for the rest of my days. Nymphs cannot do this. And no one can take this away from me.

At the very thought, my body goes cold. Could I perform such spells in Olympus? Would my magic follow me there? It's so difficult to keep that doubt away.

I make the fire go out, then light it again, banishing even its memory.

Silvie enters the room as I light the fire again and

greets me with a smile. "My queen." Her tone full of pleasant surprise.

"Silvie." I step back from the grate and match her smile. "How are you this morning?" I've grown so fond of the dark-eyed witch.

"I am well." She goes to the table and places her basket down. "And I see *you* are well."

At her side, I question if I can confide in her as I could Beatrice. Should I tell her that Hades was not there when I woke? Should I tell her about the tiny prickle of unease I still feel? As if something is wrong. It is not as if he stays in these rooms all day with me. He goes about his usual habits, which do not include keeping me in the bed with him until the sun sets.

I'm free to go as I wish as well…within the confines of the castle, but still, something feels very wrong.

I decide against it. There may be nothing to worry about, and as much as I trust Silvie, I do not want her to have reason to tell others—which others, I do not know—that Hades left the room, and I lost my composure.

"I'm grateful for the power of fire," I say in reply. "I owe that to you."

Silvie shakes her head, blushing slightly. "I am only showing you what is already within you."

I think Silvie is both right and wrong. Some powers may have been inside me—I was born of a goddess, after all—but those powers do not exist in the Underworld. However, there are *other* powers, and it is because of Silvie that I have found it and learned to wield it. It is because of Silvie that there are enchanted bells at the threshold to the room.

I am about to tell her so when the bells chime gently.

Silvie looks first. It takes me another moment because I am still deciding what to say to her, but I turn my head as soon as my mind catches up.

"My lord," Silvie says. "Excuse me. I did not know you would be returning."

Silvie scoops up her basket and bobs her head, but Hades holds up his hand. "Stay. I will have need of you."

"Of course, my lord." Her demeanor with Hades is quite different. Less friendly and more subservient. Hades doesn't seem to notice, and I don't quite know what to think of the difference.

Silvie does not leave the room, but she goes to stand near the door, quiet and unobtrusive.

I almost feel as though I am alone with him.

It is hard to look anywhere but at his tall, handsome frame and the possessive heat in his eyes as he moves toward me, stopping a few feet away. He looks me up and down as if he is trying to make a decision.

Or as if he has already *made* a decision, and now wants to see if it will suit me. My heart beats faster, fluttering up into my throat. My palms grow clammy, and I don't love the unease that comes over me. I keep my back straight and my chin lifted, though what I feel waiting for him to speak is not fear or anger.

A smile quirks the corner of Hades's mouth, and he meets my eyes at last. "You will sit beside me at court."

I had wanted to answer without missing a beat, but when I open my mouth, words escape me. He's kept me hidden except to a spare few.

You will sit beside me at court.

The announcement echoes in my mind. This can only mean one thing.

"You would let them see me?" My voice is thinner than I would have liked, but there is nothing I can do to change it. I'm too shocked. Stunned.

"To rule beside me, you must sit beside me and rule, no?" he proposes.

A thrill runs through me, one I've not quite felt before. A power that has not taken hold before. The room seems to bend at the heady feel.

Who is the woman who has such thoughts? Have I truly changed so much? I did not feel it happening, but I suppose it must have.

Who is the man who would have me sit beside him for all to see?

Has *he* changed, as well?

Hades nods, as if this is nothing. "It is a small court today. It won't take long."

"What exactly does it entail?"

"Souls who the judges disagree on. We will preside over their judgment."

"Understood." I do not know what else to say as my heart hammers with a vicious need to be freed.

"Silvie," Hades says, turning to her. "A maiden is

waiting with a gown for my queen in the hall. Please gather it for her."

Silvie does so, returning a few moments later with a gown draped carefully over one arm.

That is not all Silvie is carrying.

She is also carrying a crown in both her hands. I step to the side to let her pass, unable to keep myself from the gilded crown. Silvie sets it carefully on the table, then drapes the gown over a chair in the far corner of the room. Her head stays hung low although her posture straight.

When I turn back to Hades, his dark eyes are lit with amusement. "Dress. I will wait for you."

"Will you?"

Hades takes a long step toward me, and I go to him. "Yes," he answers. "I will be out in the hall."

I tilt my face up, my heart pounding, and Hades leans down and kisses me. I've never felt the need to please him as I do in this moment. To stand beside him as if I know what I am doing. Hades breaks the kiss, and I bring my fingertips to my lips, my breath shallow. I grip him before he can leave me.

"Are you sure?" So many thoughts scour my mind. All the what-ifs.

"It is time, my queen. I am sure." Something flashes in his eyes that I can't place.

Despite my fears, I feel myself falling.

Falling in love.

Or maybe it is deeper than love. Maybe it is a love I did not know existed until I came to the Underworld.

"Dress," he says again, in a low voice meant only for my ears.

Then he turns and leaves, closing the door behind him.

I whirl toward Silvie and the chair. "The *court?*"

"Indeed, my queen," Silvie says evenly. "Come now. I will help you." It's evident her demeanor has changed. I do my best to mirror what she offers. The seriousness of the situation.

The new gown is made with a rich, luxurious silk that falls over my body like water.

I watch Silvie adjust the gown in the mirror, pulling the ties in the back, each drape becoming more exquisite under her hands.

But then she lifts the crown over my head and settles it down.

One blink, and I am transformed. There is a grounding that settles the anxious parts of me. Almost as if I was waiting to wear it. Like my soul once had it before.

The crown has not changed anything about me. It does not have magic.

And yet, it possesses me, more than I possess it.

"Beautiful, my queen," Silvie murmurs. "You are fit for court."

"Am I?" I catch her eyes in the mirror. Enchanted bells and fires in the grate—those are small things. How could they be anything else in comparison to passing judgment in the court of the Underworld?

"You *are,*" Silvie says more firmly. "Is there anything else I can do for you, my queen?"

"What should I expect?"

"Sit beside him on your throne. Watch and wait. It will not be hard, I assure you. Hades will guide you, my queen. He will not lead you astray. Likely he will ask you your opinion. You are quite capable of giving such things," she adds with a smirk.

With a huff of humor, I agree.

Silvie escorts me to the door. As promised, Hades is waiting on the other side—along with a cloaked guard. The only one of his men I recognize is Minox. The others do not offer me their names and they change frequently.

Hades's eyes are hot and dark when Silvie opens the door for me. He offers me his arm. "My lady."

I put my hand on his arm. "My lord." I nearly ask him to allow me to simply observe today, but I bite my tongue, mindful of the audience. I know not what comes but intrigue has captured me.

"There is no need for nerves. It is your rightful title," he states as if reading my mind.

Hades escorts me down the hall, all the while I stand tall and keep my head still so as not to compromise my crown. He leads me to a wall that opens with a wave of his hand. As it was locked with a magic that disguised it. There are three more guards waiting outside the court. All three dressed the same, with black cloaks tied at their throats and hoods up nearly covering their faces with the shadows they offer. I can make out slight differences in their faces although they don't offer enough to recognize them.

In awe, I enter the massive room beside him.

"My lord," one guard in front greets us with a bow of his head. "My lady."

"Call her queen," Hades says abruptly. "I prefer the sound of it."

"Yes, my lord. My queen." The guard bows more deeply this time.

Hades leads us past, and the guards fall into step behind us. They stay close enough to offer protection, but far enough that we still have a bit of privacy. All the while the nerves run through me. My hands are nearly numb. The stone floors are slightly worn from centuries of passage. The ceilings high and lit from candles that draw the eye up. And in the room that echoes the click of our footsteps sit what must be a hundred pews in four equal rows and at the head of the room, the raised thrones and several seats.

The thrones themselves are decadent. With velvet lining in a deep red set within the carved wood. The backs are at least ten feet high, and the edges of the feet carved and touched with fire to give a burned flamed look to them. Both of equal height, but flames varying between the two so that it appears the fire starts from the left throne and carries to the right. It is quite obvious the throne at the left is newly made. It's wood fresh and the red velvet plush.

My throne, I nearly whisper.

It feels incredibly real, this procession. It feels like

I am meant to be at Hades's side with guards trailing after us.

Or am I only tricking myself so I can cling to bravery?

I do not know.

"You will speak as you please, you will show the audience that you are here to rule, understood?" he murmurs as he leads me up the steps to the thrones.

"I will," I answer him quickly without thinking.

"You almost sound like you believe that, Persephone. Be careful," he warns. "Our thoughts are powerful, and yours even more so."

This, said so casually, renders me speechless once again.

Should I tell him about my vision of my mother? About her threats and her agony of losing me.

How much time for questions do I have before we will be in court and passing judgment on the souls of the Underworld? Before he shows the world that he thinks of me as his *queen?*

In the end, I cannot form the question, and my heart beats too hard for me to speak.

I keep my mother's warning to myself. For I do not know what is real and what is only in my mind, but at this moment I stand tall beside my lover and attempt to be his equal in a room that feels so very familiar and yet one I do not know I belong in.

chapter 23

Hades

LET WORD SPREAD THAT SHE STANDS BESIDE ME with a rightly deserved crown. Let Hecate hear whispers from the army of the dead. I pray it travels to every realm. With purpose and a renewed sense of thrill, I lead her to her throne.

Entering my court has never felt like this. Not once.

The pride is unexpected, as is the anxiousness of their reaction.

Stepping through the doors with my queen at my side is unlike every other time I can recall, and the sensation is not entirely comfortable. Mostly, this is for my own behalf.

With a sharp gasp, I turn to look at her. Fucking beautiful. She's breathtaking in the crown made for her.

I take great pleasure in Persephone's company. I

would prefer to see her spread out on the sheets beneath me, but out of the corner of my eye, she is all regal beauty.

Whispers rise as we move toward the dais.

The gathered attendants lean close to one another, speaking in low voices or whispers. Though I cannot hear the words themselves, the tone is audible.

The tone is kind. The tone is slightly awed, as if they are surprised to see her at my side.

Many of these attendants have seen Persephone out on the path. The few who I have allowed in the castle. They have come to like her. To respect her.

Now they will stand in astonishment, as I do every time I walk into the rooms we share.

It is like watching the sun rise in the realm of the mortals or if Elysium were to come down to meet the darkest pits of hell. It would be difficult to explain Persephone's beauty to one who had never seen such things. They might think, in their ignorance, that it was nothing more than exaggeration.

It is not.

Persephone holds tighter to my arm, and we step up onto the dais at the opposite side of the room. Two thrones wait for us. I guide Persephone into the one on the left, if one is facing the dais.

I take my seat and Persephone is at my right hand, where she should have been before and will remain. I will ensure it.

She is trembling. Nerves, I think. I brush my

knuckles along the back of her hand and she glances at me. Her beautiful eyes wide and full of awe.

"Your kingdom awaits, my queen," I tell her, and she offers me a short nod in acknowledgment. I can practically hear her heart racing from here. There's nothing to concern her. She will participate as much as she'd like to and nothing more.

Persephone's hand slides into mine atop the thick armrest between our thrones.

She's here, my heart says, though my eyes can see this perfectly well. *She is here, and today you need not remember all those eternities you spent alone.*

"We will begin," I announce, my voice reaching the very back of the hall.

Voices rise slightly, then the first of the new souls is brought in and we fall into the well-worn routine.

It is the same pattern as always, and yet it feels like the first time. Each soul is a precious being. One under my rule and their eternity at my discretion.

With Persephone's hand in mine, I am the same god I was before. And I am a god I have never met.

It is not a matter of fairness. From my first breaths in the Underworld, I knew I would rule with balance, and that with it would come judgment from others. Scathing hate from those receiving a punishment that is inescapable. Heartless is a word I hear often. There is no one in the Underworld who can claim that I was unfair or unjust. Except for liars and those who still fail to see their sentencing here is mirrored in their free will in the mortal realm.

Persephone does not inspire whimsy in me for a task like this. She doesn't inspire rage or a severe harshness. She simply sits beside me to observe and in that, she inspires additional patience. As I treasure the moment of her first court in her throne. The first witnesses to her crown.

Court proceeds as such: the guard states the name, verdict by each judge and then allows the soul a moment of appeal. When the judges do not agree, that is where I am needed. Screams and cries are silenced with a wave of my hand. The first soul, a murderous thief screams out, tears streaming down his face when sentenced to a hell of listening to the screams of his eight victims, then the cries of their loved ones, then the silence of the funeral. Over and over again for a hundred years. At which time, he will be resentenced. The moment his scream begins, my hand is waved and the black tarp is placed over his head, silencing the cries as the man is made limp by the magic, and he's taken to his new home.

I glance at Persephone whose lips are parted in what appears curiosity and then her gaze catches mine. For a moment, something flickers between us. Something unprecedented. But then the next soul is announced.

After some time, Persephone's hand relaxes in mine.

After a few more souls, the doors open to admit another.

This time, I wait.

The silence spreads across the hall. All the whispers and murmured conversations cease from the audience.. The new soul waits, her head bowed, her eyes on the floor. A murderer, but of her captor. For weeks she contemplated, she could have run and left another upon her escape. Instead she ended the murderer and released the other prisoner. There was some deliberation among the judges given her obsession with how she would kill him. In his sleep with boiled sugar water. Painful. She craved his suffering.

The woman's bottom lip wobbles as she stands before us silently. When asked her plea, she simply requests mercy in this life because she had none in the last.

Persephone squeezes my hand in a silent question.

I squeeze back. There is her answer.

She does not look to me for further debate, and I do not look at her. I give her the time she needs to consider the soul before us.

Persephone hesitates for one more moment, as if giving me a chance to stop her.

I do not.

She takes a deep breath, her grip tight on my hand. It is another thrill. Her softness and strength are there in her touch. Her compassion. I feel so much coming from her.

And I do not want to draw away from it. I do not want her hand to leave mine.

"You will go to Elysium," Persephone says without a word from me, her voice as clear and steady as mine.

"There, you will spend time in rest and contemplation until you are ready to return to the mortal realm for a new life. You will be safe there for as long as you wish. You may lay down your burdens."

The soul exhales, her voice thick with relief. "Thank you, my lady," she murmurs. The audience murmurs as well, the sound reaching us. The guards do not hesitate, they allow Persephone the sentencing and move forward without pause. Excellent.

This is exactly what I intended. Persephone to rule, confidently beside me. I pray whispers reach the ears of Hecate. For the Titan will judge me as I judge the souls before me. I am sure of it.

More whispers follow. They get louder until the next soul is brought in.

This soul is already tormented.

As the judgments are heard and the soul is granted their moment to plead, I request of Persephone, "Again."

She glances at me with wide eyes before nodding in agreement.

Persephone does not take as much time to speak once silence settles in the court.

"You will go to the Asphodel Meadows," she proclaims. The soul sobs. "There, you may drink from the River Lethe. You may be reborn again."

The attendants murmur among themselves, approvingly. A subtle smile lifts my lips into an asymmetric grin.

All of them together could not approve more than I do.

I want to whisper this in Persephone's ear, but the next soul is brought in.

Once again, the court goes silent.

This soul is compelled by evil. The room is suffocated with it. The stench is evident. It is obvious from the bristling feeling in the air. An evil sinner. One who does not regret what they have done. One who takes pride in their malice.

I know Persephone will see this, too.

The twist of apprehension I feel is only for her, not for myself.

She does not hesitate when I turn to her and nod for her to give her sentencing. My queen delivering a sentence of pain… Will she do it?

"You will face the torture of knives." There is no malice in Persephone's voice. "They were chosen by you in your previous life, not by me." She does not take pleasure in passing this judgment. What shocks me most is the note of empathy. "You cannot be allowed to forget what you have done. Think upon it well."

"How long?" I ask her. The three judges could not agree and thus the reasoning for his summons here.

She glances at me, but then back to the soul who screeches in anger. "A thousand years," she states lowly and I tell her, "louder."

"Your sentencing is a thousand years," she answers, her voice strong and the crowd goes silent as the soul is hushed with magic and draped in the tarp.

My breath catches as the soul is led out.

Yes. She is every bit a queen fit for this realm. Although she readjusts in her seat and unease is written in the way she picks at the hem of her sleeve, she did not cower. She was just. I am obsessed with her ruling.

I take over the judgments to let her breathe, but keep her hand in mine. She whispers a soft, "thank you," when I take over.

I pray she knows how well she did. How honorable and righteous her judgments were.

This will tell everyone in the room and soon everyone in the realm, how much I value Persephone. How much I trust her. How much power she holds and not only because I offered it to her.

When she sits forward to offer her own judgment, I let her. Some souls she seems eager to deliver a verdict, too. Mostly women. We trade off seamlessly. Persephone herself was the one who made herself this way. She took on the mantle of queen and sat on the throne beside me. She has already taken responsibility into her hands, and her judgments are entirely her own.

When the last soul has been brought in, judged, and sent out again, I stand up, Persephone's hand still in mine.

"We are finished here today," I announce. For this court. For today. With Persephone, I am only beginning. I am only *just* beginning, and I will not allow it to be ripped away from me. I cannot. "May the days bring peace and gratitude for each of us," I offer as a parting word and keep my hand on Persephone's as she rises.

"You may leave," I command to the room and guide her to walk beside me as the court rises.

Pride would be overwhelming if not the aching of my cock demanding attention. She is glorious. Gorgeous and fair, my equal and righteous half to the courts. Fuck, those lips. I will never forget today. I will pine for these first moments of her power being realized for centuries to come.

The voices on either side of us as we leave the court are filled with praise and thanks and *goodwill*. I ignore them all, pushing past the stone door and leading her down the hall with haste.

We make it only three steps past the threshold before I guide her to the wall and kiss her.

I am too filled with pride to walk back to my rooms. I am too filled with awe to do anything but kiss her. I need her now. In this moment. Her flesh on mine. Her warmth and the sound of pleasure spilling from her lips.

She gasps the sweetest sound and then my name is spilled from her before she deepens the kiss, her hands reaching under my robe and gripping my back to pull me in close.

Persephone's sweet mouth forces my lust to turn to need. Her hands lift and find my shoulders, and mine find her waist. I'm so hard that my whole body aches for her. It is a pain I would accept much more of in order to be close to her, but I do not need to.

My queen pulls herself up, braced against the wall, and I slide my hand up her gown and under her thigh.

She lifts one of her feet and hooks it around my hip, her pale neck arched for me. Persephone's crown *clicks* and *scrapes* against the wall. I hope it leaves scratches for all eternity. I hope the evidence of her as my queen never fades, no matter what may come to the Underworld. No matter what war may threaten us.

I cannot think of any future war with her body moving against mine. She rolls her hips, brushing against my hardened length that is already leaking precum through our fabrics. Her skin is so soft, so fucking perfect, under her gown. A groan of primal need leaves me and in that moment, she moans the softest sweetest sound fueling me for more.

I hitch it up to her hip and kiss her with desperate need as I explore the warmth between her legs with my fingers. She's already wet for me and lets out a needy noise into my mouth I can't deny.

"I need you," I growl.

"Yes," she pants. "*Yes.*"

I want her as desperate as me. I crave her falling apart.

So I work my fingers over her clit, rubbing circles that deliver the sweetest sounds from her. At first, Persephone presses her mouth into the fabric of my robe to muffle her cries, but she forgets, and I do not care who hears her. I cannot spare even a thought for anyone else. The only thing I am aware of when Persephone is soaking my fingers with her desire is that I must give her more pleasure—

And that no one has disturbed us. Not even my guards have come out of the court, though I know they must be hovering inside the door. It would only serve my cause for them to hear and bear witness to what she does to me and what I do to her.

In this moment though, I don't care for their opinions or presence. This is my kingdom, and she is my queen.

I lower my mouth to Persephone's neck, kissing her there, sucking her there, and angle her over my cock. I get myself free from my clothes and in a haze of her sweetness, get her positioned to take me and pull her down onto my length in a swift thrust of pleasure. I bury myself to the hilt, feeling nothing but ecstasy.

Persephone lets out a loud, low moan as she takes my cock, then arches her back.

"Oh," she says, and works her hips. "Oh, oh—Hades!" She cries out my name and I fucking love it. Harder and harder I rut ruthlessly, needing more. Craving her moans to turn to screams of pleasure.

Persephone is fucking *mine*.

And no one else is going to have her. Not a fucking soul could take her from me. God. Titan. Or anything or anyone. She is mine. Forever.

chapter 24

Persephone

A hum of satisfaction leaves me as I grip the luxurious sheets. I'm rewarded handsomely for staying at Hades's side.

I did not expect to feel so treasured. A greater goddess would have been able to see what was hidden behind Hades's power and rage from the beginning. Would she not? I heard stories of his power, his judgment…but not of this side of him. The sensual needs of a god.

I arch up underneath him, into his touch, as his breath whispers along the side of my neck, hot and humid. I've lost track of the amount of time he's spent circling my clit with the pads of his fingers. Hades's touch was so soft at first that I did not think he could make anything from it.

I was wrong.

Because the longer he moved his fingers, the more deeply I fell into the sensation.

This is a true reward—to be allowed to dwell in pleasure, riding the waves until they peak and crest, and I come on his fingers. Once. Twice. I lose track.

How could my feelings for him not grow?

They do. They catch like a wildfire.

And I can tell—I can feel—that his feelings are growing as well.

Those emotions transform into something like peace.

Something like being at home.

The days have passed and my cup flows over.

As the morning light peers into the bedchambers, he strokes his fingers between my legs until my thighs tremble, then pushes into me without a word, thrusting into me until he comes with a growl. His heat inside me is like another fire, sending every nerve ending to a scorching burn, and it makes me so needy for him that my desire refuses to settle even after Hades has come. It takes a few more orgasms quaking through me before at last I sprawl on the pillows, naked, sated, and bared to him. The only thing I am wearing is Hades, stretched out next to me with one arm across my waist.

He lifts his head and kisses between my breasts, following a path down the front of my body, leaving opened mouthed kisses. Goosebumps follow in his wake.

"My lady," he says, then kisses me again. "My goddess. My queen. I have a gift for you."

"What gift?" I blink up at the ceiling. It must be a joke of some sort. What more could he possibly give me after the pleasures of this morning? There can be nothing left in all the realms.

"I have arranged for you to meet with the Fates."

He brushes a kiss under my belly button, his breath warm and sensual. It is difficult to think when he kisses me like that. It could so easily become *more,* and I would accept it gladly.

Eventually, his words make it past the delicious haze subsuming me.

A chill comes over me. The last meeting of the Fates summoned to my mind.

"The *Fates?*" I say and put my hands on either side of Hades's head and pull him up so I can see his face.

"Yes," he confirms, and kisses me sweetly. He smiles against my lips as I struggle to understand why. Why have me meet the Fates. Those who stated I would be a nymph and no more.

"I do not know that I wish to see them," I confide in him

"What you were before, you are no more. You will meet them as the queen you are," he tells me, and the smoothness and certainty of his voice nearly convinces me.

"I met with them. They wish to see you as well."

My heart hammers but he assures me. "It is a wise decision to consult the Fates."

My mind riddles with so many questions. Most of

which take me back. I do not wish to ask the same questions. I do not wish to even think of that fear. I am different now. And I do not know what I would even ask of the Fates. All the while the questions in my mind lead back to my mother, back to Olympus, but not back to who I once was.

We bathe and dress in a blur of kisses and touches, then Hades offers me his arm and escorts me to the path.

It is the same path I have walked before. After a short distance, Hades must sense that I am questioning our destination.

"When I must meet with the Fates, I do so on neutral ground. There is a forest glade in which they dwell. It appears to be part of the Underworld, but it is not. It is not part of any realm, which makes it suitable for private conversations."

A branching path appears a few steps ahead of us.

"Here," Hades says, and steers us onto it.

We follow that path until it opens into a forest glade, just as Hades said it would. The dwelling in the center is not large, but it is elegant. Its white walls remind me of Olympus. Perhaps this place is why Olympus looks as it does. Perhaps the Fates were the inspiration. It is so different here compared to the other times I have met with them. They do not know time and space, for they are fate.

Hades takes me to the large iron-decorated wooden door and opens it for me. We step inside together, all the while my blood rages in my ears. My pulse quickens. I do not know what to ask. But I think of my mother. I think of the vision I had.

The room inside is comfortably dim in comparison to the daylight outside. There is a certain stillness in the air, as if time itself is being held in place.

There are the Fates—three beautiful women, each in dark gowns, each sitting on a chair like a throne on the opposite side of the room. Each holds a golden thread gracefully in her hand, or crooked over a finger, or pinched between thumb and forefinger. Those threads glow, giving off light that reminds me of fireflies in a summer garden.

"I will be here, just outside, when you are finished." Hades bends to kiss my temple, then leaves, closing the door behind him.

I approach the Fates with my head slightly bowed to show my respect for them. I hope my racing heart is not obvious.

The Fates rise from their seats, gold threads in hand. "Persephone."

I cannot tell which one of the sisters has spoken, or if it was all of them at once.

"I do not know why I have been given this gift," I admit.

"We have a message for you." My heart jumps to my throat. A message? It would be the first one I have received in the Underworld. *From my mother? My father?*

"I would like to hear it. Very much."

The Fates pause, then speak again in that strange chorus of a voice.

"You may thrive in death as much as you would have thrived in life," they say. "But neither life would be complete, regardless of which you choose."

What? That is not any message I had expected. All the warm, hazy feelings that stumbled upon me drop to the floor and are replaced with cold confusion.

"There is no way for me to have a complete life here? Is that what you're saying?" I whisper, thinking of the powers I lost. The longing for them back has not withered as my flowers surely do.

"That is not what was said," they answer calmly. "You must listen."

"I will listen," I murmur attempting to remember what they said word for word.

I cannot quell my frustration, and it seems the Fates don't feel any at all. I fold my hands together and clasp them tight to keep from making fists. There is no running from fate, and I do not know that I am entirely ready for mine. It feels as though I've just found footing again and that they're here to throw me off balance.

"I miss my mother," I say finally, the grief of missing her twisting in my gut. It is easier to ignore it when I am in bed with Hades or at his side in court, but she is my *mother*. I had never been apart from her before I came to the Underworld. All that separated us were the secrets I kept from her. I wish she knew I was well. I wish I could see her again. Tears prick at the back of my eyes, and I swear whatever magic exists in the bedchambers has been broken in this room, for I feel like a child again.

"She misses you as well." The Fates sound reassuring, though their words only make me miss her more.

I do not know what to say, but I gather myself as much as I can.

"Tell me again, please," I ask. "So that I may remember this message."

The Fates tug at the strings in their hands.

"You can thrive in death in the Underworld as much as you can in life on Olympus." They speak more slowly this time. "But neither life would be complete."

A lump aches in my throat. "How am I to be complete, then?"

What they are saying makes no sense. Two halves of a life? How could I choose between them? In the Underworld, I have *some* control over my powers. On Olympus, I have my mother, but my powers will go and surely I will be swept aside.

"To simply be," the Fates reply. "You do not need to choose."

I let out a harsh laugh as tears slip from the corner of my eyes. "But you have just said that I will never be complete no matter *what* I choose. That doesn't make any sense."

"It does, my queen," the Fates say. I want to scream at how calm they sound. "Find your power. It is then that fate will find you."

Hades

I know Hermes is in the Underworld the moment he arrives. I had been returning to Persephone, who came down the path some time ago, but when I sense Hermes on the path, I change directions and go to find him before he can find her.

Whoever granted him passage will hear from me next.

It is not difficult to locate the god of war and conductor of the dead. His eyes are on the side of the path as he walks in loping strides, and he is not attempting to conceal himself. He guides souls to the River Styx, he is not permitted on these grounds though. He should not be here, and I can only imagine why he's ventured this far. *Zeus.*

"Hermes."

The youthful god boasts an athletic yet slim build under his cloth tunic. His winged sandals mark him as the messenger. He rubs his beardless chin with one hand, grasping his gold staff with the other.

He turns at the sound of his name, a smile on his face. "Hades." His tone is one of greeting. As if I do not know better. His arrogance is infuriating.

"I did not know you planned to visit my realms."

"I am here at the behest of Zeus," Hermes

announces. He's always honest…when it suits him. "Tell me. Where is your queen?"

"Not available to you." My tone is harsh intentionally, although the god does not change his demeanor.

"I've come to convince Persephone to return to Olympus," Hermes says. Apparently there is no need for subterfuge.

"You will not," I say flatly.

Hermes glances around the grounds. "She was here. Wasn't she?" He stares at me a moment. "Persephone," he says as if I need reminding.

"Do not speak her name," I warn. "Lest you wish to get her attention." Anger bristles inside of me and I imagine her in her throne, her righteous anger.

"Persephone?" Hermes says. Chills run down my spine at the thought of him taking her. "She is here, then. Here in your realms."

"She will not return," I tell him firmly. "She is my wife."

Hermes squares his shoulders and faces me. A moment passes and it's then I realize my hands are in such tight fists that they pulse. "I would like to see her and speak to her myself."

I put my two fingers in my mouth and let out a sharp whistle. Cerberus will hear it wherever he is in the Underworld and he will come to my side.

Hermes narrows his eyes. "You have called the three-headed dog."

"Yes. And he comes…. You can go now."

"I do not wish to go. I wish to see Persephone so that I may speak with her."

"Then you will want for much," I offer him and settle on a calm exile of the god. "No one will take her from me."

Hermes darts a glance toward the river where Cerberus will come from. He knows this all too well. His voice lowers as he attempts to reason with me. "Someone needs to confirm her presence, Hades. Time has passed. Gods and goddesses grow uneasy."

"I think it is you who should feel uneasy."

"Fine." He bows a farewell toward the castle and moves quickly. "If you insist on war, I will not stand in your way." I follow Hermes down the path. He turns back to warn me. "You should know, the dead are many now, and it is your doing and your doing alone." I search his eyes for deception, but find none.

The dead are many.

It takes me a moment to realize he must mean the mortal realm. *Demeter.*

We leave the glade behind, and he disappears onto the main path just as a crack of lightning rends the sky in two.

The decision is made for me, then. I will not follow him farther.

I go back the way I came, toward Persephone.

I am nearly back at my home when she appears on the path ahead of me, her brow furrowed with worry.

"Hades." She hurries to me and takes my hand. I

curl my fingers though hers and keep us moving. I want to be within the walls. Persephone cranes her neck to look over her shoulder, then looks up at the sky. "What was that?"

"It was nothing."

As if to taunt me, another thunderous crash of thousands of screams are heard overhead. It is loud enough to ring in my ears. Persephone stops on the path, staring up at the dark crack that has been left in the sky. This one lingers for several beats, only beginning to fade against the brightest light of the sun.

Slowly, her eyes drop to mine. "What *was* that?" Persephone asks again. "It is not my father." She states although there's uncertainty there.

"That is the sound of mass deaths and the imbalance of life and death."

"What does that mean?" she questions, her eyes wide and her body breathless with worry.

I stare up at the sky, wanting to deny Hermes' judgment. "More of the dead are coming."

chapter 25

Hades

IT HAS BEEN DAYS SINCE HERMES CAME TO THE Underworld.

It seems like an eternity and at the same time, no time at all.

It's like she's slipping away and there's nothing I can do about it. I know it to be so. With every wretched thunderous cry in the darkness above, thousands of souls pour into the river who should not be here. They overwhelm the judges. They drown in the river with fear. And the balance has been upset. The pain is immense.

Agony is felt by all. It's a suffering the worlds have never known.

And yet, every moment that I am with Persephone is precious. In the bedchambers what lies beyond this space does not matter. It does not exist.

But whatever the Fates said to her left its mark. She does not seem to recognize herself.

In the days since they met, Persephone's powers—and her control over them—have improved a great deal. Even the amount of power she keeps close to herself is greater by far. When she walks past the torches, the fire blazes as if they cannot contain themselves. When she stares intently at a fire in the grate, it burns hotter. When we walk among the shade of the trees, the sun shines stronger through the branches, warming us from the inside out.

The power calls to her although I do not know if she's aware. She seems lost in contemplation.

Persephone's attention has turned back to Olympus.

She speaks often of the roses there. Several times a day, her expression goes distant. Agony has met me in such ways though I try to deny it.

"The roses will surely have wilted," she says one afternoon, the corners of her mouth turned down.

The next morning: "They used to pray to me, you know. The mortals. I heard their prayers on Olympus. I cannot hear them in the Underworld."

The day after: "I cannot make the roses bloom again, Hades. I cannot answer the prayers of the mortals. What good is power if I cannot use it for those who pray to me?"

I have no answers for her, and it only adds to the despair that grows within me. My queen struggles, and I can only distract her. I can only offer what I have in the

Underworld. For the most part, it is enough. She needs to only release what once was.

As I prepare to open the door to the bedchambers, a weight seems to settle in the pocket of my robe. Curiously, I check it and find the seeds of the Underworld. The pomegranate seeds, at least a dozen of them. Lifting one, I observe the shiny translucence of it, the delectable dark red and burgundy shades.

For a moment, I think to squeeze them into her wine, and then shame falls upon me given what happened before. Putting the seeds back, I open the door to find Persephone standing at the lone window, looking out.

She is a vision. My queen.

She is not preoccupied with the changes to my rooms. Persephone hardly seems to notice them. But they *are* there. More soft rugs decorate the floors. The fire burns higher in the grate. Our bed is piled with pillows and blankets. The finer things that can be softened *have* been softened. It is a sanctuary now. A place to rest as well as retreat. Whatever her heart desires, Silvie brings at once. Wine and chocolates. Candles and crystals. She entertains herself with so many books of histories that stacks now line either side of the window. I shall build her a library. It does not escape me though that pages have been torn out and folded into flowers and lilies that sit atop the stacks of books.

Quietly I approach. When I place my scepter down, leaning it against the table where her half-drunk goblet of wine rests, she glances at me. The warmth in her cheeks and the smile that greets me reminds me that all is well.

I need only give her the seeds, a voice in the back of my head reminds.

I go to her, put my hands on her shoulders, and bend to kiss her cheek.

"It is dark," she says softly.

"It is Samhain." I press another kiss to her cheek.

Persephone lifts one hand to find one of mine and twines our fingers together. "Winter is coming," she says softly. "It will be dark for some time."

"It will," I agree. Her eyes soften and within them the colors swirl. Her softness has not left her, although she strengthens with her power. "Walk with me."

I take her down the path to the fields of Elysium, then spread a woven blanket made of the finest dark green threads that was left there by the crystal clear river and help her sit. The moon is just beginning to rise. Persephone leans against me, watching the sky. For now, it is quiet—almost lonely, and Persephone is quiet.

It begins shortly after. One soul, then another. Persephone studies them, her lips slightly parted. Coming home to the Underworld.

"There is beauty in the dark," I say. "It is when the light of the souls is clearest."

"It *is* beautiful," Persephone agrees. "The veil must be very thin."

"It will reach its thinnest very soon."

"There are so many," Persephone whispers. "So much light. So much beauty."

"It is not a sin to take joy in that."

"I can hear their pleas," she says, pain in her voice.

"Answer them."

Persephone leans closer, her hand tight around mine. "My powers do not work here."

"Which powers do not work?" She has not tried. She may have power yet that she has not discovered. "You have more power than you know, my love."

"Do I?" Persephone meets my eyes in the glow of the souls. "Because it does not seem that I have enough to be both parts of who I am."

"You do."

"You could not possibly know that," she murmurs. Whatever plagues her is troubling. Again, I think of the seeds.

I take her in my arms and kiss her, lingering over each press of her lips on mine. Persephone opens her mouth to me, letting out quiet moans.

"Take me to bed," Persephone begs. "Please."

I take her back to my rooms in near silence and seal the door behind us. I put my fingers under her chin and tip her face up. Tears stand on her cheeks. Is it from the beauty of Samhain or her worries about Olympus? I do not know. All I want is to give her what she needs to dry them. To hold her head up high.

"You do not believe in your powers, my queen."

"What can they possibly be worth when I have lost half of who I am?"

Anger simmers at her words. She keeps saying that. But what once was is gone. She is not meant to be in Olympus. She is more powerful here. She is safe beside me. She is meant to rule!

"Everything. It is worth everything," I answer her solemnly. It is time. *Past* time to make good on what I said to Zeus. Tonight the veil is thin, and the power of souls and life and death mingles between the realms. It is a sign that we should mingle ourselves in that same way. "I have one more gift for you, my queen." The ritual must be done.

"What is it?" Persephone whispers, intrigued and hopeful. It is obvious if she does not believe in herself, she does believe in what I tell her.

I wave my hand, and the room transforms. Persephone glances to the side, then turns around to look. No longer black obsidian, this room bares one purpose. The soft color palette of rose and peach in the luxurious velvet drapes add to the opulence and sensuality. A hundred candles or more take up the floor space and add a warmth no fire could provide. In the antique mirror on the other side of the room, our reflection stares back at us. My darkness to her light and yet, we are perfect for one another.

"Hades," she says.

"I crave to be bonded with you," I murmur into her ear. "I need you to know that you are powerful enough to be bonded to me. You are my queen, and I am your king. Let us make that true in every possible way."

Persephone turns once again, her eyes searching mine. Her hand lays across her chest as if she must physically contain her heart. "Bonded? For eternity?"

"Forevermore."

There is a moment when I think she might shake her head. When she might reject me. Distrust me. It would be like surviving in that pit of darkness again.

It would be worse.

But Persephone lowers her hand and kisses me sweetly, dearly even.

"Yes," she says, breaking the kiss, her eyes still closed. Then she opens them, staring up at me like I'm her savior, not the villain who stole her away, lied to her father, and will soon offer her the seeds that will bind her here forever.

"Yes," she murmurs and kisses me again. Whatever pain lays deep in my chest is numbed by her affections. By her love.

I undress her by candlelight, lifting her gown and undergarments off her soft skin as carefully as if I am dressing her for court. With each inch of her delicate skin that is revealed, my heart beats harder. The aching emptiness at the core of me is no longer a void that could consume everything. It is my hunger for her, and only Persephone can fill that space.

When I am finished, Persephone takes her turn undressing me, biting her lower lip as she concentrates.

Her hands glide along my skin like fire. I cherish the moments she lingers.

Neither of us is wearing anything when I take her hand and bring her to the bed; the white fur covers the four poster, dark-wood bedframe with silk drapes that glisten in the candlelight filling the room.

"My queen."

Persephone nods to me, trembling slightly, and accepts my help up onto the bed. Persephone lays back, her hair flowing out around her head.

I lean down and kiss her gently, taking my time and knowing all too well what will happen after tonight's deed is done. The knowledge is heady as is the floral scent of Persephone which envelopes me as I kiss her neck and then the soft spot just beneath her ear and then nip her earlobe.

My lips. Hers. Heat. Passion.

But there is more.

Flames spring to life around the bed, surrounding us. The magic of the Underworld has come to oversee the ceremony. That is the only witness we need, other than the two of us.

"This is an ancient ritual," I murmur into Persephone's ear, stroking between her legs as I do.

"How will I know what to do?" she asks with all sincerity.

"I will guide us. And if I could not, the magic would guide us. This part—" I pull her earlobe between my teeth and breathe. Persephone shivers underneath me. "Will not be difficult for you."

Her arms rest around my neck and she kisses me, tasting me, testing my lips, while I stroke her until she's hot and tight on my fingers and writhing, her hips rocking along with my touch, begging me for more. I do not rush. Completing the ritual on Samhain will add blessings to our bond, but I will not move forward until she has shaken off all the sadness of the past weeks and succumbed to pleasure. There is no sign of anything but the goddess who is only submissive to me and rules over all others when I kiss her again.

She is mine. Truly now and once the ritual is done, forevermore. Whether we part or not. She will always feel my love and I hers. She will always feel my pain, and I hers. In every life, we will be together, our paths destined to cross with the prayers that we will find one another, or else our fates will not be complete.

I sink two fingers into her and find the rough spot that makes her moan with abandon then stroke it in a slow rhythm until she's gasping, unable to make a single coherent sound.

By then, my body demands hers. I would deny myself forever if the ritual called for it, but it does not.

It calls for me to have my queen just as I like.

Persephone spreads her legs for me, wrapping them around my waist as soon as I have begun to enter her. She welcomes me, pulling me as close as she can and rocking her hips at a slow pace that quickens as my pleasure rises.

She feels like fucking heaven. The pleasure is unimaginable. Waves of heat crash down upon us with every thrust and I struggle to hold back my groans of unadulterated lust.

There is so much sweetness in her. So much heat in her body. She was made for me. She is the only place I will ever find solace or comfort.

It is at this point that I push myself above her, my pulse rampaging.

Persephone opens her eyes, panting, and looks into mine.

"Trust me," I tell her, catching my breath as I do.

"I do." Her lips are swollen from our kiss and her cheeks and chest flushed.

I have to lean away from her to reach the athame, a pagan knife, on the bedside table. It is silver and twinkles in the light, polished to a high shine, and the tip is razor-sharp.

"Give me your hand."

Persephone offers her hand out without an instant of hesitation.

"Yours and mine forever bind," I pronounce, then prick her palm with the tip of the knife.

A single drop of blood wells up.

I bend my head to lick it off Persephone's hand, repositioning myself as I do. The taste of her blood—salt and iron—is divine. Black and white smoke curl out of the grate and circle over us on the bed.

The two shades of smoke separate. The black goes to me. The white goes to Persephone. But the boundary does not stay firm as I thrust into her, again and again, needing her more in this moment than ever before. The smoke teases between us. It cannot find its place.

I will show it where it belongs. I will show *her* where she belongs.

Her blood—my spend. That is what the ritual demands. That is what will bring the smoke together. That is what will bind us.

Persephone grips me to her, pulling my body into hers. "Yours *and* mine," she moans.

That pushes me over.

I grab her throat out of instinct. Fucking her with reckless abandon as I squeeze her delicate neck. Her hands rise out of instinct, her eyes locked on mine. She grips my wrists and struggles to say something. My hips thrust even deeper and harder, and I release her. She gasps for air as her head falls back and an orgasm like none before rocks through her body. Power consumes me as I lower my head to her neck and piston myself between her legs, desperate for my own release.

I come hard, my vision fleeing from me and going dark with the intensity. Persephone clenches around me, her arms tight around my neck, holding on through another strong orgasm.

Somehow I'm able to prick my palm and I offer it to

her. In the haze of pleasure, she licks my palm, and the requirements of the ritual are done.

The separate plumes of smoke wrap around each other, twisting and swirling until the black and the white are one and the same. They can never be separated again.

Persephone can never be separated from me.

It is a high, intense peak. Knowing it is done. She is mine in all ways the gods revere, I let my forehead lean against hers, struggling to catch my breath.

Persephone does the same. Her hands stroke over my cheeks and on the back of my neck. My queen.

The question comes as if from a great distance and within my heart at the same time.

Perhaps it is a question I have been longing to ask.

"Persephone." I roll my forehead gently against hers. "Do you love me?"

"Yes," she breathes, her hands on my nape now.

"You would never betray me, would you?" I question as the thought comes to me. The thought of her ever leaving me. "You wouldn't leave me? Not after this?"

"Never," she whispers. "I'll never leave you."

Persephone's hands are much smaller than mine, and yet such power dwells in them. Such power dwells in every word, but especially her *yes*.

"Persephone," I say again, unable to stop myself. "My lady. My queen. My love. My goddess. You are every name that can come from my lips. You own everything I do and everything I am."

"Everything you are?" Persephone asks, her eyes shining.

"You misunderstand, Persephone." I draw in another breath. The magic of the bond overwhelms me, but not as much as Persephone. "You are my everything. *Everything.*" I close the last inch between us and kiss her hard on the lips. That is the taste of my queen. That is my Persephone. "To me."

chapter 26

Persephone

IN THE MORNINGS, I SPEND TIME SITTING AT THE table in the quiet period before Silvie comes, sensing my powers and thinking about what the future holds. Many mornings, I look through the book Silvie brought me. Books on magic and witches, the history of gods, and what has been and what is foretold to come. I cannot say I understand all of what is written and much seems contradictory, but I'm taking it page by page, reading carefully. Studying it as I release the idea that I'll ever go back home.

Perhaps it will be like coming to understand my powers in the Underworld. We went over many small pieces of knowledge over and over again before it finally clicked into place.

I do not know if my mother and father think I've gone on my own. If they search for me or not. I do hope they are at peace and perhaps the Fates have told them I am well. There is a soft agony deep in my heart that even the love Hades gives me does not soothe.

Silvie still does not think she was the one to teach me magic, but this is not true.

She taught me something that might be more important than how to sense the powers available to me in the Underworld. Silvie taught me patience. She taught me that commitment must be stronger than fear. I would never have been able to set aside my own panic and study if it weren't for Silvie.

That is what I am doing on the morning I feel the pull. Reading in an attempt to understand and to escape and to find peace that evades me.

It's after Samhain, so the days are shorter, even in the Underworld. The sun takes more time to rest below the horizon. Silvie comes to join me a bit later, as if the whole of the Underworld has adjusted to the sun. Because Silvie does not come early, I have more time in the mornings to sit at the table with the gentle light of a lamp and the book, letting my mind wander over the pages as I might wander through the gardens, touching the words with my fingertips without trying to make them into something they are not.

I am only getting to know them.

I ignore the tug at first. There is much magic in the Underworld, and it is not unheard of for me to feel it as it moves. I did not recognize such things when I first arrived here. Even with my powers at full strength and a deeper understanding of how they worked in various realms, I was too terrified to have noticed a sensation like this. Like the crackling behind the obsidian walls. I no longer fear it. I only wish to know what causes it and why Sylvie and Hades do not appear to hear it like I do.

It comes a second time, and I ignore it again. Magic is unpredictable. I have learned much about my powers in the weeks that I have been in the Underworld. That does not mean I know everything. And what the Fates told me was unsettling. There is a choice to be made, apparently—and it is impossible to make the right choice. Lightning cracked across the sky not long after I left them. More souls are flooding into the Underworld.

The Fates did not offer to take a message to my mother. They only told me she misses me as well, along with what seemed like a prophecy I could not understand.

The third time the pull happens, I close the book and put it on the table, then close my eyes.

Something isn't right.

But what?

I open my eyes with a deep breath, then look around the rooms as dispassionately as I can. I have had blankets, pillows, and soft rugs brought in. I make a point of keeping the fire bright and hot. I cannot change how the sun rises and sets, nor would I want to, but I have made this place welcoming.

There is nothing wrong that I can see.

Silvie?

It is a bit earlier than she usually comes to join me, but I don't feel a sense of dread about her. I might, if she were in great danger. We have spent enough time together that I know the feel of her magic, and I care about her enough to notice if something terrible had happened.

When the tug comes again, I concentrate on it as hard as I can.

It is like a calling.

My magic—or the magic of the bond I have with Hades—is calling to me.

I rise from my chair and find a simple cloak to put over my dress, then leave my rooms. At the end of the hall, two guards leave their posts and follow after me. I do not mind if they accompany me wherever I am being summoned.

If what has gone wrong is some kind of catastrophe, then at least I will have them with me. They are sworn to protect me, after all. And I am still so new to the Underworld and what lies beyond the castle.

And if there is nothing awry after all, no harm done. They will have done their duty and stretched their legs.

I follow the tug out along the path. More time had passed than I realized. The tug comes again, spurring me onward. I focus on following it, keeping my mind clear, like I do when I read from the book with its ancient spells. I travel through the maze-like stone halls, not quite paying attention to where I am, as I'm focused on the pull and not losing it. I do not want to read trouble into this feeling if there is none. I do not want to panic before there is reason to. But it calls to me with necessity.

At last, the call in my magic guides me off the path and into the outer fields of Elysium.

I follow it across a narrow valley to row of old oak trees. They're beautiful with ancient bark, and one of the few plants that resides in the Underworld. They were a gift long ago from one god to another. Beyond the trees is a clearing with a stream running through it.

Hades stands near the stream, his arms at his sides. At first, I think he is alone.

He is not.

The nymph blends in with the trees around her. The fabric of her gown looks like dappled bark until she moves and the fabric rustles, and it is a gown again. She wears a wreath of autumn leaves on her head. Long, blonde hair flows down her back, wavy and shining. She looks caught between the seasons—green and dappled in places on her gown with the darker shades of winter gradually taking over.

I raise my hand, and the guards come to a stop.

"Hades."

Hades turns to look at me, and a smile spreads across his face. His eyes light. "My queen."

"I had a warning." I move to his side and put my hand in his. "Did you have need of me?"

"Always," he says in a low voice, his eyes darkening. But before I can leap into his arms—and I *would*—he lifts his head. "I was delayed."

"Were you?"

"Yes. This nymph engaged me in conversation."

The nymph has not gone. She peeks out of the trees at us, her bright eyes jumping between Hades and me.

A tug that feels more like fire than a call springs up in my chest. "In conversation?"

I meet Hades's eyes. He gives me a calm, even look that soothes some of the fire.

Some—but not all of it.

The nymph takes a few steps out of the trees. What is she thinking, getting closer? Possessiveness like I've never felt comes over me. It would make more sense to me if she had turned and run at the first sight of me. A pink flush to her cheeks says the conversation was not a simple exchange of greetings. Her hands move to the buttons on the front of her dress—visible one second, then lost in the dappled pattern the next.

Her fingers work, and her buttons close.

I'm genuinely surprised for a few beats. This nymph unbuttoned her dress? She saw Hades on the path and decided to unbutton her dress?

Anger grows and with it, a heat in my palms. Hades stands by my side, laying a hand on my shoulder, and whispers at the edge of my ear, "It does not matter what others may try. I am yours and yours alone." My eyes do not leave the nymph as he speaks. "I told her such and I believe she understands now."

The fire rages in me. But it is not chaotic, it is eerily calm. I do not address him. Foolish god.

"What is your name, nymph?" I question. My voice does not need to be loud. The magic between me and Hades seems to amplify my powers, and his hand in mine amplifies my sense that *yes*, something was wrong, and *yes*, it was this nymph.

He may have said no, but I do not for one moment believe that she took it to heart.

"Minthe, my queen," she answers. Her voice is sweet, like a breeze in summer leaves.

It does not strike me as innocent. She knew what she was doing when she unbuttoned her dress. Power surges inside me. It is the magic, telling me in no uncertain terms that I am where I need to be. My very purpose grows within me here.

"And you met my king on the path," I say, although my tone is question-like.

"Yes," she answers.

"And you unbuttoned your dress."

Minthe's gaze flicks to Hades before reaching me. She admits, "I did, my queen."

"And you thought…what? That you'd take him to bed with you?"

Minthe says nothing for a moment. "It was an offering for the god, my queen. One he refused. My mistake."

She made an offer to Hades, who has not let go of my hand.

Who *will* not let go of my hand. Who meant it when he said his love would always be greater than his anger, and meant it when he said I owned every part of him, and meant it when he said *always*.

Anger and rage turn to something else. Something cold deep within me. Something almost unfeeling.

"I don't find that acceptable," I murmur. And although her gaze leaves mine, mine stays on hers and when she looks back, she's caught in it.

Hades brings my hand to his lips and kisses my knuckles gently before releasing it. As if a blessing to do as I wish. Minthe freezes as I cross the space between us. Her eyes go wide, then faraway, as if she has accepted her fate.

She closes her eyes as I lift my hand and press it against her head.

I do not think. I simply do. "My queen!" She begs at first but in my touch, she is silenced. Her wide eyes stare back at me with terror. Minthe's head drops down under my hands almost instantly and keeps dropping. I kneel, following the shrinking figure to the grass.

I change her from one form to another. Taking the essence of Minthe and guiding it into a new way of being. One that will let her feel the pleasures of existence, but not the freedom of wandering through the woods, unbuttoning her dress for any king of mine who happens to walk by.

Leaves tickle my palms, and I open my eyes, then open my hands.

A tiny, perfect plant with velvety leaves sprouts from the ground. It smells fresh and cool and soothing even.

I imagine her leaves plucked and seeped into hot water would make an excellent tea.

"Mint," I say, feeling like I'm telling the plant its own name. "It shall be called mint. That is only fair, I suppose."

Look at that. I made life in the Underworld that pleases me. A pleasure like none I've felt before flows through me, eerily calm.

As Minthe was in her nymph form, she is beautiful as a mint plant. Though slightly out of season, her leaves are green and fragrant, and her stalk is well-formed and strong. Soon, there will be other mint plants around her. More of her sisters will grow in the summer. My smile fades. That cannot happen here. No new life will grow. But others can be made as such. Others who betray me. Slowly, the warmth returns at the thought. Perhaps I shall have gardens in the Underworld after all.

Hades steps beside me, and he offers his hand to me.

I take it and let him help me to my feet, my face hot.

His hand wraps underneath my chin, and he tips my face up to his, claiming my mouth in a possessive kiss filled with heat and gratitude.

He kisses me so deep and long that I have no choice but to put my arms around his waist and hold him tight.

"Are you well, my queen?"

"I am pleased," I tell him in a whisper.

I get dizzy with the taste of him and the powerful magic of the bond, which must be celebrated. I've never felt so much approval in magic before. I did not know it could *give* so much approval.

Finally, just when I'm about to forget the forest entirely, Hades breaks the kiss and puts a hand at my elbow to steady me.

"Thank you," he says, his voice raw.

"It was nothing." A shaky laugh escapes me. "What else could I have done? You're mine now."

"My goddess, I am yours," says Hades and bends down for one last kiss before we return home. "Rage and possessiveness look beautiful on you."

chapter 27

Hades

THE KNOWLEDGE OF THE SEEDS WEIGHS ON me as I leave the bedchambers as quietly as I can. I've left Persephone in bed, dreaming, in the tangled sheets, because she deserves to enjoy her pleasure. My queen does not need to scramble out of it like a prisoner. She can lounge in the afterglow of the many times I made her come with my hands and mouth and cock for as long as she pleases this morning.

With the onslaught of new souls and chaos at the River Styx, I'm needed to survey the court. I don't wish to worry her. As far as she knows, nothing is out of the norm. She has not much to go by and so I keep what's occurred away from her. No one is to speak of it. No one is to know that souls are being destroyed faster than they can be judged. They wither to nothing as her flowers do in Olympus. Threats from Zeus and those who do his bidding aren't heard by anyone but me and Minox.

If she sits at my side for this session, I'll have to explain the nervousness and fear permeating the air at court. I'll have to explain the whispers. I'll have to explain why all the attendants seem as if they are waiting for me to direct them. To guide them because they are lost and scared. Their threads were not meant to be cut so soon.

Change *is* coming, and it will not be kind. Demeter and Zeus have struck, what awaits is my reply.

In the wide hall outside the court, several figures detach from the wall and move to intercept me before I can enter for the morning session.

It seems as if the guards and the other attendants who keep the other courts in the Underworld—for there must be many if we are to accommodate the number of souls who pass through these realms—have chosen representatives from among their group.

"My lord," the man at the front says. He wears dark robes like the man and woman who accompany him, but he is the tallest of the three, with close-cropped dark hair. "If I may?"

"Go on," I command him.

"May we speak with you for a moment?"

"Come this way." I steer them back to the wall, where we will not be so conspicuous. "What is it that you want to speak about?"

They exchange a glance. "My lord, there are far more dead than usual." The timbre of his voice shakes.

"It is winter. There are always more souls in the coldest parts of the year in the mortal realm." I offer, my forefingers running against the rough pad of my thumb. I act as if I do not know.

The leader shakes his head. "More than the heaviest winters we've had. More than we can recall in centuries."

"It came on gradually, my lord," the woman guard adds. "The higher numbers could be explained by the winter in the beginning. Now we are certain."

My hand stills and my body stiffens at her words. I take a calming breath, fighting down the strong, immediate concern that grips my chest.

"Certain of what?"

"Mortals are always the ones who pay when the gods fight, and these deaths...there is a war in the mortal realm. There must be." Her eyes are wide with despair.

The three representatives wait quietly, but they cannot hide their own worry. Balance between the realms is a delicate business. Though the Underworld appears vast—and it is larger than most mortal minds can comprehend—it *can* become overburdened with souls. Their movements through the phases of the afterlife can be unbalanced. Souls lost forever signifies the end coming. It is an omen, and one ancient souls like the men and woman before me do not take lightly.

"We will do what we must to keep the balance on our side," I tell them. "End the necessary souls."

There's a beat of shock, then the leader bows in understanding. His companions follow his lead. "Thank you, my lord," they murmur as one, then turn and hurry away to whatever courts they work in.

They will need to deliver my message quickly, because it will affect the process of judgment today.

There is another option beyond hell or Elysium.

In times of great imbalance, souls can also be ended. We will begin with souls of weak morality—those who have had more than a single lifetime and remain weak and unworthy. Their threads will be cut then burned. They will not be awaiting rebirth in Elysium or paying penance in hell.

They will simply be gone.

Sometimes, difficult choices must be made. I have not shied away from that. It is them or Persephone, and I will always choose my queen. Even if it means we will rule over a pile of ash.

I take my throne and the murmuring hushes. "Let us begin."

The doors open.

The first soul of the morning is brought in.

The day feels more like paying my own penance. My stomach churns with the choice I have had to make. I waver every moment. It had to be done. No, there was still time to wait. It *had* to be done.

This, at least, is true. How far will Demeter take it? Will Zeus allow his mortal realm to be rot with death?

I know it's for the best to begin purging now, before the surge in souls trickles over into all the realms of the Underworld. Still, it is a terrible sign of things to come.

Imbalance causes cracks at crossroads. The realms as we know them will cease to exist if such things are allowed to happen.

The balance must be maintained. The Underworld cannot be weighted too heavily, or there will be less and less reason for souls to exist in the mortal realm *at all.*

I've lived several lifetimes by the time court ends for the day.

I leave the hall behind and go to my rooms, desperate to be close to Persephone and to ensure she is still with me. Dread is cold and heavy in my gut.

Persephone is already at the door when I enter, as if she sensed me coming. She greets me right away, taking both my hands in hers and looking up into my face with real concern in her expression.

"What is it? What's wrong?" I ask her, my heart racing with the fears of what has transpired.

"I missed you," she whispers.

I lift her into my arms, and Persephone's arms go around my neck. Her softness and warmth compared to the cruelty I displayed today forces me to keep my eyes open as she kisses down my shoulder. I can breathe again when her mouth is on mine. I can reassure myself that she is here with me. Whatever else comes, I can face it, as long as she is by my side.

They will not take her from me. Even if they shatter my kingdom and release the Titans, who cannot be destroyed. Hell would be on Earth, and Olympus would not be protected. If they bring war and that is the result, so be it. I will hide her in secret depths. For I know what it is to be alone, and I know what it is to be with her.

I cannot and will not part with her.

She drops her head to kiss the side of my neck, nipping the skin and nuzzling at me in places that feel far too sensitive to be mine.

"You are not yourself. What can I do?" she asks, pulling back and looking at me from beneath her thick lashes.

She can let me take off her gown. She can let me lay her out on the bed and lick her sweet pussy until I've lost track of how many orgasms I've given her.

I take my time kissing her. Pressing my lips to hers and relishing in how her body molds to mine.

Through all this, I let her touch me. Her hands in my hair chase away any threat. I could defend the Underworld against any angry god with the strength of my love for this feeling and for Persephone.

I turn her over onto her hands and knees. Persephone tosses her head, arching her back and spreading her thighs. I kneel behind her, lost in how beautiful she is. How soft. How wet. How accepting of my fingers when I push them inside her. How welcoming she is when I thrust in.

Her power goes through my entire body. Persephone moans, clenching on my cock, and another wave rocks through me, shivering through every single inch of my body and my power.

It is so strong that I have to grit my teeth to keep my release in. I am not ready for this to end.

This is closeness that I never expected to experience. I've heard of bonds between gods before. I did not know they were overflowing with ecstasy. Like a drug more addictive than anything else. I would do anything for her. I'd let all the worlds burn.

Persephone gasps, coming on my cock again as I thrust ruthlessly behind her, my fingers digging into the soft flesh at her hips. I ride through her orgasm and then I pull her close and slow the pace. The insides of her thighs are wet with her arousal.

"Oh," she says, taking deep breath after deep breath as she circles her hips in my hands. With her cheeks flushed and her lips parted, she is breathtakingly gorgeous. Taking every bit of me like the queen she is. I need this moment with her. I need to remember how it feels to pause, even in this act, and feel every detail. I slide my hand to Persephone's belly, then delve lower to find her clit.

"Oh, yes," she breathes, rocking into my touch. She's so sensitive that it takes nothing to make her pussy clench around me. The lightest brushes have tremors racing through her thighs. I bury my other hand in her hair at the nape of her neck and pull gently, making her arch a little more for me. Her next *oh* is much longer and makes my cock twitch with aching need.

Only when she calls my name, do I find my release.

This is what it means to be lost in a woman's touch.

This is what it means to have a queen. I did not have to face my dread alone. I did not have to remain trapped in my isolation, alone in the dark.

I lie in the blankets, stroking Persephone's back for a long time before she lifts her head from the pillow and studies me, running her fingers through my hair.

"Something is happening," she says. "Isn't it?"

I give her a nod. I do not want wars between the realms to come into our bed with us. I would much rather retreat into the deepest, most hidden places in the Underworld until there was no more danger.

Persephone frowns. "And…you do not want to tell me what it is?"

"Not tonight, my queen."

She traces my lips with her finger. "But you *will* tell me?"

"You are my queen," I tell her, then drop a soft kiss to her lips. It is practically innocent compared to how I have just fucked her, but a shock ripples through me nonetheless. "You are my world. I will not keep it from you."

Persephone purses her lips, thinking. "You want to have tonight without worry?"

"I want to spend every night with you without worry."

She rests her head on my chest, her perfect body all along mine. I could spend every last bit of every eternity stroking her hair, then down her back, and feeling her breathing settle as she falls asleep.

She does not know.

Persephone falls into a dream, her limbs getting heavy. For the moment, she does not know what I have done.

I've risked the world—all of the worlds—for her.

Nothing in all my years has driven me to risk so much. Not even my own soul. I could have fought Zeus to not be trapped here but I did not. I could have lived in the seas like Poseidon or the sky like Apollo. I did my duty and took my position trapped in the Underworld.

I did not want to risk imbalance.

But now I have done it.

It is a heavy choice, but as I lay with Persephone, I know it was the only way.

She does not know how worthy of this she is. If the worlds burn and the gods destroy one another, Persephone would be worth it.

Because she is my Elysium. She is not just one version of heaven. She is not a fleeting ideal. She is the only place I will ever find rest or peace. She is the only place where touch is a haven.

My only Elysium.

My Persephone.

chapter 28

Hecate

THE SKIES AROUND OLYMPUS CRACK TO pieces. Lightning splits the clouds with hot, blinding fury. It is deafening—even more so than the wind, which whips through the elegant buildings on Olympus. Curtains snap at me like vipers. My dark purple, nearly black, robes curl around my calves, the hem kissing my ankles.

I've never seen Olympus like this before. The darkness in the skies is an omen. One I haven't witnessed since the fall of the Titans.

When it is at peace, Olympus is a realm of golden sun and navy blue night. Brilliant, colorful sunrises and stars that twinkle like diamonds. It is sturdy and strong. It seems to pin the skies in place, keeping all that it touches in balance.

Now, it is a kingdom lost in a storm. Black and gray

clouds crowd out every beam of sunlight. All they let through is the lightning, which strikes so close to me as I enter that I can smell the burning air left behind. Pausing, I consider why I'm here. I do not trust the cobblestones beneath my feet. Any one of them could plummet away underneath me at any moment.

This cannot continue. This cannot hold. Olympus will fall away underneath me, or be thrown into the sky. It will be torn into pieces, me among them. It appears only the edge crumbles now, but in time, it will cease to exist, and the crossroads will crack.

I need to find Demeter. Every doorway I peer through shows nothing but disarray. Blankets have blown off beds and landed on chairs. Vases have turned over, spilling their contents onto the floor and ceramic shards laying on cold floors.

They have fled. In the madness, they take cover.

The lightning shakes all of Olympus. No part of it is being spared. This is because Demeter's sorrow and rage are larger than all the realms of the gods.

If I can only find Demeter and speak to her, there may yet be a chance to right this. A way to change the path the Fates have set out for all of us. A way to change the decisions that have led us off that path. I do not know, but I will try.

Demeter's sobs are heard as the pounding thunder relents. They wrench my heart in two. They are sobs of pure despair. She has lost her child, and now the world will be lost to her, too.

Nothing could possibly compare to the loss of a child.

This catastrophe feels as if it is on behalf of all mothers who have lost a child. All of them, everywhere, their hearts spilling out through Demeter herself.

What mother would stop searching? None, I think. They have to be forced to give up, and even then, they never put the burden of love down.

There! I turn, my torch in hand and hounds behind me. In darkness, I follow the call of her cries down that hall of withered roses. Through that door. I proceed down the halls of Olympus, but it is the same as before. Every doorway looks in on an empty room, or it looks in on a room with people huddled in the corner, holding tightly to each other's hands and weeping.

None of them are Demeter.

I do not find her.

Demeter's voice comes from another direction, her howls piercing my ears. They are so close she *must* be here.

Then, the next moment—

Distant. Out of sight.

What foolish spell has been cast to betray me?

I halt, reining in anger as I still and wait for the world to show me the truth.

Once my mind has settled, I vow to myself that I will not loosen my grip until Olympus is saved. Until the realms are once again in balance. Life requires death and cycles come and go. We will mourn and as they do

I will hold their hand. This though…this lowly place and threat of destruction…this warrants a great threat.

I must remain in balance myself. I must look toward the future and see it with clear eyes, no matter how harrowing it looks.

"Demeter," I call, drawing my robes close to my body and standing up straight against the wind. The flames of my torch blow and my hounds gather, one on each side of me. I can withstand it. I can withstand anything. "Come to me!"

Her cries meet my ears, but they are too unintelligible to be spoken on Olympus. The lightning is too loud. The wind rages. She's speaking to me as if in prayer and every word rings in my ears. It is a prayer sent directly to my heart, and I could not ignore it even if I wanted to.

They will all freeze, she cries.

I am listening, I think in the pause she takes for breath. *I hear you, Demeter. I know it must feel that way.*

If all the mortals have perished, they will all freeze, and we will freeze with them.

We are all woven together, I think. If she cannot hear my words, perhaps she can sense the emotion behind them.

Gods will fight among themselves. They will tear us apart.

Not if we stop this! I think. *You must stop this.* I command her.

Demeter speaks again—prays again—so quickly I

know she has not heard. *We will all tear each other apart. It will be war. Prepare for war.*

"Demeter," I shout again, but her cries turn to more wrenching sobs. "Demeter, it does not need to be this way!"

She does not listen. Sorrow has made her deaf to reason. You cannot listen if you do not wish to hear, and she does not. A chill runs through me as I search again for her, quickening my pace.

It does not need to come to death and destruction. It does not need to come to fire and brimstone and buildings collapsing and lives being snuffed out. The Fates do not need to cut so many threads at once.

Whatever I think at Demeter, she must not hear me. She continues to cry. To wail. Her anger has already been unleashed.

Oh, where *is* she? I need to see her. To speak to her. To reason. She has lost, but there is much to gain.

It will not be easy. It may, in fact, be the most difficult thing Demeter ever has to do. She may hate me for it in the end, but I will make that sacrifice.

I must.

Demeter does not come at my call.

Is there anywhere I have *not* searched?

The courtyard.

I skirted the courtyard when I ran through the halls, traveling around it, but not into it. Her voice had echoed in those smaller spaces. Maybe it was echoing from the courtyard itself. Maybe she is there, summoning life from the heart of Olympus.

I rush toward the courtyard as fast as my legs will carry me and my hounds run beside me. I will catch her when she falls. I will hold her as she needs to be held. For she is a just and righteous goddess. What pain brings her here will wane. So mote it be.

It is in just as much disarray as the rest of Olympus. Petals have been torn from flowers and fly through the air. Delicate trees lay on their sides, the roots stretched to the breaking point. Branches snap and spear across the courtyard, carried by the wind.

Demeter is not here.

The only god standing in the courtyard is Zeus.

He has his back to me, staff in hand and his toga draped recklessly. Wine spills from an overturned glass as he unleashes another bolt from his staff. I know with a single glance that this is Demeter's threat coming true. Absolutely true. She will not stop it now, and calling to her will do no good. Demeter is not in any position to listen.

I had held out hope.

I should not have wasted time hoping.

I go to Zeus and call his name, letting it ring in the air as I stand tall behind him. My heart breaks for Olympus and for the mortal realms and even for myself. The magnitude of this shift overwhelms me. This is not the way it is meant to be.

"Zeus," I shout over the noise of the storm. "Where is my Demeter?"

Zeus turns and looks at me as if he cannot understand what I am saying.

I scream at him, my hounds growling at my side, "Zeus! The realms are collapsing. You can see this with your own eyes! Bring me Demeter!"

This is the last hope I hold—that Zeus can influence Demeter. That he can reach down to whichever realm she has fled to and bring her back to Olympus. Or send me to her.

Lightning flashes over us, so bright it turns the sky dark.

"You'll have to find her yourself," he says. Useless. The drunken god is useless. "She has fled me."

"If you will not hear me, I will go." I turn my back on Zeus.

"Where are you going?" he shouts after me, his powers carrying his voice through the screeching wind.

"I'm needed elsewhere." I will return to Persephone in the Underworld. Zeus does not need to know this. If Demeter will not come to me and cannot hear me, and if Zeus cannot get Demeter's attention, then I must go to where I can make a difference. Persephone must be returned.

He catches my arm, stopping me. "Don't do it, Hecate—"

Ripping my arm away I stand tall against the god of the sky. "I know what you did." The storm is too intense to say more than necessary. It cracks around us and the god stares back at me, lightning in his eyes.

He searches my face. I am certain he is trying to decide whether I am telling him the truth. "I do not lie. I am privy to what led to this."

"Do you know where she is then?" he asks, a brow arched. After a moment, he huffs a humorless laugh and then shakes his head, taking a step back. "Of course you do. Everyone will know soon enough."

More lightning rattles Olympus. Screams rise from all around me—both on Olympus and from the mortal realm as well.

"The war has begun," I shout to Zeus. I lower my voice to add, "Because you allowed it."

Zeus narrows his eyes. He has decided, then. "Obtain Persephone. By any means necessary."

"I did not come for your blessing on such things. I came for Demeter."

Zeus throws his hands up, his face flushed with frustration. "She has *gone*, Hecate. As has the sanity in the world."

"Balance will be," I insist. Another wave of lightning bolts streaks down, drilling molten holes into the very foundation of Olympus. "Promise me, before the next full moon, my daughter will be returned, although I fear she is not what she once was."

His gaze falls to the stone beneath us, and I make no promises to the god. All I insist upon is that balance will be restored. In whatever capacity that may be.

chapter 29

Persephone

THE SKY ABOVE US SEEMS TO TEAR APART.

I hold tight to Hades's hand while he moves along the path so fast the world blurs to either side of us. Fire and brimstone crack and souls scream. It is not the agony of the penance they pay but the terror of being obliterated. The voices of the gods blend with the screams for mercy. I can hear them if I focus, but Hades tries to keep his realm from collapsing, and every time we move, I lose some of the meaning.

Still, I heard mention of my mother. I *swear* I heard my mother's name. Prayers for her to help. Questions of why she has forsaken them. Pleas for forgiveness for they know not what they've done.

Just yesterday the sky was darkened but did not break. Today it has shattered. My heart races. Has our bonding destroyed the balance? Has my father discovered my betrayal? I fear the worst as I hold onto Hades, desperate for all of it to stop.

We pass by the River Styx. There are so many lanterns on the water. Not all of them are crossing smoothly. Some speed across the river at such speed that they resemble a streak of light in the air or a falling star.

Silvie and Hades's companion, Minox, are with us, following every step Hades takes.

The stone ceiling high above us rattles as if someone's on the bottom of every realm in the Underworld, pulling up pieces and throwing them all the way to the sky.

"Why is this happening?" I question and it's not Hades who answers. It's not my lover who looks down at me with sorrowful eyes.

"Because you are here," Sylvie tells me. "Isn't that right, my lord?"

My heart pounds at the confession. "My father knows?" I ask in a whisper.

"Your mother," Minox reveals. His voice deathly low and I don't miss how Hades glares at him. *She knows.* My heart shatters as well and yet it is still whole with her there. As if she holds it together herself.

Stunned, I say nothing.

From the distance the ground shakes and the castle trembles as the battlements break and tumble down stories to the ground. Shrieks are heard. It is pure chaos that has seemingly come from nowhere. But I remember the past few days. I remember how Hades would not tell me.

"You knew?" I whisper and still Hades does not speak. He offers me nothing as tears well in my eyes.

"I love you and I will not let them take you," he finally says.

"Give her leave to go, my lord," Silvie begs. There is too much magic and power whipping through the valley, it batters her hair around her face. "Our queen will find her way back."

My pulse slows as does the world around me. *This chaos.* This is because of me.

I cannot bear the destruction.

"No," Hades calls, without turning to look at her. "She belongs to me. She belongs *here*."

"My lord, there are too many dead."

Hades tightens his jaw.

"Please," Silvie starts, but we are moving again. His hand in mine, our robes tattered in the wind. Where can we even run when everything collapses? Why has it come to this?

I recognize this place in the realm—the Isle of Achilles. The water lashes at the shore, pummeling the island. The rain is so thick that I can hardly make it out.

Whatever Hades does calms the storm to a driving rain.

"Does she not miss her mother?" Silvie tries and words catch in my throat. I am torn. The Fates' warning comes back to me. I do not feel that I could ever be complete. My head spins with the chaos and the knowledge as small pieces fit into place.

It is difficult to look back at the god I love. For he played a part, did he not?

"Does she not miss the flowers?" Minox argues. It is strange to see a man I have not spoken with much make arguments about the things I must long for.

"You could allow her to simply see them, my lord." Silvie raises her voice to be heard as we move again. There is fire in the trees. "A visit would be enough. She must be allowed to—"

"They will take her from me!" Hades thunders, working his magic on the fires that plague the Underworld. Is he less powerful when he is holding my hand? He has not let go in all this time, and now his grip tightens on mine as if it is me he's saving from the fire and not the trees. "I cannot leave the Underworld. I cannot accompany her. They will steal her away!" he screams and his fear is evident.

Be careful of your thoughts, is all I can think.

Minox steps closer as the fire jumps to another stand of trees, and Hades follows it. The fire roars louder, then subsides a little.

"Hecate will return with the end of the new moon. Surely *she* can accompany her?"

"It is not the accompaniment out of the Underworld that troubles me." Hades stops on the path. It is windy here, too, with leaves filling the air and branches cracking into each other. "What if she does not return?"

"We will take her back," Silvie suggests fiercely. They speak of me as if I am an item and yet, I cannot find an argument. For my father's vengeance is harsh and my mother…to do this? I cannot imagine her state. It cannot be true. None of this is true, I will myself to change what is here, and yet when I open my eyes, nothing has changed at all.

We move again, this time landing in a meeting hall on the floor below the rooms I share with Hades. The quiet is intense after so much ear-splitting noise.

"I need to know the truth. All of it!" I demand into that silence. My voice echoes in the large space. It is not one of the courts, but it reminds me of one—stone pillars, a polished floor, a dais on one side that people could approach. "This is happening because of me?"

Hades's eyes flash. He pushes one hand through his hair. "They wish for me to live in a hell of my own making. Zeus *always* has."

I do not understand. "But these are your realms. You have power here. All this time, you have—"

"All this time, I have been living in—" Anger ripples off Hades, but he cuts himself off, turning his head at a sound.

I do not recognize it at first.

Then it gets louder. It is the sound of three dogs barking at once, alerting Hades that a stranger—or at least an outsider—has entered his realm.

"Hecate is coming," Hades declares. *Hecate.* A chill runs down my spine. Her name alone inspires something within me. Something dark and powerful.

"Why is she here?" I question in a whisper looking

out into the distance. But I know all too well. The powerful Titan doesn't come on a whim. She is strategic and only steps in when things have gone too far.

"Death." His eyes return to mine. "There is too much death, my queen. The gods have created an imbalance. Your mother—"

"My mother would do no such thing!" I cannot stop myself from silencing him.

Not my mother. She would never harm. I refuse to believe this is her doing. She would *not*. My mother has always been dedicated to keeping the realms in balance. She has given so much life to the mortal realm. She has answered their prayers! She gives for the sake of giving.

Screams rise in the distance. The dogs continue to bark. It is all too much.

Sylvie steps closer and takes my hand. "My queen, mothers would do unfathomable things for their daughters."

Before I can speak another word, Hades takes my hand from hers and places something in it. It's cold and I have an instinct to pull back.

"What are you doing?" My voice is less than a whisper. There are seeds in my hand, caught between my touch and his. I would know the shape of seeds anywhere. "What are these?"

"Do not drink the wine your father gives you," Hades tells me urgently.

"What?"

"Eat them quickly, my love. And do not eat or drink

anything from your father." My head spins and he pushes my hand up. As if to have me eat them now.

It's all too much but the look in his eyes… I cannot deny him.

Hades releases my hand, and I tip the seeds into my mouth. They land on my tongue, and I slip them between my teeth. They are tart and juicy, flavor bursting every time I chew. They are small, but there are many, and some fall to the ground with his rushed approach.

I lift my hand to my mouth, hardly feeling it, and tip another three seeds onto my tongue.

Hades strokes my cheek.

I look into his eyes, a thousand questions racing through my mind. Why is this happening? Why *now*? What more would I have to say to him if we only had time?

We do not.

The barking is louder. They are here. I am certain what once was is gone. Today marks a new era. What is to come, I am not sure. But I must continue in uncertainty.

I swallow again. "Hades." I whisper his name, already feeling as if I'm saying goodbye.

"Do not drink the wine, my love. Promise me," he orders again. "Tell me you understand."

"I will not drink the wine," I repeat, but I cannot tell him I understand. I have always drunk the wine offered at my father's table. I cannot think of a single reason why I should avoid it. But Hades's expression is deathly serious. He nods at my promise, then glances up.

The doors to the meeting hall open with a harsh bang, and Cerberus's barks fill the room, as well as other hounds that accompany Hecate. The mother, the maiden, the crone.

"Hades," I say, one more time. I cannot face what is to come without telling him *something*, but no words come. How can I possibly state what he has done for me into words? How can I tell him what our bond has come to mean to me in this short time? The days here were so long when I first arrived in the Underworld, and now it seems they have flown by.

I am not ready to say goodbye and yet, I know that I must. I do not wish to leave, and then there is a part of me already gone. It is a torment I cannot bear. It paralyzes me.

I am not the same woman I was when I came here, and it's because Hades gave me the freedom to discover myself.

I look down at my wrists, startling at the realization that there are no magical chains flickering there. Nothing binds me to Hades's bedroom. When was the last time I felt their presence? I cannot remember.

I look back up into his pained expression, speechless.

"My queen," he says.

"My king," I manage.

Then magic thunders in the room. A black cloud whirls tightly through the space, stopping only a few feet away from me.

Hecate steps out of the dark, her hand held out to

me. She is majestic. Her dark hair flowing and her eyes nearly pitch black. They mirror all that is around her. Magic flows from the powerful Titan. The mother of witchcraft and the keeper of keys.

My head bows in her presence but more so, my body wishes to be held by her. To release the pain. She takes it so willingly. Please, Hecate. I pray in silence.

I take her hand without thinking, only realizing what I have done when our hands touch.

"Come, Persephone. *Now.*"

Hecate starts to lead me away. All those times I dreamed of rescue, and now that it is here, I do not want it. Not like this. It's like being kidnapped a second time.

"Hecate wait—" I start and look back on my lover. My king and my Hades.

I want to stop everything and refuse to move another step until I have all the answers, but it is too late—we are already going, and I do not think Hecate will allow us to stop.

"You must come back to the world that is now forever changed."

Hecate leads me forward, and I glance over my shoulder to look at Hades.

He stands tall, his hand on Cerberus's head and his eyes as sharp as ever. I want him at my side, just as I was at his side at court. It does not feel right that I should go and he should stay.

"Hecate," he calls, his voice ringing through the

distance between us. Even Hecate's name is a command. "Do not leave her side. Do not betray me."

The mother, the maiden, the *crone* looks back at Hades, her eyes narrowed. There is some deeper meaning here. Something I do not understand. I have changed, yes—but I have not forgotten how it felt to watch my powers dry up without a single clue why they should do so.

She glances down at my hands—my right in hers, and my left in a fist around the remaining seeds.

"Show me," she says as tears slip down my cheeks.

Once again, I obey her. *Why?* There are no chains to hold me. And I want so desperately for someone to stop this madness. This pain. Why does agony fill me so?

"Did you eat them?" she questions.

I nod, not understanding a thing that occurs.

"Foolish girl, what have you done?" she asks breathlessly as the sky cracks above us in a powerful boom.

chapter 30

Hades

I HAVE SUFFERED MANY TIMES BEFORE, FOR FAR longer than mere mortals could ever conceive. None of that suffering compares at all to watching Persephone walk away, her hand in Hecate's and so many questions in her eyes.

It is torture that I cannot answer them. I did this. And I vow if she does not return to me, I will end it all. The only words that keep me from torment are those of the Fates. I must let her go but I fear too much. It is a sickness.

The pain is unimaginable.

It is so great that at first it does not feel like anything but an empty space.

But Persephone glances back at me one last time, and there is nothing *but* pain.

Then she is gone. Away in Hecate's grasp. Hecate will return on Deipnon. I will have my words with her then.

They are both gone, and it does not matter that Cerberus is here, nor the two inhabitants of the Underworld who have followed me all day in hopes of achieving this very thing.

I leave them both behind. I cannot find it within myself to speak to them. Not with this mortal blow to my chest.

It is the agony I have lived with all my life, only stronger. It is twice as bitter having known the sweetness of Persephone's lips. I do not know how to survive the rending ache of needing to touch her and having her taken from me. My mind is unsteady and so is my footing as my kingdom falls to pieces.

Cerberus stays at my side as I move through my home without seeing any of the halls or rooms I pass. Nothing matters. Nothing matters but Persephone, and she is not here. The screams are muted white noise and all I can hear is the ghost of her whispering my name.

I was made to be unworthy. I was *made* to have nothing of my own.

Somehow, I have made it to the door of my rooms. I push it open and go inside.

Moving has made no difference. My *rooms* make no difference. I do not truly own them. I will never truly own anything. I will have nothing, just as I have always had nothing, yet I will remain responsible for everything.

That was my reality until Persephone came to me.

Without her, it would have been my reality forever. It would have been the same as living out my existence in the Titan's stomach. Bleak and lonely and without joy.

I cling to the pillow to inhale her scent as the cries summon me. Praying for mercy. Death will come to all, and I would feel relief.

I am at the windows before I can stop myself. I draw back my fists and hit them as hard as I can. Pain echoes through the bones in my hands.

I hit the windows again, screaming in anger. It is a satisfying sound. The walls around the windows rattle with the force of my blows.

But the windows do not break. For this was made a prison for her and it is where I rightly belong.

The Underworld will not let me out no matter how much I want to follow Persephone. I cannot leave no matter how hot my anger burns.

In my memory, I return to the mirror. Olympus is blinding. It is endless and white behind Zeus. Too bright, and purposely so. I go back to the night she was taken. Back to what Zeus said. Back to when I knew this was the only way...

THREE MONTHS PRIOR AND THE NIGHT PERSEPHONE CASTS THE SPELL

"I will her to turn mortal," Zeus says. I must bite my tongue to keep from tearing him apart. Turn *mortal?* My queen? How can he think so little of her and fear her at the same time? "I have heard the prophecy that says my offspring will be stronger than me. This is a win for both of us. I shall turn her mortal, it has already begun and shortly there will be no power left in her. She will not overpower me, and she will go to you. You will make her a fine partner and king. I only need a little while longer."

Zeus should have known there was no way to misdirect fate in this manner. If he was so concerned about his children eclipsing his power, he should never have had children at all.

A foolish thought. No one has ever been able to tell Zeus anything. He simply assumes he will bend every prophecy to his preferences without facing a single consequence.

That is not how any realm works. There is always a consequence.

I stand firm in the mirror, my jaw tight but my expression unmoving. I do not wish a mortal for my wife. I want her. I crave her. I've watched her for months. She is to be a queen at my side. Zeus wishes her away and for me to take her. Why harm my wife? I cannot allow it.

"I want to have Persephone forever," I tell him.

"Forever you shall. She will be mortal. She shall perish as they do and will be sent to your realm. You need only wait a little while longer, no?"

"I don't want her as a mortal soul in the Underworld. I want her as the goddess she is."

He scoffs.

Anger bristles through me. How dare he question my desire. How dare he attempt to change the perfection Persephone is.

"For what purpose?" Zeus asks with shock and humor.

For what? What are goddesses for, but to rule? What is a goddess like Persephone *for,* but to have everything her heart desires and every possible power at her fingertips? What is *my* Persephone for, if not to be worshipped as the queen she is?

"To rule beside me," I say, barely able to keep my voice in check. Zeus already knows that I will not do his bidding without appropriate payment. Without a deal that benefits *me.* But I cannot let him think he can use Persephone to control me. "She is meant for me, and she is meant to rule."

"Very well," says Zeus, as if it does not matter what becomes of Persephone. "She shall be a nymph very soon as her magic wanes, you won't have to wait very long at all." As if he is satisfied to have her out of sight and out of mind. Safely in the Underworld, where he will not have to look at her and wonder if her powers are growing stronger. "We have a deal."

The anger turns to rage. Soon? How soon? The questions pile in my mind but they all lead to one conclusion. I must take her now. I have to save her.

"How?" I ask him.

"How what?" he responds as if the question isn't obvious.

"How did you take her powers?" My eyes meet his in the mirror.

"The wine of course. Poison in the wine." He answers so easily.

"I have matters to attend to," I tell him and end it.

"As do I."

The mirror goes dark.

I curl my fist in front of my mouth and breathe deeply. She is *mine*, and I have little time left.

No more dwelling on Zeus. I turn away from the mirror and leave it behind, moving down the halls to my rooms as quickly as I can. Minox steps out of an alcove up ahead of me, but disappears into shadow when he sees that I will not stop for him.

I need her. *Now.*

A small voice in the back of my mind whispers to me as I stride down the hall.

You could have had her for infinite time, it says. *If she was a mortal soul in your Underworld, you could have kept her forever.*

I wave away that suggestion like I would wave away a cloud of smoke. Persephone was not born to be a mortal in my realm, the thread of her life snipped by the Fates for any number of reasons.

She was born to be a goddess.

And she was born to *rule.*

I open the door to my rooms. In comparison to the hall, it is bright, though not overwhelmingly so. The fire burns hot in the grate, casting flickering shadows over everything. Those shadows will caress Persephone's skin like a lover.

I steel myself against the rush of arousal and approach the bed.

With the fire crackling and the rustling of the sheets, I can imagine her here. She turns over in my bed. There's a sultry sinful look in her dark eyes, filled with lust as she peers back at me. The innocence is still there as she pulls the silk threads to her chest and her pouty lips, slightly swollen from pleasuring me, slip open at the sight of me towering over her.

My Persephone. My queen.

Her chest rises and falls with heavy breaths.

I know her so well. Every curve of her body already. For months I have watched her as she slept. I have been in her dreams, cloaked in darkness.

A deep groan of discontent bellows up my chest. The voices of warning hiss at my impatience.

She will be mine in every way. Every possible essence of her will bear my mark.

Time, the warning echoes in the back of my head. *In time…she will be yours.*

In time.

I come back to the present hell, my forehead cool against the glass, and straighten. My realm stretches below the window, but it is empty.

Oh, it is filled with souls. Bursting with souls. There are too many of them. The balance has been thrown off.

But without Persephone, it is empty.

The crackling of the fire in the grate sounds like a mockery now. It's taunting me with the idea of Persephone in my bed. If I look at the bed in the reflection, desire so fucking strong hits me and being without it could be the end to me.

I back away from the window and fold my arms over my chest. Cerberus pads to my side, sitting close so that I can reach his heads. I stroke each one in turn, biting back wave after wave of emotion.

This is what has to be done.

I *knew* it would have to be done when all of this began.

And it began, as so many tortures do, with Zeus.

He wanted Persephone weak and then dead. He offered her to me as my queen for he did love her, but he feared her more than he cared for her.

So he poisoned her. Even knowing him, I was stunned. How much time was left?

I was too selfish, and too stubborn, to let that happen so easily.

Minox entered and before he could speak, I commanded him, "Take her in the night. Go now."

"My lord—" Minox began.

"Aphrodite has opened the realm. She made a deal

with a demon. I cannot enter but you can. You must. Tonight. No more time can pass."

"My lord...I have never ventured to Olympus. If caught—"

"If caught, you will die. If you do not return with her this evening, I shall kill you myself. You will go. Now."

I would have Persephone as the goddess she was. I could not allow Zeus to harm her.

PRESENT DAY

I cast my intention in the obsidian wall, in which her power lies.

With a hand against the cold crystal I pray: *Let her recover from the poison that had seeped into every part of her. Give her the time and space and guidance she needed to discover the powers within. Bring her back to me. Let her grow in my realm as Zeus did not allow her to do on Olympus.*

From my realm, I cannot see her, and that causes me more grief than Zeus can possibly know. I stare up at the sky, which has been splitting and raining down souls for days, and imagine that I can speak into Hecate's ear despite the distance between Olympus and the Underworld.

"Do not fail me, Hecate," I call to her. "If Persephone

does not return to me, Demeter's reign of death will be met with my reign of destruction."

For the good of all and to the harm of none

May vengeance and justice be a healing path
May it be quick; may it be severe
May we all receive what we deserve
May it be screamed for all to hear

So mote it be

His in the Fire, book 2, coming 2026.
Available to pre order on my website now!

Want to know which Greek God or Goddess you are, scan the QR code below and take my quiz! There will be some special sneak peeks and bonuses sent out to you via email before *His in the Fire* releases!

about w winters

Thank you so much for reading my romances. I'm just a stay at home mom and avid reader turned author and I couldn't be happier.

I hope you love my books as much as I do!

More by Willow Winters
WWW.WILLOWWINTERSWRITES.COM/BOOKS

www.ingramcontent.com/pod-product-compliance
Lightning Source LLC
Chambersburg PA
CBHW021710160626
46733CB00044B/6
9798885927918